MURDER AT THE WILD HAGGIS BOOKSHOP

JACKIE BALDWIN

Storm
PUBLISHING

This is a work of fiction. Names, characters, businesses, places, events and incidents are either the products of the author's imagination or used in a fictitious manner. Any resemblance to actual persons, living or dead, or actual events is purely coincidental.

Copyright © Jackie Baldwin, 2025

The moral right of the author has been asserted.

All rights reserved. No part of this book may be reproduced or used in any manner without the prior written permission of the copyright owner. This prohibition includes, but is not limited to, any reproduction or use for the purpose of training artificial intelligence technologies or systems.

To request permissions, contact the publisher at rights@stormpublishing.co

Ebook ISBN: 978-1-80508-842-4
Paperback ISBN: 978-1-80508-844-8

Cover design: Dawn Adams
Cover images: Dawn Adams

Published by Storm Publishing.
For further information, visit:
www.stormpublishing.co

ALSO BY JACKIE BALDWIN

A Grace McKenna Mystery

Murder by the Seaside

Murder at Castle Traprain

Murder at Whiteadder House

The Highland Bookshop Murders

Murder at the Wild Haggis Bookshop

Dead Man's Prayer

Perfect Dead

Avenge the Dead

In memory of my dear friend, Julie Fotheringham.

ONE

BETH

Beth put down her ancient copy of *Pride and Prejudice* and sighed with pleasure. Although she loved all sorts of different books, this was one of her comfort reads that never failed to delight. Jumping to her feet, she placed it back on one of the two bulging bookcases on either side of the stone hearth. She glanced at her watch, hurriedly gathered up her leather satchel then turned to the mirror in the hall to pull her long curly hair into submission before sticking it up in a messy bun. The face that stared back at her was ghostly pale with a smattering of freckles across her nose and cheeks. It was not unheard of for her to get sunburnt in the time it took to hang washing out on the line.

Poking her head round the living room door she spied her black cat Toby giving her a stern look from the sideboard. Used to inspiring terror in the mean streets of Glasgow he was slowly adjusting to a more rural life in the Scottish Highlands. He had taken to following her along to the shop at times, which had initially worried her until she realised that he was used to far heavier traffic in the city than he'd ever find up here. The customers looked forward to seeing him. She dropped a kiss on his massive head then pulled on a wool coat over her navy tweed skirt and slid her feet into her trademark sensible shoes. The air in the house was distinctly cooler than usual. No wonder, as it was already into October. She'd need to turn the heating on tonight.

Closing the door to her small, whitewashed cottage behind her, her green eyes widened with pleasure as she took in the beauty of the morning accented by the autumnal colours. The cold pinched her cheeks but the sun was shining, the birds were singing and the deep blue sea sparkled. A bubble of optimism floated up inside her. Walking along Gallanach Road, she breathed the salty sea air deeply into her lungs. She could never tire of this view, she thought, as her eyes swept over the tranquil bay to the misty smudge of the outlying islands.

The huge black and white Calmac Ferry to Mull, berthed in the harbour, suddenly blasted its horn to signify it was about to leave, making her jump. She glanced round to make sure no one had noticed. An amused pair of eyes smiled at her over a garden gate. The elderly woman was wearing faded dungarees with a colourful scarf knotted at her neck.

'You'll get used to it, lass,' she soothed before sticking out a slightly grubby hand for Beth to shake. 'Maggie McCrae. It's Beth, isn't it? You're the one who's bought Thistle Cottage.'

'Yes, that's right,' said Beth, tentatively returning her smile. It still unnerved her that everyone she met seemed to have an idea of her business. She was used to the anonymity of Glasgow.

'I've been hearing that you've given the bookshop a whole new lease of life,' Maggie continued. 'I must pop in some day when I'm getting my shopping.'

'You'd be very welcome.' Beth smiled, giving her a small wave as she set off once more.

As she turned left onto the main shopping area, she headed straight for the bookshop which was located just off George Street. Her heart swelled with pride as she took in the two-storey green building with its pointy gables. The hand-painted sign depicted rolling hills and a cheeky haggis wearing a Tam o' Shanter hat with a pair of bagpipes tucked under its arm. It never failed to make her smile. Her gaze turned to the vibrant display of books in the window. She couldn't believe that it was really hers; it had been her dream from being a tiny child to own her own bookshop. Other girls might have a scrapbook detailing their ideas for a dream wedding but hers had been a scrapbook devoted to her first bookshop. Now all she had to do was make it a success in order to hang on to it. She pushed the door open.

TWO

The smell of coffee and books tickled her nose. Hurrying through to the kitchen at the back of the shop, she quickly opened the containers of chocolate chip cookies she had prepped at home and placed them in the fan oven. Soon their delicious aroma would spread around the shop, enticing her customers to linger.

'Morning, Lachlan.' She waved at the man adjusting the books on the reclaimed timber shelves as she walked back through into the main part of the shop, stooping to straighten one of the colourful rugs that were scattered throughout. Lachlan had been the manager of the shop before her, but the owner of the business had decided to sell up and retire to Spain. The other members of staff had been young and easily secured other jobs. Although only in his late forties, he had worked in the bookshop for most of his adult life and hadn't found anything else by the time she took over. It had seemed sensible to take him on to manage the shop as she hadn't had the faintest idea how to do it herself. Although he was generous with his knowledge and worked hard, she knew he often bit his tongue over what he no doubt termed her 'outlandish notions'. The previous incarnation of the bookshop had done well enough, but Beth rather thought the owner had been a bit stuck in the past and was eager to make some changes now it was hers.

'How many are you expecting tonight for this shindig?' Lachlan asked, his features arranged in a frown as he pushed up his glasses. He thought she was crazy starting up a crime book club in the evenings, but she'd assured him he wouldn't need to be involved with The Armchair Detectives Club.

'Just five, plus myself,' she replied. 'I thought I could start with those and then, through word of mouth, increase it up to a maximum of ten.'

'You'll be lucky,' he grunted, shaking his head.

'I think it's a really smart move, actually,' her assistant Morna called, emerging from the back stockroom and fixing Lachlan with a stern look. 'Everyone has to buy the book from us in advance as part of the ticket price so if they didn't show up it would be an epic fail and total waste of money for them, but we've still made a sale.'

Even though she was grateful for his expertise, Beth did wish Lachlan could be a bit more positive at times and less a prophet of doom.

'Beth, have the extra books for Fan Fiction Night come in yet? I can't see them anywhere,' asked Morna.

Beth smiled at the fierce-looking young woman before her. She had her own unique style and the thick layers of makeup, black eyeliner and piercings served as less of a fashion statement and more of a suit of armour, she suspected. Ferociously intelligent, she was a dedicated gamer. Beth had given her a free rein to build up the science fiction and fantasy side of the business and she was doing a wonderful job.

'Sorry, Morna, the delivery came in just as we were about to close. They're in a corner of the staffroom underneath the new curtains for the children's area.'

Morna rolled her eyes, though it was hard to tell underneath all the makeup. She was always borderline insubordinate but never crossed irrevocably over the line. Beth suspected she was struggling with some issues in her personal life. She always seemed so tightly coiled. Despite being well spoken with the kind of refined accent typically gained in a boarding school, her clothes were cheap and her shoes worn.

The bell tinkled once more and her youngest recruit, Chloe, came hurrying in, huffing and puffing. Time keeping was not her forte, partly due to her frenetic social life. Just hearing about her wild nights out was enough to curl your hair.

'Morning, everyone,' she called out in a soft Highland accent, earning her a ferocious scowl and a pointed look at her watch from Morna. On the surface, Chloe was an unlikely person to find working in a bookshop – the word 'bling' came to mind when one looked at her. Beth saw Chloe as a magnificent bird of paradise compared to her own drab sparrow, plus she was wonderfully entertaining for the rest of them. Well, maybe not for Morna. Those two were oil and water, and viewed each other with mutual distrust and suspicion.

'Hi, Chloe, once you're sorted could you post on our socials about tonight's crime book group?'

'Already on it,' she replied. 'That's why I was late,' she added, shooting a glare at Morna. 'I've made these cool graphics using Canva and posted them on our Facebook page, X and Insta.' She pulled out her phone and scrolled down before presenting the screen to Beth with a flourish. 'See?'

'Those are amazing, Chloe, I love them!' said Beth. What she knew about social media would barely fill a postcard, but it was child's play to Chloe, who seemed to spend as much time online as she did in the real world.

'I also made a TikTok.' Chloe stalked over to Morna and showed her.

'Not bad,' she conceded grudgingly.

Encouraged, Chloe gushed, 'I could do some for your section if you like?'

'You'd do that?'

'Sure.' Chloe shrugged. 'It's all one bookshop, isn't it?'

'That would be cool. Er... thanks...' said Morna, sounding like the word was stuck in her throat.

The door opened. 'Morning, all.' Dave the postman grinned, handing across a pile of letters and padded envelopes to Beth. 'That's your lot for today. I swear my bag's been getting heavier and heavier since you took the shop over.'

'Hey, Dad,' called Chloe, walking over. 'Mum's on a course tonight. Are you cooking or do you want me to stop by the chippie?'

'How does my cheesy chicken sound?' he asked.

'Perfect.' She grinned. 'I'll do the dishes. Any gossip from your round?'

'None that I care to share,' he shot back, doing his best to look mysterious.

After he had left, Beth marvelled at their easy relationship. Her own relationship with her father, such as it was, had been fraught to say the least.

Chloe was an avid reader and devoured young adult and romance titles. Her current passion was 'romantasy', which was edging dangerously into Morna's territory. She was also much smarter than the airhead persona she liked to cultivate. It felt good to have the young ones in the shop. At thirty-four, Beth knew that she wasn't old, but her tastes were more middle-aged than they should be. She had never been as carefree as Chloe. Her life experiences had shunted her down a very different path.

She had converted one of the large stock rooms previously filled with sets of old lawbooks that no one would ever want into a light and airy café with a Nespresso machine and preloved leather sofas where customers could take the weight off their feet and relax with some home baking. On one wall the shelves were filled with a curated selection of books with staff reviews posted underneath with funky magnets, which were also available to buy. The others contained crafts and artwork for sale by local artists.

Lachlan had been scandalised when she first proposed getting rid of the law room – or 'his treasures', as Beth liked to secretly think of them. 'These books are of historical value!' he had spluttered. Gently, she had explained that now that legal session cases and case reports were online, it was virtually impossible to sell them, given the amount of room they took up and that they were no longer being printed.

The day passed like any other, with customers wandering in to browse the shelves or ask for something specific. Some stayed for a cup of tea and a chat. As the sun began to set and pink tinged the early evening sky, Beth gently shooed the last couple of stragglers out and closed the door behind them. Her staff weren't long in following them out of the door. It was time to get ready for the first meeting of the Armchair Detectives.

As she moved through to the café, she removed the canapés that she had made last night from the fridge and stuck them in the oven to bake. She had put on quite the spread for the inaugural book club meeting, desperate for it to go well. To create a fun atmosphere, she'd used blue and white crime scene tape to outline a dead body on the floor and ordered themed blood-spatter serviettes and plates. The white wine was cooling in the fridge and a bottle of red stood open on the large oval table Lachlan had helped her move in from the front of the shop. She'd even brought in her own crystal glasses from home which sparkled under the spotlights. For effect, she'd also positioned a number of deep red candles in black dishes which emitted an exotic scent. She heard the door open and, eyes sparkling with excitement, she moved through to the shop. This was going to be an amazing night! She could feel it in her bones. The first social event she had ever organised. Her new life was opening up in front of her and she couldn't wait to live it.

THREE

Beth stood at the front door making sure that it was only the members of the book group who entered, then locked it behind them as they made their way in a throng through to the café area, as directed. Once she had shepherded the last straggler through, she stood at the head of the oak table and nervously cleared her throat. The talking continued. She cleared it again, feeling a nervous flush creep up her cheeks. Finally, and now a little cross, she reached behind her to one of the shelves for a weighty tome and dropped it onto the table with a satisfying bang. Instant silence.

'Welcome to the first meeting of The Armchair Detectives, everyone,' she called. 'Tonight, we're going to be discussing *Murder at Crowton Hall* by Josephine Barclay, a cosy mystery with gothic undertones. Let's start by introducing ourselves then we can discuss the book before breaking for wine and nibbles.'

'Do we have to?' moaned a man she recognised from earlier visits to the shop as Mike Carter. He sighed and leaned back in his chair with a hint of ennui.

Beth bridled. He was tall and lanky, late forties, with long floppy dark hair, and wearing cords and a tweed jacket. 'Yes, we do,' she said. 'Why don't you go first, Mike, and get it out of the way?' The others looked at him expectantly.

'Fine. I'm Mike Carter. I teach English at the high school for my sins. I read widely in the crime fiction genre. I have to say, this book was dismal.'

'We'll come onto the book later.' Beth smiled through gritted teeth. Glancing at the vibrant, beautifully made-up woman next to him, she nodded encouragingly.

'My name's Veronica Kerr, Ronnie for short,' she said, dimpling. 'I run Glow, the beauty parlour a couple of doors up from here. It's not normally such a mess in front of the shop, but some idiot tourist managed to demolish my garden wall last week. I mainly read gritty crime thrillers, but I have to say, I really enjoyed the book.' She turned and glared at her neighbour pointedly.

'I'm not surprised *you* enjoyed it.' Mike sniffed.

'What's that supposed to mean?' Ronnie snapped back, eyes narrowed.

'Er, moving on...' said Beth, gesturing to the elegant older woman on the other side of Ronnie. She hadn't expected her book group to be so feisty.

'I'm Harriet Brown,' she said, her intelligent blue eyes flicking round the table, sizing everyone up. 'I used to be headteacher of the local secondary school. These days I'm all about gardening and books. The book was... interesting. I'm quite an eclectic reader.'

'Did you two work together?' asked Beth, looking across at Mike.

'In a manner of speaking,' replied Harriet, her cool gaze sweeping over Mike who, Beth noticed, refused to meet the older woman's eyes.

Oops, thought Beth. *Clearly no love lost there.* They had probably all come across each other in some capacity in a town this size. The introductions were really for her benefit.

'Dan Guthrie,' said a young man who looked to be around thirty. 'I'm a writer. My first crime novel is due out shortly,' he added almost apologetically, dropping his eyes. Everyone apart from Mike gave him a spontaneous clap. Beth noticed Mike rolling his eyes.

'That's wonderful!' Beth exclaimed.

'Can we please get on?' sighed Mike. 'We're meant to be here to discuss the book, not network.'

Beth ignored him, though he was making her increasingly uncomfortable. 'And last but not least...' she said to the attractive brunette on her right. Despite her looks, she had a hard edge to her that Beth found intimidating – she could give even Ronnie a run for her money in the glamour stakes. *I really need to up my game,* Beth thought, wincing.

'Darcie Baxter,' the woman said in a clear strong voice with a Glasgow twang. 'I'm an investigative journalist currently working for the local rag. But not for long!' she added with a mysterious smile. 'I've rotted up here long enough. I've discovered a secret that's going to propel me back into the big leagues. Glasgow, here I come!'

'Intriguing,' said Beth, though all of a sudden she felt a bit sick and clammy.

'I love all kinds of crime fiction, but my favourites are those where someone will go to any length to cover up a secret. We've all got them, haven't we?' she said, pinning everyone around the table with a knowing smirk. Clearly, she was just bursting to let the cat out of the bag, but the journalist in her reined it in.

Mike snorted behind his hand, covering it with a cough. What was his problem? Beth hoped he didn't come back. He seemed rather hostile for what was meant to be a simple social event. Was it her imagination or had the evening just taken a darker turn? Everyone suddenly seemed frozen in their seats, staring down at the table as though they wished themselves anywhere but here. *This is not going well.* Beth panicked. She had to move things along, loosen them up a little bit.

'So,' she said brightly. 'What did we think of the main character, Fletcher Monterey?'

'Two dimensional and dull as ditchwater,' announced Mike, folding his arms.

'Well, I liked him,' pronounced Darcie, also folding her arms.

'In fact, I *really* liked him, if you get my drift,' she said, waggling her eyebrows suggestively.

Everyone, apart from Mike and Dan, laughed and nodded in agreement.

'How about you, Dan, since you're the expert in our midst?'

'How is *he* an expert?' demanded Mike. 'Does he have a degree in English Literature?'

'He's an expert because he's written a crime novel of his own,' retorted Beth. 'Besides, you've already had your say.'

There was an awkward silence. Beth bit her lip and willed somebody to say something.

'Mike's right,' said Dan with a nervous grin. 'I still have a lot to learn. However, I disagree with his assessment of the main character. I thought that, overall, he was quite nuanced. He was strong and led the investigation through his sharp wits, but he also had his flaws and demons to slay along the way. He was damaged, but compelling and charismatic.'

'Thank you, Dan. And what did you all make of the plot?' asked Beth, starting to relax a little.

'The red herrings kept me on my toes,' said Harriet, pushing her chic ash-blonde bob behind her ear. 'I thought I knew who the killer was a few times. I did guess in the end, but only after the author made me work for it.'

'It kept me up way too late,' complained the salon owner, Ronnie. 'I kept thinking just one more chapter, but the chapters were so short and enticing I couldn't help myself. It was worth it though' – she grinned – 'but I did *not* enjoy the bags under my eyes the next morning.'

'The mark of a good book.' Beth smiled. 'We've all been there.'

'Well, I thought it was pitifully transparent,' announced Mike, his voice already grating on Beth's ears. 'I think we need to choose something a bit more challenging next time.'

The discussion carried on for a while with everyone but Mike seeming to have enjoyed it. Beth was developing a tension headache. Surreptitiously, she glanced at her watch then brightened.

'Well done, everyone, that was a lively debate. I think we can agree that most of us enjoyed this month's offering. It's time to take a break, so if a few of you wouldn't mind helping me bring things through from the kitchen, we can have wine and nibbles whilst we get to know each other a little better.'

'Assuming we want to...' said Darcie, a sarcastic edge to her voice. 'Just joking!' she added with an abrupt laugh, jumping to her feet. Beth didn't know what to make of her at all. She definitely had a spiky side to her, signalling she could be dangerous or unpredictable if you crossed her. Yet she was sharp and quick-witted, too, as if she might even be fun when you got to know her better.

'She didn't sound as though she was joking,' murmured Ronnie in Beth's ear, as she moved round to help. 'I'm sorry Mike has been such an arse tonight. You've worked so hard to make it a success. I love the crime scene tape on the floor. Might get a photo of me in that later for Insta, though it's not exactly on brand for my beauty parlour.'

'Oh, are you one of those influencers?' asked Beth. 'My staff have dragged me kicking and screaming on to social media, but I don't understand it at all, really.'

'It's a good way to promote your business,' said Ronnie. 'Every business these days needs to set up a brand. Take me, for instance, I like nothing better than closing the curtains and slobbing out in leisure wear with no makeup, but you'd never catch me in public like that.' She gestured to her immaculate appearance. 'How could I expect people to believe in my salon and products if I don't present myself well at all times?'

'That sounds exhausting!' exclaimed Beth. 'That sort of stuff makes me feel like pulling out my own fingernails.'

'Don't despair,' said Ronnie, giving her a shrewd, assessing look. 'You're kind of "on brand" already with the sexy librarian look.'

Beth snorted with laughter. 'The young ones are a great help. They're all over the social media stuff.' By now everyone was mobilised, taking plates and glasses back and forth. Everyone except Mike, it seemed.

Ronnie stomped through in her high-heeled boots. 'Little Lord Fauntleroy, get off your skinny arse, we're not all your bloody handmaidens.'

Mike jumped as though he'd been shot, then got up with a sour face and started helping. Soon, they were all moving round the table and, as the wine flowed, they became more chatty. Darcie had a raucous laugh and told wicked tales of the famous people she had interviewed for her paper and what they were really like. She was a force of nature, thought Beth, happy to take a back seat now that the main work of the evening was done. Even Mike finally had a smile on his face. It made him look totally different. He was enthusiastically chatting to Ronnie who was now literally fluttering her eyelashes at him. Maybe she should take a leaf out of Ronnie's book and go for some beauty treatments. She'd never worn makeup, but now might be the time to experiment. She loved Darcie's huge gold hooped earrings... *no, who am I kidding? No one would be interested in a drab mouse like me.* Stifling a yawn, she glanced at her watch. Goodness! It was later than she thought. Time to bring the evening to a close. It had been a long day.

'Thank you all for coming to our inaugural meeting,' she interjected into a lull in the conversation. 'I hope it'll be the first of many. The next one will be in two weeks' time on 15th October. Details of the next book will be put on our Facebook page.'

She busied herself making sure all the coats and umbrellas were claimed by the right people, feeling a gush of pleasure that it had gone really well. Even Mike looked almost cheerful as he got ready to leave, chatting away to Darcie and Ronnie before coming over to thank her.

'Not bad,' he proclaimed, 'not bad at all,' before wandering off.

Beth supposed that constituted high praise despite his surliness at the start.

Ronnie was next to go, giving her a warm hug. 'Fab night, Beth. Looking forward to the next one. If you ever fancy a glow up, you know where to come!'

'I might take you up on that.' Beth laughed, having no intention of doing so.

She noticed that Darcie was hanging back, as if to catch her on her own and her stomach plummeted. She waved off a few half-hearted offers of help as the others said their goodbyes and trickled out the door one by one.

Once they had left, Darcie walked over to her. Beth held her breath.

'I admire what you've done with the place,' Darcie said, her expression hard to read. 'Thanks for a great night. See you next time.'

Beth was at a loss. She had the impression that Darcie had been about to say something else but had changed her mind at the last minute. Smiling, she waved her off and rushed back to the kitchen to compose herself, exhaling with relief. She'd been worried about nothing.

She set about clearing up as the sound of their chattering voices receded into the night. Eventually there was silence, and she felt her shoulders come down and her body relax. She dug out her headphones, selected some soft rock from her phone to energise her and put it on full blast, her head bobbing away. Although she was tempted to leave the dishes until the next day, she managed to power through until everything was shipshape. Finally, feeling tired to her very bones, she turned off the music and the kitchen light before making her way through into the adjacent room with a cup of tea before heading home.

She stopped abruptly, her eyes scarcely able to process what she was seeing. Blinking rapidly, she briefly wondered if she might be hallucinating. There was a body lying on the floor neatly positioned inside her crime scene tape. Frozen in shock, her cup and saucer slipped from her bloodless hands and shattered on the floor, splashing hot tea onto her legs. She rushed over, desperately hoping it was an elaborate prank. She tugged on an arm and the head rolled to face her, lifeless eyes staring up at her. Her mouth opened in a scream...

FOUR

Beth yanked the door to the shop open when she heard the reassuring voice of her lawyer Harris Kincaid on the other side. She quickly ushered him in, locking the door behind her. Although he was a few years younger than her, his calm demeanour was always a comfort in trying circumstances. Tall and lanky, he had sensitive features and a quiet intelligence.

'Thank you so much for coming,' she sobbed. 'I didn't know who else to call and, well... there's a dead body in my shop. I figured I might need a lawyer.' She bit down hard on her lip to stop it wobbling like blancmange. She had to get herself under control. She was a grown woman... who had a dead body in her bookshop. The hysteria kept bubbling up inside her like a kettle on the boil.

Harris gave her a wry smile. 'I think you're allowed to be upset, Beth, in the circumstances.' He patted her arm awkwardly then switched into professional mode. 'I take it you've called the police?'

Beth nodded miserably. 'They're on their way.' She looked out the window and saw a flashing blue light approaching. No sirens. What would be the point?

'Any chance it could be a natural death?' he asked.

Beth shook her head. 'See for yourself,' she said, nodding towards the room where the body still lay.

'I can't go in,' Harris said. 'Best not contaminate the scene. I'll take a quick look from the doorway.' Looking a little green, he walked over and craned his neck.

'See what I mean?' said Beth.

He returned to her side, looking worried. 'It's murder all right. The body is perfectly positioned inside the crime tape shape on the floor. Beth, this could be very serious.'

'What do you mean?' she said, aghast. 'I didn't kill her. Why would I?'

'Now, I don't want you to panic,' he said, taking her warm hand in his cool one. 'But the police will, at least initially, consider you to be a suspect.'

'But... that's ridiculous!' she burst out. 'All I did was hold a book group. Whoever did it, it wasn't me. It must have been someone else from the group that killed her. You do believe me, don't you?'

'Of course, I do,' he said, dropping her hand like he'd only just realised he was holding on to it.

Beth wanted to take his hand again. It made her feel safer somehow. There was a loud bang on the door. They both jumped.

'Police! Open up!' demanded a harsh voice.

Harris let out a low groan.

'What is it?' asked Beth, turning round on her way to the door.

'It's Detective Sergeant Logan Hunter. Not the most reasonable of men. Our paths cross in court on a regular basis.'

The banging resumed and Beth hastily opened the door. Two police officers strode in, both in plain clothes.

'Detective Sergeant Logan Hunter and this is Detective Constable Rhona Quinn.'

The man speaking to her was tall and burly, with the physique of a rugby player. His dark grey suit was rumpled and his tie slightly askew. His brown eyes were bordering on hostile and Beth felt more than a little afraid as she looked into them and discerned no warmth whatsoever.

'And you are?'

'Beth Cunningham,' she said, her voice low and quiet, her tears spent for now. 'The body's through there.'

'Stay here with DC Quinn,' he commanded, as he strode away into the adjacent room. A couple of minutes later, he was back, his face even graver now. He shook his head at the unspoken question in his colleague's eyes.

There was a muted knock on the door.

'That'll be the duty police surgeon,' he explained, as DC Quinn opened the door to admit a stooped elderly man with kind eyes.

'Dr Kennedy!' Beth exclaimed.

'She one of your patients?' asked the sergeant, jerking his head in Beth's direction.

'You know I can't comment on that,' the doctor said with a frown, turning to give Beth a quick wink.

'Fine,' sighed DS Hunter. 'Body's through there. I need you to pronounce life extinct. We're looking at a murder investigation.' He turned towards Beth. 'As this is now a crime scene, you'll need to vacate the premises until further notice.'

'But... this is where I work,' said Beth, uncomprehending. 'It's a bookshop. My staff will be here in the morning. I have customers...' She sat down heavily on a nearby chair. Did that police officer just roll his eyes? How dare he? Her face flushed with anger, and she sprang to her feet only to have Harris steer her out the door by the elbow.

'We'll meet you at the police station,' he said over his shoulder.

'The police station? But I want to go home,' she muttered, that treacherous lip wobbling again as she strived for control.

They emerged into the cool night air and Harris turned to her. 'Look, Beth, I know this is hard but surely you want to help the police find out who did this? If we wait until morning before you give a statement, the trail will be getting colder with each passing hour.'

'When you put it like that—'

'And to be honest, you don't really have a choice.'

'I don't?' she asked, bewildered.

'No. The only reason you're going with me and not being escorted in a police car is because he trusted me, as your lawyer, to get you down there. Now, you don't have to answer their questions but, assuming you have nothing to hide' – he shot her a sharp glance – 'it's probably best to cooperate.'

'This is a nightmare,' she groaned, rocking on her heels. 'That poor woman. Who could possibly have wanted her dead?'

'Oh, you'd be surprised,' he said, his mouth set in a grim line.

'What do you mean by that?' she asked.

'Nothing,' he said, shrugging it off. 'Come on, let's walk there. It's only a few minutes away and the fresh air will do you good.'

As they set off walking, another police car arrived, closely followed by a large police van. As they rounded the corner off the High Street, they saw a black hearse gliding through the silent streets in the direction they had come from. Beth shivered. Death had stalked her mother for months before she had succumbed. She hadn't expected to encounter it again so soon.

All too quickly, they turned into Albany Street and arrived at the police station. Beth's breath caught in her throat. It reminded her of a time in her life she'd rather forget.

Sensing her hesitancy, Harris paused beside her. 'Ready?' he asked.

'As I'll ever be,' she muttered and pushed open the door.

FIVE

The desk sergeant, a grizzled man of around fifty, had clearly been advised to expect them and they were immediately shown into an interview room that smelled of pine disinfectant with an undernote of sweaty feet. They sat side by side behind a table that was bolted to the floor. By now it was nearly eleven o'clock and Beth would have given anything to be tucked up in a warm, cosy bed where none of this nightmare had happened. Her thoughts flew to the dead body and she gave herself a silent rebuke. How could she dare moan when their life had stopped dead like a broken watch. She resolved to do everything she could to aid catching the killer, no matter what the cost. This was personal. She glanced sideways at Harris. As the lawyer her mother had engaged to deal with her estate and arrange the purchase of the bookshop and cottage, he had really taken her under his wing. Although he was very reserved and she struggled to know what he was thinking at times, she felt that he was someone she could rely on and turn to in a crisis. And this certainly qualified as a crisis, she thought, squirming in her uncomfortable plastic seat. She hoped it wouldn't be that unpleasant sergeant who came to question her. There was something about him that made her hackles rise.

The door swung open and her heart sank. *Speak of the devil.* In waltzed Detective Sergeant Hunter with Detective Constable Rhona Quinn in his wake carrying a tray with four cardboard cups of tea and a tray of rich tea biscuits. *No expense spared.* Unlike her rumpled colleague, DC Quinn didn't have a hair out of place.

'Sorry to keep you waiting,' DS Hunter said, not looking sorry at all. 'Harris, Miss Cunningham is merely giving a witness statement unless you know something that I don't? Is your presence here strictly necessary?' he asked, jutting out his chin and glaring at him.

Harris glanced at Beth, acknowledging the truth of what the policeman had said but, after correctly interpreting her desperate Save Me eyes, he turned back to DS Hunter. 'Regardless of that fact, I feel it prudent to stay given that the deceased was found in Miss Cunningham's shop whilst she was the only one present. Just in case things take a turn...' he said with a pugnacious glare of his own.

'Fine,' snapped DS Hunter.

DC Quinn handed the teas round. She was tall and angular with a pixie cut framing her sharp features. Catching Beth sizing her up, she raised an eyebrow.

'Now,' said the sergeant, turning his dark eyes towards her, as he readied his electronic device to note down her statement. 'Firstly, can you formally confirm the identity of the deceased?'

'Yes,' said Beth. 'Her name was Darcie Baxter. I understand that she was a journalist who worked for *The Oban Times*.'

'Thank you. Now, if you can tell us what happened tonight at the bookshop, in your own words.'

Taking a deep breath, Beth recounted all that had transpired at the book group, together with the names and addresses of all those who had come that evening which she'd had the foresight to bring with her. The questions seemed to go on and on and she could feel herself start to zone out as fatigue bit into her.

'So, you're telling me that to the best of your knowledge, everyone left the premises apart from you? You didn't think to escort the last person out and lock the door behind them?'

'Well, no,' Beth said. 'It's Oban after all, and I wasn't planning to be long. I mean, it's not like I have to worry about robbers or anything...'

'You'd be surprised,' DS Hunter, said, looking at her like she was a sandwich short of a picnic. 'Your client is perhaps a little too trusting,' he said to Harris. 'If I were you, I'd help her wise up and fast.'

'I don't need help with managing my client, thank you,' Harris retorted, and the two men glared at each other with unconcealed dislike.

'Excuse me...' said Beth indignantly. 'I hear what you're saying, Sergeant, and no doubt your job has given you a somewhat warped view of the world, but the consequence couldn't exactly have been foreseen. That someone would murder one of my customers and place the body in my crime scene tape...' To her horror, her voice broke and tears suddenly rose up in her eyes like an unbidden tsunami. It was all just too much.

DS Hunter regarded her through narrowed eyes, then pushed back his chair and stood up.

'That will do for now, unless you can think of anything else?'

Beth shook her head, causing a few tears to spill over and run down her cheeks.

'Then you're free to go,' he said. 'I'll escort you out.'

Beth welcomed the cold, fresh breeze outside and drew in a deep lungful of air.

'I'll walk you home,' said Harris. 'I could do with stretching my legs after a day spent behind a desk.'

'Thank you,' said Beth. 'I hope that's the last time I have to set foot in that place.'

'I do, too,' Harris replied. 'But I wouldn't count on it.'

SIX
MORNA

The next morning, Morna woke up to the sound of her alarm going off. Bleary eyed – she'd stayed up later than she should have gaming – she reached for her phone. As she opened a text from Beth, she snapped awake instantly like a jolt of electricity had jerked through her body.

What the hell? Someone's been murdered in the shop? Is she serious? That's crazy!

Hurriedly she jumped in the shower and got dressed in her usual uniform of black jeans and black T-shirt. She thought about breakfast, but decided she didn't have time given that her boss lived much further away than the shop. Grabbing her hoodie and sliding her laptop into a backpack, she pulled the door to her flat shut behind her and ran down the steps. As she stepped out onto George Street, she could see a police incident van parked further down on the left, just before the turning to the shop. Her steps slowed as she reached the corner where she would normally turn up to go to work. The whole side street was cordoned off by police tape. A group of people had stopped to gawp. Her anger sparked as she saw that several had their phones up, avid to capture anything they could upload to social media for a few clicks.

'Morons,' she muttered. Harriet, her old school headmistress, stopped by her side. She was carrying a string bag with some rolls, a paper and a pint of milk.

'What on earth's going on here?' she asked, her bright blue eyes alive with curiosity.

Morna shifted from one foot to the other, feeling awkward. 'Haven't you heard? Darcie Baxter was murdered last night in the shop. It happened after book group while Beth was clearing up in the kitchen.'

'Good heavens!' gasped Harriet, rocking on her heels. 'I can't believe it.'

Ronnie, the proprietor of Glow, came running over from a few doors down, her face white, dark circles under her eyes. Her lipstick was smudged and there was a stain on her blouse.

'Morna, how's Beth? What a thing to happen! That poor woman! Would you look at all these vultures? Turns my stomach, so it does. They need to get a life!' she said, raising her voice and throwing a contemptuous glance in their direction. 'I've been up half the night with the noise that lot were making.' She jerked her thumb in the direction of the police and the crime scene investigators in their white coveralls. 'You know how that tourist numpty demolished my front wall last week? Well, the police knocked me up to tell me they needed to test all of the fallen bricks for blood residue. It gives me the creeps just thinking about it.' She shuddered.

'Did they find anything?' asked Harriet.

'Not as far as I'm aware. Probably some nutter up from Glasgow did it, that's my theory anyway.'

Dave the postman walked up to Morna with a bundle of mail. He looked worried.

'Morna, love, can I give this lot to you? They're not letting me in the shop.'

'Yes, sure,' she said, stuffing it in her backpack. 'I'm on my way to see Beth now.'

'Chloe told me what's happened. Darcie was such a larger-than-life character. I can't wrap my head around the fact that she's gone, let alone been murdered.'

'You knew her then?'

'I was her postie for the last few years. Always gave me a bottle of malt whisky at Christmas. A right twinkle in her eye, she had. All that zest for life stamped out in a moment.' He glanced at his watch. 'My wife, Jean, is giving Chloe a lift along. If you hurry down, you might catch them.'

'I don't know where Chloe lives,' she confessed, staring down at her shoes. Although they'd been working together for a few months now, she hadn't been tempted to see her colleague out of work hours. They were just too different.

Unfazed, Dave pulled a notebook from his pocket and scribbled it down. 'There you go, love, I reckon you'll get there in time if you get a wiggle on.'

Morna thanked him, waved to the others and headed off at a brisk pace. Chloe, it turned out, lived on a council housing estate on the outskirts of town. As she turned into the street, she noticed how cramped the houses were with their small patches of garden and rotary clothes dryers. A world away from the lavish surroundings she had grown up in. Chloe's house was painted white with the same red door as its neighbours. A tabby cat sunned itself on the wall, ignoring her. She wasn't sure about this. Wasn't it a bit of an intrusion? Maybe she should just go ahead on her own.

Suddenly the door was flung open and Chloe rushed out, followed by a smiling woman who Morna was surprised to recognise. It was Jean, one of the nurses from the local doctor's surgery.

'Morna! Dad texted to say you were on your way. That poor woman! It's all around the town. I woke up this morning to find my phone had blown up. It's all anyone is talking about.'

'I'm not really one for social media,' muttered Morna, feeling uncomfortable.

'I don't blame you, Morna,' said Chloe's mum with a warm smile. 'Load of nonsense, isn't it?'

'Muuum!' exclaimed Chloe, sounding about twelve.

'Anyway, get in, the pair of you. I've popped some croissants and things in a bag for Beth. Poor love probably hasn't had the chance to nip out to the shops.'

Morna thanked her, feeling a pang as she thought of her own parents and their unfeeling ways. Chloe was rich in ways that she didn't even realise.

Jean started the car and they pulled out of the street. Things had certainly taken a turn. She thought she'd landed on her feet when she secured this job after years of minimum-wage work in various pubs and restaurants. Now she wasn't so sure.

SEVEN

BETH

Beth started awake on hearing the doorbell. Rubbing her eyes, she dragged herself out of bed. Her head was pounding and she'd forgotten to switch on her alarm. Throwing on her tatty old dressing gown, she stumbled down the stairs and flung open the door, blinking rapidly as her eyes adjusted to the sunlight. Her staff looked at her, mouths agape, especially Lachlan, before recovering themselves.

'Come in,' she said, attempting a watery smile and conscious of the fact that she had yet to brush her teeth or take a shower.

Chloe rather unexpectedly flung her arms around her, causing her to stagger backwards and crash into the wall.

'You poor thing!' she exclaimed. 'No wonder you're all over the place. I would be in absolute bits!'

'I'll pop the kettle on,' muttered Lachlan, clearly uncomfortable and desperate to escape.

'I've brought croissants from the bakery,' piped up Chloe.

Morna scowled. 'Beth, go shower and get dressed. I'll set up my laptop in the sitting room. Lachlan will do breakfast, and Chloe can go on our Facebook page and other socials to let folk know that the shop is temporarily closed but that everyone can still phone and email us if they need something.'

Everyone went a bit slack jawed to see Morna taking charge but then rushed off to do her bidding.

Thirty minutes later, their socials had been updated and Beth was polishing off the last croissant. Glancing up, she saw her staff staring at her expectantly, which prompted a coughing fit as a bit of croissant abruptly went down the wrong way. They were right. She was the boss and it was up to her to lead them all through this crisis. Somehow.

'How can they be sure it's murder?' asked Lachlan, his forehead creased with worry. 'Isn't the most likely explanation that she just collapsed from a stroke or a heart attack?'

'They can't be sure. Not yet anyway,' conceded Beth. 'However, the body was arranged inside my crime scene tape. I mean, what are the odds of that, right?'

'Not the smartest move,' opined Morna.

'No.' Beth shrugged. 'I think it was just too tempting for the killer, which hopefully will be their undoing.'

'Have the police got any leads?' asked Morna.

'They'll know more after the post mortem. In the meantime' – her voice wobbled – 'I rather think I might be a suspect myself. I was the last person to see her alive after all.'

'Apart from the killer,' said Chloe, agog.

'Detective Sergeant Hunter certainly gave me a grilling,' Beth said. 'Not the nicest man. Mind you, given the circumstances, it's perhaps not surprising.'

'Darcie always was relentless in pursuit of a story, but I'd never have believed someone would want her dead over it,' said Lachlan.

'You knew her then?' asked Beth, leaning forward.

'Our paths crossed a few times,' he said. 'She was desperate to break a big story that would get her out of the Highlands and back in one of the big city papers. The last time I saw her she was throwing out hints about something she'd discovered that could be her passport out of here.'

'When was that exactly?' asked Morna, turning her steely glare upon him.

'A week ago,' he said, looking more dejected by the minute. 'We... er... had dinner.'

'I see,' said Beth faintly. Another connection with her bookshop. This was the last thing she'd wanted to hear.

'I suppose the police will want to talk to me?' Lachlan continued, running his hands through hair that was already sticking up on end.

'Maybe, said Beth, shooting him a sympathetic smile.

'Now that I think of it, she did make one or two cryptic comments while she was at the book club,' Beth said. 'Maybe she was taunting someone there that night? Someone who was willing to kill to stop it coming out?' Unlike myself, thought Beth.

'Who was there?' asked Chloe. 'Maybe we'll already know some of them.' Toby the cat had made himself at home on her lap and was purring up a storm whilst she gently stroked his big head.

Beth fished in her bag from last night and they solemnly passed the list between them.

'Well, I know Ronnie,' said Chloe.

'Of course you do,' muttered Morna.

'And what's that supposed to mean?' Chloe asked, scowling at her.

'Just that you're never away from that place.'

'The beauty parlour?' asked Beth. 'I've never been in there, or to anywhere else like it. I don't even know what goes on in these places, really.'

The two girls glanced at each other, eyebrows raised.

'What, never?' asked Chloe, her tone scandalised. 'How is that even possible in this day and age?'

'Maybe she doesn't see the need to conform to patriarchal notions of beauty,' muttered Morna.

'Not this again! You're such a hypocrite, Morna,' snapped Chloe. 'You wear just as much makeup as me, *more*, in fact. So, it's only okay if you're trying to look all *alternative*?'

'This really isn't getting us anywhere,' said Lachlan. 'As I've said, I knew Darcie. Quite well, in fact.' He went a little pink. 'I don't know Ronnie, but I know everyone else on the list. Dan Guthrie, the novelist, was a regular customer of the shop though I have to say he didn't buy much in the way of fiction. Mike Carter has been in and out of the shop for years.'

'He was a bit unpleasant to Dan,' said Beth. 'I wonder why?'

'Mike can be a bit bitter and twisted,' said Lachlan.

'That's no motive for killing Darcie, though,' said Beth. 'You two went to the local school, didn't you?' She looked over at the girls.

'I did,' said Chloe.

'Did you have Mike Carter for English?'

'Yes,' said Chloe. 'I liked him. He'd a very sarcastic sense of humour, but at least he didn't play favourites. I do remember hearing him and Harriet Brown having a shouting match one day back when she was headteacher. She said if he didn't resign, she would find a way to end him.' She shrugged. 'Nothing came of it though.'

'Hmm... what about you, Morna?' asked Beth.

'Only for fifth and sixth year,' Morna replied. 'I did have him for English. I thought he was quite cool at the time. He was open to fantasy and stuff, unlike some of the others.'

Beth noticed that she had wound some hair around her finger and was subtly tugging on it. Clearly thinking about her school days was stressing her out, even though it was a long time ago. *Time to change the subject.*

'Obviously, the police will be looking into everyone who was there that night, but let's not forget that the door was left unlocked for at least half an hour whilst I was clearing everything away and washing up the dishes. Someone could have been waiting for her to leave and then hid her body back inside to conceal it from passersby. It's entirely possible they didn't even know I was still in the kitchen. Although I was listening to loud music, I had my earphones in to avoid disturbing the neighbours. I also had the door to the kitchen closed to prevent the heat getting out.' Beth shivered. It was only now sinking in that had she entered the room just a few minutes earlier, not only might she have caught the killer in the act, but they might have murdered her, too.

For the rest of the morning, the team worked at Beth's scrubbed pine kitchen table that she'd moved with her from Glasgow. It was a comfort to have reminders of her previous life surrounding her. Toby scowled at them from the dresser for disturbing his peace before getting bored and stalking off to the sofa for a nap, a beady eye flickering open every so often.

Around noon, there was a loud rap at the door making them all jump. Beth went to answer it, her heart hammering. As she opened the door she was faced with a grim-faced DS Hunter with his sidekick DC Quinn. His dark eyes were hard as flint.

'Detective Sergeant Hunter, do you want to come in? I was just going to put the kettle on...' She tailed off as his lips visibly tightened. Her stomach roiled. The way he was looking at her, something was very wrong, and she had a feeling she knew what it might be.

'Beth Cunningham, I'm detaining you on suspicion of the murder of Darcie Baxter. You do not have to say anything but anything you do say may be taken down in evidence and used against you in a court of law. Do you understand?'

Beth sagged against the wall, as her legs nearly went from under her. It was happening again and she was powerless to stop it. Her staff had come out into the hallway, their faces a mix of shock and confusion, mirroring her own.

'Please lock up behind you, and can someone feed Toby before you go?' she said to them, nodding at the keys on the table. 'Lachlan, can you call Harris Kincaid and tell him what's happened? Ask him to meet me down at the station.'

DS Hunter then placed her in handcuffs, took her by the arm, and frogmarched her to the waiting police car. She was dimly aware of a few neighbours stopping to gawp at them. This was a nightmare. One that showed no signs of releasing her anytime soon.

EIGHT

Beth was dry-mouthed with fear, which was in no way alleviated by the cup of tea she'd been brought by DC Quinn, who was looking at her differently now. Clearly, they knew about her past. That was the only explanation she could think of for why they had suddenly detained her. When she had moved to Oban, she'd dared to believe that the events of twenty-one years ago could finally be put behind her for good. Yet she could hardly complain. Wouldn't it, after all, be karma? Didn't she deserve to have this new, happy life snatched away from her? The door opened, drawing her back from her turbulent thoughts and in walked Harris Kincaid. A lump rose in her throat just looking at him. He was so good, so decent. Would he still want her as a client once he learned who she really was, and what she had done as a scared kid?

'Harris, thank God you're here.'

'Of course,' he said, with a small smile. 'Why wouldn't I be? You're my client.' He took a seat beside her at the table.

'They'll be in shortly to question you under caution,' he explained. 'You don't need to answer any of the questions they put to you, but it might be better to get ahead of this from the outset.'

'You know then?' she asked in a small voice.

'I do,' he said, his voice grave, his eyes kind. 'I've always known.

Your mother told me in case it ever became an issue. How you had changed your names and moved from Aberdeen to Glasgow.'

'What must you think of me?' Beth whispered, forcing the words out from between trembling lips.

Tears threatened to fall, but she dashed them from her eyes. She was fighting for her survival now and couldn't give in to the wave of emotion that threatened to drag her under the surface. She had to fight back.

'As you were so young at the time, and in those particular circumstances, I doubt that'll be the only reason they're looking at you,' Harris said thoughtfully. 'A bigger concern is that it gives you a motive. Darcie Baxter hinted to everyone there that she was going to expose a secret. The press are always fascinated by child killers. It could have made quite the juicy story.'

Beth groaned. 'I'm doomed, aren't I?' she said, slumping down further in her uncomfortable, black plastic seat.

'It makes you a person of interest, but they're going to need more than that to make it stick,' he said. 'And they know it. The only way they can obtain corroboration is if you inadvertently provide it. Don't do that. After confirming your name, date of birth and address, all further questions should be met with the same answer. "On the advice of my lawyer, I have no comment." Got it?' he said urgently, his eyes staring deeply into hers.

She nodded mutely, the feeling of déjà vu sending a puddle of acid into her mouth which she swallowed back down with a gulp.

'If you stick to what we agreed, they're going to have to release you in a few hours. Don't be goaded into digging your own grave. Stick to the plan.'

Beth jumped as the door opened forcefully and DS Logan Hunter entered. His presence filled the room and made Beth shrink into herself even further. DC Rhona Quinn followed in his wake and quietly closed the door behind them. The air seemed thinner with them in it and Beth could feel her breaths becoming faster and shallower. A sour smell caused her to wrinkle her nose until she identified the source. It was coming from her. The smell of fear. It took her straight back to the horror of that earlier interrogation when she was only thirteen. Then, too, a tall dark man had stuck his face aggressively in hers and demanded answers she did not have. She forced herself back into the room, the beep of the recording machine as regular as a metronome. DS Hunter was glaring at her across the cheap bolted-down table. He must have asked her a question. His colour was heightened and his lips compressed into a thin tight line.

'On the advice of my lawyer, I have no comment to make,' she stumbled, her voice sounding forced and unnatural.

It was harder than it looked in the movies to say nothing at all in her defence, especially when DS Hunter was doing his level best to goad her. She shot Harris a beseeching look. He sent her a warning glare back and slightly shook his head. Sighing, she dragged her attention back to the questions which were now striking her like bullets, piercing her to the core.

Suddenly, DS Hunter slammed both hands down on the table, palms down. Beth jumped at the sound.

'You do realise that if you fail to mention something on which you later want to rely in court, your silence now can be founded upon?'

He was just trying to scare her, thought Beth resentfully.

'I am well aware and have no comment,' she shot back at him, rattled nonetheless.

He sat back in his seat, clearly frustrated, and gestured to DC Quinn to take over the questioning. Her demeanour was more sympathetic and Beth welcomed the respite.

'Look, Beth, I appreciate how difficult all this must be for you,' she said, her voice low and musical unlike that of her boss which grated on her ears. 'You must have fought so hard to come back from what happened to you all those years ago when you were still a child?'

Beth nodded, tears springing to her eyes.

'Sorry, could you answer for the tape?' DC Quinn said gently.

'Yes,' she said.

Harris nudged her ankle with his foot, admonishing her to be on her guard. Beth was by nature polite to her core and found it even harder not to respond to these ever-so-gentle questions. She was desperate to unburden herself to a sympathetic ear, but now was most definitely not the time, she reminded herself.

'Oban was meant to be a fresh start, wasn't it?'

'Yes,' she said, still guarded. It surely wouldn't hurt to offer a little more information? 'After I was released from the secure unit, I never went back to school. My mother had multiple sclerosis. I became her carer until she died.' Another kick from Harris. She felt like kicking him back but refrained. This wasn't about Darcie and it felt good to talk. After all, it was her story to tell.

'That must have been tough,' said DC Quinn, her eyes encouraging. 'Yet you seem to have made a success of your life since moving here. I hear the bookshop is doing well and you've been positively welcomed into our community?'

'Yes,' said Beth, feeling suddenly emotional.

It was true. Her life since she moved to the Highlands had been beyond her wildest dreams. A home of her own, a modestly thriving business, even people she felt she could tentatively call friends for the first time.

'So, you were prepared to do *anything*,' said DC Quinn, her eyes hardening, 'even kill, to avoid Darcie Baxter, an investigative reporter, exposing your secret?'

'What? No!' cried Beth, realising all too late the trap that she had just walked into. She shot an anguished look at Harris, but it was too late. The damage had been done. She had all but confirmed to the police that she had a strong motive for wishing Darcie dead.

When she was eventually allowed to leave the police station, Beth and Harris went to her cottage rather than his office as she couldn't stand the thought of people staring at her. She was under no illusion that it would be all round Oban by now that she was a suspect in the case. As they walked into her cosy kitchen, she was touched to see that despite the events of the morning her team had cleared up before they left. Trying to regain control of her emotions, she took her time preparing the tea tray, finding comfort in the normal routine. Rummaging about in her tins she managed to find some homemade shortbread to go with it. Nonetheless, as she settled on one couch with the coffee table between them, her hand still shook as she lifted the teapot to pour. Harris put his hand over hers and quietly took it from her. He had the long slender fingers of a pianist or artist, she thought, unlike her own short stubby ones.

'I'm sorry, Harris,' she said, taking a sip of tea and scarcely daring to look at him. 'I know you said not to talk but it's harder than it sounds.'

He gave her a faint smile. He looked exhausted, she thought.

'Don't worry. They'll need more than that for the Procurator Fiscal to consider bringing the matter to trial. They nailed the good-cop-bad-cop routine in there. You're not the first to succumb to DC Quinn and you won't be the last.'

There was admiration in his voice, and she suddenly wondered whether it was purely professional.

She cleared her throat. 'Erm... so, what do we do now? Could I actually go to prison for this?'

His eyes slid away for a moment, which was answer enough.

'It won't come to that. I know that you didn't do it. I would stake my professional career on it.'

'You might have to,' she muttered despondently.

'As far as the police are concerned, they reckon they've established means, motive and opportunity. They may not be inclined to look very hard for other suspects. One weakness in their case is that the murder weapon hasn't been recovered yet.'

'I'll come clean with my staff tomorrow and tell them exactly what's been going on.'

'Are you sure that's wise?' he asked, looking worried.

'What choice do I have?' She shrugged. 'It's high time I owned my past rather than try to run from it.'

NINE

Beth turned the sign to 'Closed' at lunchtime. They'd been rushed off their feet all morning. The shop had been buzzing. Although they'd sold a whole load of books, she had the strongest feeling that most people had come in to gawp at both her and the murder scene. Her first task on entering this morning had been to scrub off the blood from the wooden floor with soap, disinfectant and water. She had felt sick to the stomach, but it still had to be done. No matter what Darcie had done or been about to do, she hadn't deserved to be murdered for it. Her staff for the most part had quietly gone about their work, seeming reluctant to engage her in conversation. Hardly surprising when the last time she'd seen them she'd been led off in handcuffs. Would they stand with her or turn against her now? It was time to find out. She'd scheduled a meeting for when the shop closed for lunch and brought sandwiches and cake in with her. As she made a pot of coffee and a pot of tea, she noticed they were all sitting around the table staring into space, their expressions giving nothing away. Oh well, here goes nothing, she thought. Placing the tea and coffee down in front of them she sat in her customary seat at the head of the table and cleared her throat, her insides twisting into knots.

'I'm sure you must all be wondering what yesterday was about...' she tentatively began.

'Just a bit,' said Morna drily.

'I'm sure there's a reasonable explanation,' said Lachlan.

Beth shot him a grateful glance before continuing. 'I was detained for questioning in relation to Darcie's murder. The reason they fixed on me is because twenty-one years ago, when I was thirteen, I killed someone.'

There was a collective intake of breath, and three pairs of eyes widened as they stared at her. Even though it was her lived experience, part of her still felt that the events from her past weren't quite real, as though the trauma that she had gone through at that time had caused a profound dissociation.

'What happened?' asked Lachlan quietly, a faint reserve in his eyes now.

'I was at school in Aberdeen. There was a girl there – her name was Jill Montieth, in case any of you want to google it,' she said, with a touch of rancour.

Chloe immediately picked up her phone then put it down again, flushing, as Lachlan gave her a nudge.

'Anyway, I was a shy little thing, a mouse not a lion. I don't know why she targeted me, but she was relentless, picking me apart, piece by piece like a vulture. Nobody dared to talk to me. I had one friend, my best friend, who I'd been close with since primary school. She tried to stick up for me, but they were so vile to her she couldn't withstand it and stopped talking to me as well. That hurt. A lot. The bullying was both physical and mental. I tried to tell a teacher but that only made it worse. My mum found out and went up to the school, but the headteacher was adamant there was no bullying in her school. Jill was vicious but she was pretty, popular, and could also be charming. They believed her version of events over mine. They maintained I was jealous or attention seeking. I cried every night... I more or less stopped eating. I suppose I was trying to disappear, to make myself as small as possible.'

She paused, lost in memories of the past.

'So how did you go from there to committing murder?' asked Morna, cutting to the chase, her expression giving nothing away of what she was thinking.

Jolted out of her reverie, Beth raised her eyes and looked at them all.

'They had me backed against a wall in the playground. There was no way past them. Jill whipped her phone out. "Pull her top up," she hissed. "Time everyone sees her for what she really is." As soon as a couple of them laid hands on me I charged towards Jill, desperate to get past her. I was on my way back from a tennis lesson. Instinctively I swung the racquet at her as she tried to block my way. All I wanted to do was get out of there and into the classroom where I would be safe. The wooden part of the racquet connected with her head.'

Her voice faltered. She could see it so clearly even after all these years.

'She fell backwards onto some concrete steps and banged her head. A pool of dark red blood spooled out beneath her. Her eyes were staring up at me, but they were completely empty. I froze and just stood there, staring down at her. She looked smaller than the monster that had lived in my head. Her friends crowded around her, trying to get her to wake up but she never did. I'd killed her,' she said, her voice flat, bleached of emotion. 'She suffered a catastrophic bleed on the brain.'

'But it was self-defence, wasn't it? said Chloe, her voice hesitant.

'Nobody believed me. The girls all said I'd just run up to her and swung the racquet out of nowhere because I was trying to get back at her for something. They were protecting her memory and their own skin. I felt so numb with horror at what I'd done, I barely put up a fight. Deep down, I felt I deserved whatever was coming to me. I still do. I pleaded guilty to culpable homicide and was sentenced to four years in a secure unit. When I got out, we moved down to Glasgow. My father had left us as soon as I was arrested.

So, my mum and I fled to another city and changed our names. The stress made my mother's MS worsen and she became more and more unwell. Anyway, the police obviously think once a killer always a killer. I need to find out who the real murderer is, or I have a horrible feeling that my life as I know it is over,' she said, exhaustion suddenly sweeping across her.

There was an awkward silence. Beth lifted her head and looked at each of them in turn. Their faces were guarded, giving nothing away. What had she expected? That they would all pledge undying loyalty and spring to her aid? That hadn't been her experience of life so far.

'Anyway,' she continued, 'if any of you feel uncomfortable working for me and want to leave, I will be happy to provide you with a glowing reference, which all of you have certainly earned. If you decide to stay, I must warn you that the press attention may become relentless once my personal circumstances come to light. I will give anyone who decides to leave a month's pay in lieu of notice. I'm going for my lunch now to give you a chance to discuss matters amongst yourselves.'

She rose from her seat, picked up her bag and walked out of the door, her chin lifted and her back ramrod straight. It was happening again. But this time she was going to fight. Not just for her, but for Darcie as well. She deserved to have her real killer brought to justice and made to pay for what they had done.

TEN

Beth wandered forlornly along George Street. As it was October, the number of tourists had dwindled. There was a definite chill in the air. When she'd made her grand exit, she hadn't had the forethought to bring her coat or grab a sandwich, so she slipped into The Chocolate Shop and headed for a table towards the rear where she sat with her back to everyone. She was definitely in need of some comfort food. A plate of waffles and a friendly greeting from the waitress soon made her feel a bit better and she felt her taut muscles relax ever so slightly. She was surely blowing everything out of proportion? They would need real evidence to convict her this time and, as she knew that she hadn't killed Darcie, she knew that couldn't possibly be forthcoming. Even though she hadn't been to university, her mother had always said she had a good brain. It was time to put it to use and show those police officers that they were looking at the wrong person. She would show them. All of them. She was no longer that frightened child. She was a resourceful woman with right on her side.

As she was leaving the café, her resolve flickered when she saw a group of women she recognised as customers from the shop, looking over at her whilst they muttered behind their hands.

'Good afternoon, ladies,' she said with a bright smile, as she sailed past them without waiting for a reply. Let them gossip for now. She was determined not to cave in, even if the whole town joined in.

As she opened the door to the bookshop, she didn't know what to expect. Would some of her staff have taken her up on her offer and simply left? Her heart in her mouth, she pushed open the door and saw them all still there, eating and drinking at the staffroom table as though it was just a normal day. Overcome with gratitude, her legs wobbled a little as she walked over to them.

'Thank you,' she said, a tide of emotion stopping her managing more in the moment.

'We've talked about it, and we all believe you,' said Chloe, forthright as ever.

'But we don't think anyone else will,' said Morna, somewhat raining on her parade.

'I'm afraid there's only one thing for it,' said Lachlan, looking up from a legal pad he'd been scribbling on. 'We need to carry out our own investigation and come up with other plausible suspects.'

'We've come up with a plan while you've been out, said Chloe, her eyes shining. 'I'm going to do a deep dive into the social media accounts of everyone who was at the book group that night. I'll find out who they were talking to and any posts that might flag up something they may not have wanted to get out. I'll look into any likes or comments that might be at odds with the image they project to the world.'

'I have a key to Darcie's apartment,' said Lachlan. 'I live in the same building and would water her plants when she was away. Now that the police have finished with it, we could have a nose around and see if we can find any clues they may have overlooked. I also have a fair bit of local knowledge to add into the mix.'

Morna cleared her throat. 'If we can get our hands on Darcie's phone and computer, I can hack into them and look for anything she was trying to hide. The same goes for our list of suspects. I'm fluent in a number of coding languages.'

'You... er... we have a list of suspects?' said Beth faintly, collapsing onto a seat at the table as her legs threatened to give way from under her.

'Yes,' Morna replied firmly. 'We've talked about it and come to the conclusion that it had to be someone there that night. If it was a stranger, how would they have known that Darcie wouldn't come out of the door with a few people and walk off in a group? If it was a stranger, why not just call round to her place on whatever pretext and kill her there? Even better, follow her down a dark close off the High Street at night.'

'I see what you mean,' said Beth. 'Darcie was hit over the head with an unidentified object. There was no finesse about it, which suggests it was unplanned and rushed. Whoever it was must have panicked when they heard Darcie banging on about exposing a big secret and lashed out at the end of the night in desperation.'

'So, find the secret, find the killer!' piped up Chloe.

'That gives us four suspects to concentrate on,' said Beth. 'Mike Carter, Ronnie Kerr, Harriet Brown and Dan Guthrie.'

'We need to speak to all of the witnesses to see if any of them remember seeing Darcie engaged in conversation with anyone outside the shop. It would have been easy to take her by surprise if they were chatting at the door then simply push her inside when the coast was clear,' said Morna.

'I see two different scenarios,' said Lachlan, scratching his chin thoughtfully. 'One is that she was knocked out by a blow to the head just outside the shop then dragged back inside. The other is that someone got her back inside on a pretext and then attacked her from behind.'

'The thing that really creeps me out,' said Chloe, 'is that whoever did it didn't just kill her in the heat of the moment and scarper. They took the time to position her body inside the crime scene tape. I mean, I myself will go to some length for a cool Insta shot, but most people would baulk at the idea of messing with a dying body for the aesthetic.'

'It would only occur to someone with a monstrous ego,' said Beth. 'Or...'

'A psychopath,' said Morna, her face expressionless.

Beth's heart thumped. 'Let's not get ahead of ourselves,' she said. 'The most likely scenario is that someone panicked and killed her as an act of self-preservation.'

The door handle rattled, making them all jump. It was time to reopen the shop. 'To be continued,' Beth said, jumping to her feet and running to the door, feeling buoyed up by the support of her team. For the first time, she was starting to think there might be a way out of this terrible mess.

ELEVEN

Later that night, the four of them met at Lachlan's flat. Beth looked around with interest as it was the first time she'd been in there. Lachlan was intensely private, and she still knew very little about him. Although he was a good listener and sounding board, he offered up barely anything about his personal life. His sitting room was overflowing with books, and a lot more comfortable and relaxed than she'd expected. She'd idly wondered if he would be the type to have one of everything on the draining board with everything functional and to the point. If she had to define his style she would go for retro. The couch was forest-green velvet and the coffee table was strewn with a range of well-thumbed periodicals ranging from science and nature to classical guitar.

'Do you play?' she asked, gesturing to a handsome wooden guitar propped up in a corner as she accepted a cup and saucer with a beautiful green leaf pattern on it.

'I do,' he replied, a little bashfully, which she found endearing.

Lachlan walked over to the mahogany and brass turntable and put on Ella Fitzgerald. Turning back to the room he looked alarmed.

'Chloe, what are you doing?'

Beth turned and noticed her youngest staff member snapping away on her phone.

'Just taking a few images for my Pinterest and Insta. You don't mind, do you? I promise there'll be nothing to identify you. It's just that I really love the vibe you've got going on here,' she prattled on.

'Er, vibe? I don't really see...' he foundered, turning beseeching eyes on the other two.

Morna rolled her eyes. 'Chloe, don't be such a moron. We don't just exist for your entertainment. Focus!'

'Fine!' Chloe hissed back at her, sitting down on the couch with a thump. She picked up a slice of cake and munched morosely.

Honestly, it's like dealing with a pair of kids, thought Beth, exasperated. Not that I'm ever likely to know, she added with a pang. Morna was right though. They had to focus on the job in hand.

After they'd finished their tea there was an electric silence. It was 8pm and pitch-black outside. Lachlan stood up and walked over to a dish on the mahogany dresser and pulled out a key.

'We're on the third floor here,' he said. 'Darcie's flat is the one on the left next to mine. I suggest Beth goes in first while Morna stands at the top of the stairwell to keep a lookout. There are two other doors on this floor, so, in case anyone exits from either of those, I will loiter on the landing ready to engage them in conversation until you are all safely inside. Then we'll reverse the process on the way out.'

Beth beamed at him. 'You've really thought about this, Lachlan. I feel we're in very safe hands.'

'Yes, well, let's get on with it then,' he said gruffly, walking to the door and slipping out. Beth had noticed that he found it difficult to accept compliments.

Trying to look casual, although her heart felt it was about to burst out of her chest, Beth waited a few seconds then followed him out of the door after first checking Lachlan and Morna were in position. Her hand was shaking so much the key rattled in the lock until her nerves were at screaming point, but she managed to get in and closed the door behind her. Soon, one by one, she was joined by the other three with Lachlan, as agreed, being the last to arrive. Chloe switched on the light before the others could stop her. Lachlan swiftly flicked the switch again.

'What?' snapped Chloe.

'The only person who has the right to be in here is dead,' said Morna, clearly struggling to hold on to her temper. 'If someone sees a light coming from in here, they'll most likely call the police thinking it's being burgled.'

'Oh,' said Chloe. 'Sorry, I didn't think.'

'Nothing new there,' muttered Morna under her breath.

'I'm sure it'll be fine,' soothed Beth, though she wasn't sure at all. Every nerve in her body was urging her to leave and never come back. 'We need to draw curtains and blinds then turn on a small lamp in each room before conducting our search.' She drew blue plastic gloves from her pocket and handed them out. 'It's important we don't leave any fingerprints behind,' she said, in the manner of one who broke into houses for a living.

Soon, Darcie's home was filled with soft light and they split up to systematically examine the various rooms. Beth was in the bathroom. She noticed there were two toothbrushes in the holder and was surprised the police hadn't removed them for DNA testing. Maybe they already knew who she'd been seeing? She opened the mirrored medicine cabinet and discovered a plethora of skin products promising the elixir of youth. There was no prescription medication, merely paracetamol and a multivitamin. There was also shaving cream and an expensive brand of aftershave. She headed back through to the lounge.

'I need to find her phone or laptop,' said Morna in frustration.

'The police will have them,' said Lachlan.

'Can't Harris get a look at them as your lawyer?' Morna asked, turning to Beth.

'I'm afraid not,' she answered. 'They only have to disclose

evidence if I'm actually charged. So far, I've only been detained for questioning.'

'Drat!' said Morna. After a moment, though, she brightened. 'If I could find her login details, I could maybe access her accounts remotely.'

'Her study's through there,' said Lachlan, indicating one of the two doors off the living room. Morna went off to look there and Beth followed her in. Darcie clearly didn't expect much in the way of visitors as her study was entirely given over to work without so much as a sofa bed in evidence. Her heart sank as there were piles of paper on every surface apart from a rectangular space on her desk which had clearly been occupied by her laptop. The police must have already been through all this, but Beth couldn't take the chance they had missed something as they seemed so focused on building a case against her.

The handbag that Darcie had been carrying the night that she was murdered had probably been seized by the police. It had been a distinctive red colour and by some big designer. She remembered Ronnie complimenting Darcie about it on the night. A woman like that must have more than one bag, Beth thought suddenly, maybe even more than one briefcase. Heading into the bedroom, she slid the doors to the large built-in wardrobe open. Unlike Darcie's workspace, this was meticulously organised. The clothes were colour coded and her shoes were stacked in clear plastic boxes. There were five other cardboard boxes of varying sizes. Each contained a soft bag enclosing an immaculate designer handbag. Beth knew some women treated such items with reverence, but she was more of a two-for-fifteen-pounds kind of person herself. The whole designer thing had never appealed to her. Why would you fork out vast amounts of money to a fancy designer to advertise their products for them free of charge? Barking mad in her humble opinion. The first four bags were completely empty and she nearly didn't bother looking in the fifth, which was wrapped in tissue paper. It was a handsome emerald-green satchel with the leather so soft and buttery it made you want to stroke it. As she opened it up, it, too, appeared empty. However, something about the weight felt a little off and she felt around inside until she discovered an invisible zipped pocket cleverly hidden under a flap in one of the compartments. Carefully, she extracted a slender mobile phone. It still had charge in it, but needless to say, it was password protected.

Suddenly, the doorbell rang, causing a jolt of fear. Beth raced through to the lounge where the others looked similarly terrified.

'Did someone lock the door?' she whispered anxiously.

They all shook their heads. Lachlan crept over to the lamp and turned it off. The two girls turned off the remaining lamps in the other rooms then ran back. Slowly, the doorhandle started to turn. Chloe pointed to the heavy velvet curtains and they all moved fast to conceal themselves as a shaft of light from the hallway spilled into the room. A large parcel was dropped inside the doorway by a delivery man clad in leathers with a helmet who took a photo on his phone. Then, to Beth's horror he glanced behind him and fully entered the flat, closing the door behind him. She heard a sharp intake of breath from Chloe who was beside her and gripped her arm. Beth peered round the edge of the curtain again. They had to wait and see how this played out. Was he going to steal something? Had he caught a glimpse of them after all? Two minutes later, they heard the toilet flushing and the delivery man reappeared and left as suddenly as he'd arrived.

'Ew! Gross!' Chloe sniffed. 'He didn't even wash his hands by the sound of it.'

'That's the least of our problems,' said Morna, with her signature eye roll.

'That's me done for the night,' said Lachlan, his voice sounding strained. 'I'm not cut out for all this cloak and dagger stuff.'

'I agree – we've done enough for one night,' said Beth, her legs turning to jelly as the reaction set in. 'Let's quit while we're ahead. We can discuss our findings at work tomorrow. You lot go ahead. I need to pop to the loo. I'll lock up and hand the key in to Lachlan on the way back.'

'You can use my loo,' said Lachlan. 'I'm only along the hall. I really don't think you should—'

But she couldn't wait. His words faded as Beth ran for the toilet. Fear had that effect on her. It was only as she was washing her hands that she noticed something was different. What was it? Suddenly, she had it. The second toothbrush had gone.

Everyone had left by the time she emerged. She walked over to where the parcel lay on the floor, expecting it to be from Amazon. Switching the overhead light on she scrutinised it carefully. It was wrapped in brown paper and had stamps on it but no sign it had ever been through a sorting office. Besides which, no postman she knew worked as late as this. It was the size of a shoebox. Tentatively, she lifted it up and gave it a gentle shake. It definitely had something in it. What to do? Hurriedly, she came to a decision. She locked the door and slowly peeled off the tape. Lifting away the brown tape she sighed in disappointment as a shoe box with a picture of some high strappy sandals emerged. She was just about to rewrap it when a peculiar smell made her remove the lid. Nestled amongst the tissue paper and sandals was a dead rat. Its throat had been cut. Stifling the scream that rose in her throat, she thought about what to do. The police needed to know about this, but she could hardly admit how she came by it. No, better to leave it where it was for now. Hurriedly, she reassembled the parcel and put it back where it was. She took out a clean white hankie and wiped the doorknob and key before using it to open the door and lock it. She had intended to pop into Lachlan on the way back, but couldn't face it in light of what she had seen. Hurriedly, she popped the key through his letterbox and ran lightly down the stairs. She needed to get back to her cottage and lock the world out to feel safe again.

TWELVE

At 9am the following morning, Beth entered the cool dark interior of Mortimer, Niven and Kincaid as a grandfather clock chimed, an echo from a bygone era. She arrived in reception slightly breathless from the stairs.

'Can I help you?' asked the slender older woman sitting behind a desk, starched to attention.

'Yes, I need to see Harris, er, Mr Kincaid, on an urgent matter.'

'And your name is?'

'Beth Cunningham.'

The older woman's eyes widened and her pen twitched out of her hand. Notorious already, Beth thought glumly. It was hopeless, she'd never get in without an appointment.

Miss Pringle, according to the name on her desk, bent her head to the appointment diary then smiled up at her.

'Mr Kincaid has appointments all morning, but I can squeeze you in if you don't mind waiting half an hour or so,' she said, with a warm smile. 'If you take a seat in the waiting room, I'll get Heather to bring you along a cup of tea?'

'That would be great, thanks,' Beth said, relieved. As she walked along the corridor she noticed oil portraits of stern, unsmiling men in legal gowns. It was strange to think that some or all of them were probably Harris's forebears. Taking a seat in a small room filled with uncomfortable hard-backed wooden chairs, she noticed how quiet it was. There was no background music or television screen, just the hushed unintelligible murmur of voices on serious business, punctuated by the sound of busy hands typing on keyboards when the door to what must be the secretaries' room opened. A tiny dark-haired girl who looked to be around seventeen brought her a cup and saucer on a tray with a piece of shortbread beside it. She thanked her and the girl scampered off, full of nervous energy. Eventually, after she'd seen her lawyer walk out two clients, dispatching them with a firm handshake and warm civility, it was her turn. It was strange hearing Harris in full professional mode.

'Beth! I wasn't expecting you in today. Has something happened?' He looked stressed and she felt guilty. He probably wished he'd never heard about her or her mother. He showed her into his large high-ceilinged room with huge picture windows overlooking the bay. A Calmac Ferry loomed large and receded as it set course for the island of Mull.

'I want to run a hypothetical scenario past you,' she began, as he gestured for her to take a seat opposite him with the leather desk between them.

'Oh no, what have you done?' he glared, his face tightening.

'Don't you know the meaning of the word hypothetical?' she snapped. 'I'm framing things this way so as not to put you in a difficult situation.'

'Fine,' he said, running a hand absentmindedly through his hair. 'Go on...'

'Well, if a person was suspected of committing a crime and felt the police weren't doing an adequate job, they might decide with the help of some friends to do their own investigating.'

'That would... hypothetically... be a very bad idea,' he sighed.

'Isn't everything I tell you covered by lawyer client privilege?' she asked, peering up at him from beneath her fringe.

'Well, yes, but it only goes so far,' he said. 'I can't allow you to perjure yourself in court.'

'I would NEVER!' she said, scandalised.

'Fine, now we've got that out of the way what did you want to see me about... specifically?' he asked, glancing at his watch.

'Two things. Don't ask me how I know, but Darcie was seeing someone at the time of her death. Has he been questioned in relation to her murder?'

'I don't think the police know that or he would have been questioned by now. What's his name?'

'I don't know. I've become aware that there were two toothbrushes in her bathroom. Then... er, she had a visitor who left a suspicious box.'

'What suspicious box?'

'Er, one that might have been delivered and might still be there should the police want to swing by again? It might contain a dead rat which had had its throat slit. Oh, and they may have missed a phone in an emerald-green designer bag in her wardrobe. Maybe there are clues in it. Can you indicate to the police they might want to search again without saying why?'

'Not really,' Harris groaned. 'They know that you're my client so it would be fairly obvious how I came to be in receipt of that information. However, I could request a visit to Darcie's home as part of my defence preparation at a later stage, if you are actually charged.'

'I don't think we can wait that long,' Beth said. 'I should also mention that by the time the delivery man left there was only one toothbrush left in the holder.'

'You were there at the time, weren't you? Wait! No, don't answer that,' he said, as she opened her mouth then closed it again. 'I don't know what the devil is going on. A murder of this sort is highly unusual in this part of the world. I can't help feeling you're putting yourself in danger if you keep trying to uncover what it's all about. Darcie Baxter was evidently investigating something deeply unsavoury. It could have been anything. Something like you have just described has all the hallmarks of organised crime.'

'Agreed, but what choice do I have?' she replied. 'Unless I find the real killer, I'm going to be imprisoned for something I didn't do, and Darcie's real killer will never pay for what they've done. Someone killed her to protect their secret. Who's to say they won't kill again to prevent it coming out?'

He sighed. 'I'm going to have to tell DS Hunter. There's no way I can keep this from him. Hopefully, he'll see the bigger picture rather than focus on your illegal visit to Darcie's home. Was it just you that was there?'

'Yes,' said Beth firmly. She didn't like to lie but there was no way she was going to drop the others in it as well.

'Who have you got helping you?'

'My staff are helping me gather information on our various suspects.'

'What can I do?' he asked. 'Bearing in mind I can't get involved to the extent that it would compromise my ability to defend you in court.'

Beth thought for a minute. 'Can you find out if any of the people who attended the book group that night has a criminal record?'

'That, I can do,' he said, making a note on his legal pad. 'It's a matter of public record. Refresh my memory as to their names and give me their addresses and dates of birth if you have them.'

Beth reached into her shoulder bag and passed across a list to him. 'I only have their current addresses and no dates of birth, I'm afraid. You work in the courts most days. Is there anyone on that list that rings a bell for any reason? It might not be a criminal case they've been involved in. Maybe a divorce or civil claim?'

He glanced at it. 'Nothing springs to mind but I'll have a nose around and see if I can turn anything up. The police are keeping their cards close to their chest on this one but in the absence of another credible suspect they're determined to construct a case against you, have no doubt of that.'

'You do believe me, don't you?' she said, staring at him anxiously.

'What I think really doesn't matter,' he replied. 'I'm your lawyer and I'm going to do my best to ensure you're acquitted of any charges they decide to bring.'

'That's not what I asked,' she muttered.

'It'll have to do for now,' he replied, his gaze softening. 'Don't worry, Beth. I have your back on this, I promise. One thing is clear though. The killer and the person who sent the parcel may not be one and the same person. Why send what is effectively a threat to someone you have already murdered?'

THIRTEEN

As Beth turned the sign on the door to 'Closed', she heaved a sigh of relief. It had been a trying morning, although the till was overflowing. Lachlan, Chloe and Morna looked as exhausted as she was, as each of them joined her round the table with their individual packed lunches. Toby startled them by jumping down from the top of a nearby bookcase in case there was anything tasty up for grabs. She let them eat in peace for a few minutes then cleared her throat.

'I went to see Harris and told him about our little foray into Darcie's flat last night. Don't worry, I said it was only me. No sense in dragging you lot into this mess.'

'I still feel slightly ill thinking about that,' said Chloe, looking queasy. 'It was well dodgy. Delivery men don't come in your door. He should either have left it outside or with a neighbour.'

'And the way he waltzed in and used her loo, too. What if she'd come home?' said Morna.

'Perhaps he knew she was already dead,' said Lachlan.

'Unlikely,' said Beth. 'Did any of you notice anything on his clothing to suggest he worked for a bona fide delivery company?'

'Well, no,' said Chloe. 'I was hiding behind the curtain with my eyes shut praying. I must've got through ten Hail Mary's by the time he left.'

'I didn't know that you were religious?' said Morna.

'I'm not,' said Chloe. 'But it was an emergency and I'm religious in emergencies.'

'Of course you are,' said Morna, managing a simultaneous head shake and eye roll.

'Anyway,' said Beth, interrupting before the girls started one of their interminable squabbles. 'There's stuff I haven't had the chance to tell you about. When I went to the loo, I saw that someone had removed the second toothbrush. I have to ask, was it any of you? I don't even need to know the reason,' she added awkwardly.

'Eww, gross.' Chloe squirmed. 'Not a chance.'

'Likewise,' said Morna. 'No one would do that unless it contained DNA evidence linking them to the victim.'

'Lachlan?' asked Beth.

'Do I even need to answer that?' he sniffed, looking uncomfortable.

'Of course not,' she said, leaning over and patting his hand. 'So, if it wasn't any of us, and it was there when we arrived, then it's possible our mystery delivery man removed it.'

'You didn't actually open the item delivered, did you?' said Lachlan, sounding worried. 'I don't want us to be tampering with evidence.'

'Yes, I did. Don't worry, I wrapped it up again really carefully.'

'The police will know,' Lachlan groaned, putting his head in his hands. 'I feel like I'm going to end up with an ulcer at this rate. I'll bet you didn't think to wear gloves either?'

Beth fidgeted, remembering that she hadn't replaced them after washing her hands in the bathroom.

'Anyway, back to what I was saying. At first, I thought it was just a regular delivery. It was a shoe box with a picture of some strappy high-heeled sandals.'

'Maybe whoever it was used a box they just had lying around,' said Chloe excitedly. 'That would point to it most likely being a woman.'

'Was there a receipt inside?' asked Morna. 'If so, maybe whoever it was could be tracked from that?'

'What was the size and style of sandal?' asked Chloe, ever the fashionista.

Beth slapped her head once more. 'I never thought to even look. I'm no good at this investigating malarkey,' she berated herself. 'Mind you, when I explain what was actually in the box, I doubt that you'll blame me.' Her eyes troubled, she looked at her staff, who were all leaning forward, poised for the big reveal. 'It was a pair of high strappy sandals but with the addition of a dead rat.'

'I suppose it could have got in there by accident?' offered Lachlan.

'No, I'm afraid not. It clearly didn't die of natural causes,' replied Beth.

This news was greeted with a stunned silence.

'It was maybe a warning to Darcie not to write the newspaper article,' said Morna.

'It was definitely a threat,' said Beth. 'A deliberate attempt at intimidation. Maybe the secret Darcie was going to expose had nothing to do with us. Maybe she was about to blow the lid on some organised crime boss or corrupt politician?'

'But that would mean,' Lachlan said, his voice cracked, 'that her life was snuffed out for no good reason at all. That makes it so much worse.'

Beth reached over and patted his hand. 'We'll get justice for her, Lachlan. Someone will be held to account for her death and suffer the consequences.'

She just hoped it wasn't going to be her.

FOURTEEN

This is a really terrible idea, thought Beth, as she took her seat at the crowded table. They'd all voted to have the scheduled meeting of the book group as it was the only way they could obtain credible access to the suspects. This time, though, her staff had joined in, ostensibly because they were crime fiction fans, but also to help her with providing nibbles and keeping the wine flowing. The seating was far from casual as they'd each been assigned people to try and develop a closer relationship with, which in turn should give them more of a chance to include them as a suspect or to strike them out from consideration. Lachlan was given the task of watching how they all interacted as a whole and to jump in if someone was struggling. Surprisingly, everyone they contacted had been eager to attend. Beth had thought they might run a mile, but seemingly what had happened to Darcie Baxter was all they really wanted to talk about. The book under discussion was the psychological thriller *Mirror Image* by Tessa MacPherson, which they'd selected at that last fateful meeting two weeks previously. They were all completely wired. Beth was feeling a little lightheaded from her second glass of wine.

'I'd like to propose a toast,' said Ronnie, startling everyone by jumping to her feet.

'To absent friends,' she announced, tearing up. 'Darcie, if you're looking down on us now, we want you to know that you're missed. It's not the same without you.'

'To absent friends,' murmured Harriet Brown and Dan Guthrie, rising awkwardly to join her.

Mike Carter, the English teacher, remained seated and rolled his eyes.

'You hardly knew her,' he snapped. 'All this fake emoting is pathetic. What's next? Going to get the Ouija board out?'

'You're all heart,' muttered Ronnie, sitting down and glaring at him.

'At least I don't allow myself to be led around by my feelings like a bull with a ring in its nose,' he said, staring the beautician down.

Beth could feel the air crackling with hostility. Her staff looked at a loss. Chloe, in particular, was white as a sheet. This had been a terrible idea. She jumped in to try and regain control.

'Thank you, Ronnie. That was a lovely gesture and one that I'm sure Darcie would have greatly appreciated. We've gathered here tonight to discuss *Mirror Image* by new writer Tessa MacPherson. What are your initial thoughts? Let's move round the table starting with you, Dan, as our resident author,' she said lightly, startled to see a look of utter malevolence flit across Mike's face as he looked at the younger man.

'Well, if I'm honest, I thought it was a bit derivative,' Dan said. 'I managed to finish it but there was nothing new explored in it that could differentiate it from others of a similar ilk. The characters were unlikeable which is often the case in this genre, but that made it harder to care about the outcome. The plot was dull, and I guessed the "twist"' – he waggled his fingers – 'fairly early on.'

Chloe, who was next to Dan, opened her mouth to speak, but Mike rudely talked across her.

'Oh, come on, Dan. You've been a writer for all of five minutes and you think that gives you the right to dismiss all psychological crime fiction in favour of your own woke nonsense?'

'That's not what I actually said.' Dan glared. 'In any event, I can't imagine how you know my novel is "woke nonsense" since you haven't even read it.' He turned to the others. 'In the last week, I've had a bit of a pile on of vicious one-star reviews online and my book's not even out yet.'

'Don't worry, I'm sure the negative nellies will soon be drowned out by the flood of positive ones after the public get their hands on it,' said Chloe, patting his arm reassuringly.

'The thing is, my publisher thinks it's one individual that has set up a ton of accounts to try and sink my book before it's even off the starting block.'

'Disgusting troll,' said Morna. 'I can take a look if you like? I'm quite handy on the tech front.'

'Would you? I'd be really grateful. At the moment it's all I can think about.' He had the grace to look sheepish. 'Well, that and what happened to poor Darcie, of course. I hadn't expected this publishing malarkey to be such an emotional rollercoaster.'

'This is meant to be a book club, not Oprah,' sighed Mike. 'Can we move on, please?'

'Of course,' said Beth brightly. 'Where were we up to? Chloe?'

'Well, I absolutely loved it! I think the whole mirror play gave it a bit of an edge which I'd never seen done in a psychological thriller before. It really creeped me out. I couldn't decide if the main character was losing her mind or if someone was messing with her. The twist, I thought, was brilliant and I definitely didn't see it coming. I loathed the husband from the get-go. Talk about mansplaining,' she said, with a pointed look at Mike. 'I was blown away when I discovered that the wife was manipulating him and not the other way round.'

Harriet jumped in. 'I have to say it was a bit overblown for me. I'm more inclined to crime novels that present a puzzle for me to solve. All this rummaging about inside people's heads made me feel quite queasy. It was too messy by far for my taste. You couldn't trust anyone, which made for quite an unsettling reading experience.'

'Couldn't have said it better myself,' said Mike, nodding in agreement.

'High praise, indeed!' murmured Dan, shooting Mike a hostile look.

'I enjoyed it as well,' said Ronnie. 'It was like being inside a nightmare. All those ferocious mind games. And as for the mirror scenes? Those literally gave me nightmares. I had to immediately start a different type of book to take the taste away, if you know what I mean.' She shuddered. 'I liked that both characters got their comeuppance, but not in the way that I expected.'

The discussion raged back and forth as the wine flowed. Beth rushed around delivering more nibbles and was surprised to see that it was already after nine. It felt good to have had such a positive meeting after what had happened the last time. A sudden thought stopped her in her tracks: the night wasn't over yet. Darcie hadn't come to harm until *after* the meeting had ended. She could feel panic flare and reminded herself to breathe and act normally. She certainly wasn't going to reprise her role in the kitchen until she was satisfied that the remaining book club members had left the premises and were safely on their way.

'Dan and I are going for a drink in Aulay's Bar, if anyone else wants to come?' Morna said, going a little pink and glaring at Chloe, to her amusement.

'Sorry, I have other fish to fry,' said Mike.

'A hot date?' asked Chloe, who always went where others feared to tread.

'That would be telling.' Mike smirked. 'Would any of you ladies like me to escort you home? After all, the killer is still at large. You can't be too careful.'

Or we could be looking at him, thought Beth, trying to suppress a shudder.

'Did any of you know Darcie before you met her at book group?' she asked casually.

'I knew her,' said Dan, putting on his leather jacket and wrapping a trendy scarf round his neck. 'She reviewed my book and had done a feature on me for publication day. We'd been out for dinner a couple of times.'

'Let's get out of here,' muttered Morna in his ear. He grinned at her and Chloe danced forward to open the door for them.

'Don't do anything I wouldn't do!' she called after them. Grinning, she locked the door again.

'You really must stop baiting poor Morna like that,' scolded Beth.

'But it's such fun!' Chloe beseeched her, causing Beth to hide a smile beneath a yawn.

Beth was nonetheless a little concerned about Morna waltzing off with Dan. As far as she was concerned, he was still a suspect. Although she consoled herself with the thought that after being seen so publicly with Morna, harming her would be the last thing he would want to do. At the end of the day, she was a grown woman and, as such, her choices must be her own.

The remaining people drifted through, chatting animatedly.

'The offer still stands,' said Mike, pulling on a threadbare tweed jacket. His eyes flicked round the remaining women in turn, but none would meet his gaze, murmuring quiet excuses.

'No one's actually scared of *me*, are they?' he asked, incredulously.

'No! Of course not!' Beth exclaimed, adding *they just don't like you* in her own head. 'Your kind offer is very much appreciated, but I need Chloe and Lachlan to stay behind to discuss the rota for next week.'

Harriet stepped forward as peacemaker. 'Well, I'm sure Ronnie and I would be grateful for the company. Thank you for offering.'

Ronnie didn't look convinced but quickly shrugged on her red trench coat and forced a smile.

Beth let them out, locked the door behind them and froze, waiting for a scream, something to suggest that all was not well.

Such a sound didn't come and the voices of her customers gradually receded along the High Street. She noticed Lachlan and Chloe relaxing their shoulders at the same time. 'I'll stick the kettle on,' she said, walking through to the kitchen.

FIFTEEN

Ten minutes later, with a hot cuppa and the last fairy cake sitting on her plate, Beth felt a wave of fatigue settle her further down in her seat.

'Well, what do we think?' she asked Lachlan and Chloe, who looked as drained as she was.

'I've just remembered... you do know that Mike is a frustrated writer, don't you?' asked Lachlan. 'I think that he's beside himself with jealousy that Dan is being touted as the next best thing with the backing of a top agent and publisher whilst he himself has got a drawer of unpublished short stories and poems.'

'Do you know that for sure?' asked Beth.

'Well, yes, I do. We used to be in a writing group together,' he mumbled.

'A writing group!' exclaimed Chloe. 'You clearly have hidden depths, Lachlan.'

'It was a long time ago, fifteen years or so. Put it down to youthful pretensions.' He grimaced.

'So, Mike would be about the same age that Dan is now?' pondered Beth. 'No wonder he's so bent out of shape about the boy wonder.'

'I can understand his point of view,' said Lachlan. 'When you get to our age, doors slam behind you but not many open. It can be hard to accept the slow decline of middle age.'

Beth wondered whether this rather bleak world view was brought about by the indignity of now having her as his boss. Maybe she hadn't done him a kindness as she had thought.

'Don't worry,' he said with a warm smile, perceptive as ever. 'I'm perfectly content with my lot.'

'We'd be lost without you, wouldn't we, Chloe?' Beth said.

Chloe nodded in agreement. 'One hundred per cent!' She frowned and turned to them both. 'Do you think that Mike could be the one who's been sabotaging Dan's books with the one-star reviews?'

'Very possibly,' said Lachlan. 'If Morna can dig around and prove it, we could ask him quietly to remove them if he didn't want us to tell Dan.'

'It still doesn't give him a motive to kill Darcie though, even if she'd got wind of it,' mused Beth. 'It's hardly front-page material given that Mike's a complete unknown. It would be different if he was a bestselling author himself. It's happened before and to far more famous people. Nobody would bat an eyelid now.'

'It's still a sordid little secret though, when you think about it,' said Chloe. 'Maybe he has other sordid little secrets that would destroy his life if they came out?'

'You said you had him for English at school, Chloe,' said Lachlan. 'No gossip? Rumours of inappropriate behaviour?'

'No, nothing as far as I'm aware. He was dry as a bone. Though, to be fair, he did get most of us through our Higher English. If there'd been something going on like that, I'd have heard about it for sure. I was plugged into the grapevine.'

'What about Harriet Brown, the headteacher?' asked Beth.

'She's a bit of a strange one,' said Lachlan. 'Her husband passed away ten years ago. He was wealthy, but rumour had it he was tight with money. Despite being a headteacher, she never dressed or conducted herself in the manner you'd expect. It was odd.'

'Maybe she just wasn't materialistic,' offered Chloe. 'But now you mention it, I do remember something. Believe it or not, I was a good girl at school so I didn't come across her much. But there was a bit of gossip about a purple velvet coat. One of the other teachers had put a fancy coat into a charity shop as she'd lost hope of fitting back into it. A week later the head rocks up to school wearing that exact same coat. No one dared say anything. But everyone thought it was a bit odd that someone in her position and on her salary would need to get her winter coat out of a charity shop.'

'Maybe she was just being eco-friendly?' offered Beth.

'After her husband died, Harriet inherited a ton of money and Ronnie says she's now never out of the beauty salon. She's the most pampered woman in Oban with gorgeous clothes, so I don't think that was it,' said Chloe.

'I remember her husband was found outside a pub at closing time with a head wound,' said Lachlan. 'It was no secret that he liked a drink, so it was assumed that he'd had a fall and cracked his skull open.'

'You don't think that she *killed* him, do you?' asked Chloe in horror. 'Darcie was killed with a blow to the head as well. Maybe she'd found something out and was going to expose Harriet. Goodbye couture, hello orange jumpsuit?'

'The orange jumpsuit is American jails,' said Lachlan, a fount of knowledge on most things. 'Think washed-out grey trackies in Scotland.'

Beth's head had begun to throb. She couldn't think straight but she knew she had to proceed carefully. 'Look, everyone, I really appreciate all the help tonight. I couldn't have done it without you. That said... airing all our wild theories in here between ourselves is one thing but nothing must leave these four walls. Is that understood?'

Lachlan and Chloe nodded seriously. Beth noticed Chloe stifling a yawn. 'Get away home, the pair of you,' she said. 'Lachlan, can you walk Chloe back to set my mind at ease?'

'Of course,' he said. 'But what about you?'

'I can always get a taxi,' she said to reassure him, though she had no intention of doing so. It was an extravagance she couldn't really afford, and she didn't want to get into the habit. 'I've some bits and bobs I need to finish up and then I'll get off. Text me when you're both back.'

She secured the door, then collapsed onto a comfy leather armchair in a corner of the shop. The old building settled around her with a few creaks from the wooden floorboards and gurgles from the ancient pipes. They weren't all that much further forward, but she had faith that with the combined talents of her team they would get there. She just hoped that it was in time. Wearily, she forced herself to her feet and started tidying up. She was almost finished when she was startled by a loud bang on the window. Had one of them forgotten something? She flew to the door and drew back the bolt but kept the chain on as she peered out into the darkness. The smell of the sea drifted up from the harbour, borne on the mist. A fine drizzle moistened the air. It was pitch black outside and no one seemed to be there. She opened the door wider. There was nothing there. The distant sound of laughter and Scottish music drifted towards her.

Probably just kids, she rationalised, moving to close the door. A flash of white caught her eye. It was a piece of paper attached to a small boulder with an elastic band. Someone had tried to put her window in, but it was safety glass so they'd been unsuccessful. Trembling with fear, she looked all around her then picked it up and retreated back inside. With shaking hands, she removed the band and opened out the white piece of paper.

In crude capitals were the words inked in red:

THIS ONE'S GOT YOUR NAME ON IT, NOSEY PARKER

She turned the rock over in her hand. It did indeed have her name on it. Her old name, from before she'd changed it...

Feeling dizzy, she hurriedly called a taxi. There was no way she was walking home now. To heck with the expense. Before the taxi arrived, she dug out a plastic bag from the kitchen drawer and dropped the items in it. She then opened up the safe and placed the bag inside.

Another thump on the door had her squealing in terror.

'Taxi for Beth Cunningham?' a cheery voice shouted. Weak with relief, she opened the door and locked it behind her.

SIXTEEN

The next morning, Beth was waiting anxiously at the top of the steps up from the High Street when the lofty wooden door swung back on its hinges. Miss Pringle let out a small cry but recovered her composure quickly.

'Miss Cunningham,' she said, twisting her thin lips into something approaching a smile. 'I don't believe you have an appointment?'

'No, I'm sorry but it's really important I see Mr Kincaid. You see, something happened last night that I urgently need his advice on.'

Miss Pringle sighed. 'Very well, his first appointment has rung to cancel so you'd best come in and I'll speak to him. But please don't make a habit of it. We can't just have people turning up willy-nilly. The whole system will collapse.'

'I won't, I promise,' she said, with what she hoped was a winning smile. As she followed Miss Pringle's stiff back up the stairs, she wondered if her life would ever return to normal or if she was going to end up with a one-way ticket back to prison.

She was shown straight into Harris's room. Today the harbour beyond his massive windows was shrouded in mist, hiding the outlying islands from view. Although it was now after nine, the dark clouds and swirling fog outside made the office seem gloomy with an air of melancholy. Once she was seated, Harris switched on the light and the shadows were instantly dispelled.

With her usual relentless efficiency, Miss Pringle arrived with a tray of tea and biscuits.

'Thank you, Miss Pringle, I really don't know what I'd do without you,' Harris smiled.

'Och, away with you, Harris,' the older woman smiled, looking as though she was tempted to give him a cuff around the ear. She closed the door quietly behind her.

'She started here straight out of school as the office junior,' he confided. 'By the time she was in her early twenties, she was my grandad's personal secretary. So, I inherited her along with the rest of the place.' He glanced around him ruefully.

'Did you always want to work here?' she asked.

'Heavens, no! I had grand notions of forging my own path with an Edinburgh firm, but I could see my dad was struggling. He was too proud to ask for help, so I moved back anyway. Having been away for a while I could see the attraction of a slower pace of life and a room with a view.' He laughed, gesturing at the window behind him. 'I'm assuming this isn't a social call?' he said, picking up a pen and leaning forward.

'No,' she said, tears prickling, as she remembered the stark terror she had felt last night. She dug around in her large shoulder bag and extracted the plastic bag containing the rock. Carefully, she pushed it across the table towards him and he examined it carefully without removing it from the plastic.

'What's the story?' he asked, looking worried.

'Well, we had another meeting of the book club last night,' she confessed.

'Do you think that was wise?'

'Not particularly wise, but necessary if I'm to identify the real murderer. Anyway, everything had gone well and the rest of them had gone off in pairs with the door locked behind them. Half an hour later, there was a loud bang on the window. When I opened the door there was no one there but I found the note attached to that stone. Whoever it was is trying to warn me off. They must have got wind of the fact I'm investigating the murder.'

'You mentioned that everyone who attended left in pairs,' said Harris. 'Either none of them are involved or someone managed to double back on themselves after walking away.'

'But what do I do about *this*?' she asked, pointing to the plastic bag. 'My first instinct was to take it to the police to prove to them that there's someone else out there doing this, who is likely responsible for murdering poor Darcie. But, on the other hand, I also don't want to stir it all up again. I know that Sergeant Hunter is hell-bent on building a case against me. He might think I've made the whole thing up to deflect attention away from me. What do you think I should do?'

Harris sighed. 'I do see your dilemma, but I don't think you've got a choice, really. There could be fingerprints on it that might lead to the killer. Equally, the writing and the ink could all proffer clues. Did you pick it up with gloves on when you first found it?'

'I should've done,' she admitted. 'But to be honest I was in too much of a flap to even think about it at the time.'

'Which means that if the killer took precautions and wore gloves themselves, then yours might be the only fingerprints on it.'

'It's a chance I'll have to take,' she said, her mind made up.

'Would you like me to come with you?' he asked. 'In case you run into any bother with the good detective sergeant?'

'No, it's fine. I'll call you if they try and hang on to me though. Sorry to barge in this morning.'

'Be careful,' he warned. 'The killer clearly sees you as an obstacle to getting away with murder. I don't want you walking anywhere on your own, least of all late at night. You have my number. If you're worried at all then don't hesitate to phone me, day or night.'

'Do you give all of your clients this gold star service?' she teased.

'That would be telling,' he said, tapping the side of his nose.

SEVENTEEN

Heading into the police station, Beth experienced a strong sense of foreboding. When she'd been released from the secure unit, she'd vowed to never darken the door of a police station again. Now she had been dragged into a huge mess which, this time, was not of her own making.

As she approached the counter in reception, she hoped against hope that DS Hunter was not working today. The lanky young constable greeted her with a cautious smile.

'I'd like to report a crime,' she said. 'At least, I think it's a crime. It's most likely related to a murder case you're working on. One in which I'm apparently the chief suspect.' She burbled on, so nervous she was unable to stop herself.

'Er, name?' he said, looking startled, as well he might.

'Beth Cunningham,' she said. 'Someone left this for me last night.' She heaved the boulder out and placed it on his desk with a thump.

His eyebrows shot up once more. 'If you'd like to take a seat, I'll see who's available,' he said, disappearing from view so that he could tell the person on the other end of the phone that a looney tune had arrived in the station. Not DS Hunter, not DS Hunter, she prayed, her fingers crossed fervently. She heard footsteps. A pair of shiny black shoes presented themselves in front of her downcast eyes.

'Not DS Hunter, what?' he said, staring down at her with his customary frown.

Oh no! She must have said it aloud. 'Er, nothing. I came to hand this in.' She held up the bag. 'I went to see Harris Kincaid this morning,' she added, as though invoking his name would have a magical effect on the surly officer. It didn't.

'Right,' he said, looking bored. 'Come this way, Miss Cunningham.' She stood up, her shaking legs causing her dress to flutter as she followed him. As soon as he had keyed in a code and she was through the security door, she immediately felt trapped as it clanged behind her. He showed her into a small interview room that smelled of the obligatory disinfectant and smelly feet. There was no DC Quinn this time. He examined the boulder and its paper wrapping silently whilst it was still in the bag.

'Mind if I hang onto this?' he asked.

'No, of course not,' she snapped. 'I wasn't planning on placing it on my mantelpiece.'

'Tell me how this came to be in your possession?' he asked, turning his dark eyes her way.

'Well, we had another book group meeting at the shop with the... er... remaining participants and three of my staff members. It all passed off without incident. The meeting ended at 9pm. I made sure that everyone was paired off as they were leaving, so that no one was walking home alone, just in case.'

'Who were you paired with?' he asked.

'Er... no one. I had the clearing up to do. I'd locked the door behind the last people to leave and then got on with the washing up. About twenty minutes to half an hour later, I heard a loud bang. Obviously, I was careful. I attached the chain before opening the door but there was no one there. I was about to close it again when I noticed the boulder.'

'Did you handle it without gloves?' he asked.

'Of course I did. I didn't see the message till I looked at it properly so I'd no idea it might need preserving. As soon as I realised it was a threat, I popped it into a bag from my kitchen drawer.'

'I see,' he said, implying by his tone of voice that he'd taken everything she'd said with a large dose of salt. The man was impossible!

'It had my former name on it,' she said. 'The only people up here who know about that are my staff, Harris Kincaid and yourselves. For obvious reasons I tend to keep my former identity hidden.'

Sergeant Hunter looked exasperated. 'So, basically the whole town probably knows by now. People talk to each other up here. Was there anyone at the book group that night who wasn't at the original meeting?' he asked.

'Only my three members of staff. Here are their names and addresses,' she said, tearing a page out of her notebook, having anticipated he might want to talk to them.

'Please tell me you're not trying to conduct some half-arsed investigation into Darcie Baxter's death?' he said, clearly hanging on to his temper by a thread.

'I'm not going to sit idly by whilst you build a case against me for a crime I didn't commit, based on something I did when I was barely into my teens,' she almost shouted.

'You could end up being charged with attempting to pervert the course of justice if you hinder this investigation in any way,' he snapped back at her.

'My second threat in twenty-four hours,' she said with a hollow laugh.

He leaned right across the desk and glared at her. 'It's not a threat, it's a promise,' he glowered. 'I can assure you that we're following any and all lines of inquiry into the murder, so perhaps you're the one making lazy assumptions?'

She was surprised into feeling guilty. Did she have him all wrong? Time would tell.

'Am I free to go now?' she asked.

'I'll show you out,' he said, rising to his feet. 'And, please, leave the investigating to us. You're only going to place yourself, and possibly others, in danger.'

The unspoken words *'unless it was you all along'* dangled between them unsaid.

EIGHTEEN

It was nearly eleven by the time Beth arrived at the shop. She paused outside as she often did to take in the sage-green and cream painted exterior with its cheerful hanging baskets and cheeky haggis, but it was the gold painted letters above that always gave her a frisson of pride. "The Wild Haggis Bookshop", then in smaller letters to the right: "proprietor Beth Cunningham". But for how long? she wondered, swallowing a sudden lump in her throat as she pushed the door open and stepped inside.

The smell of freshly baked scones made her mouth water. Fortunately, one of the staff had got them out of the fridge and stuck them in the oven for her. They greeted her cheerfully. Toby came running over, miaowing loudly as if to tell her off for arriving late. Smiling, she crouched down and scratched his ears, triggering some loud purring. She wondered whether to tell them all about the latest development, not wanting to dampen the mood, but figured she'd better as the police might follow it up. It would look odd if she hadn't mentioned it. But first, she needed to check that their journeys home had been uneventful.

'Did you learn anything from Dan in the pub last night?' she asked Morna. Her normally taciturn assistant flushed bright red and ducked her head beneath her long fringe before answering, much to Chloe's amusement.

'I talked to him about Darcie and asked if she'd been seeing anyone before her death. He said she'd hinted at an ongoing relationship but didn't let on who it was.'

'Somebody local?'

'Impossible to say.' Morna shrugged. 'He said some people thought she and him were an item, but they just got along well. She used to refer to him as her toyboy to wind him up. If there was a relationship with someone else, he suspected that it was a clandestine one, maybe because they were married?'

'I take it he walked you home afterwards?' asked Beth.

'Yes, he insisted on it,' she said, with a small smile.

'And did you invite him in for coffee?' asked the irrepressible Chloe.

'None of your beeswax.' Morna scowled. 'Now is this interrogation over so I can get back to work?' She stormed off to her section.

'Oops, might have hit a nerve there,' said Chloe, mischievously.

Beth shook her head at her. She hoped that Morna knew what she was doing. 'I had thought that you and Morna would get along, given that you're relatively close in age and both grew up here.'

Chloe looked incredulous. 'We're nothing alike. Morna was born with a silver spoon in her mouth and had every opportunity thrown her way. She didn't exactly "grow up here" either. Her parents have this massive estate in Argyll and sent her to some posh boarding school down south. She only came to Oban High School for the last two years.'

'Then why is she living in a one-bedroom flat in George Street?' said Beth quietly.

Chloe shrugged. 'Who knows? But one thing I do know is that it's *her* choice. Maybe she's just a masochist?' With that, she tossed her hair and moved behind the counter ready for the customers approaching with books to buy.

Beth was troubled. Unlike Chloe, she suspected that Morna

was struggling with something too big to articulate. She worried that being embroiled in what had happened to Darcie Baxter might be even more detrimental to Morna's wellbeing. And now she seemed to be seeing Dan, who could be completely innocent or might be guilty of a heinous crime. She would have to monitor the situation. Maybe DS Hunter was right, and she should leave the investigating to the police? The trouble was that she couldn't trust him to be both diligent and impartial. Harris clearly didn't like him either. Whether that stemmed from personal or professional reasons Beth had no way of knowing.

All morning there was a steady stream of customers. At one point the store was swamped with tourists with time to kill before getting the ferry, who were hoovering up guidebooks. She'd also stocked a number of tote bags with Scottish expressions on them which were flying off the shelves. Morna had rather taken exception to them on the grounds that it was commodifying their language, but Chloe had muttered disparagingly in Beth's ear, 'I don't know what she's banging on about. She doesn't even *sound* Scottish.'

Perhaps that was part of the problem? thought Beth. Maybe the poor girl felt alienated from her culture and her peers after being sent away at such a young age?

Chloe, on the other hand, clearly came from a lovely home. Her mother was a nurse and her father a postman. They'd popped in a few times to buy stuff since the shop had opened and their pride and joy in their daughter was unmistakeable. Chloe was rich in so many ways, but didn't yet have the wisdom to understand that fully.

After the tourist rush was over and the shop put back to rights, Beth wandered through to the back office where Lachlan was catching up on some admin relating to their suppliers.

She closed the door behind her and sat down in a comfortable armchair in front of the weathered old table he was working at. He looked at her, his eyes wary. That wariness told her all that she needed to know.

'Lachlan,' she began gently. 'Were you and Darcie a bit more than friends?'

His face flooded with colour as he sat back in his chair and sighed. 'What gave me away?' he said.

'The toothbrush. It was you who removed it, wasn't it?'

'Yes, I was worried the police might test it for DNA and jump to the wrong conclusion. I didn't have anything to do with her death. I loved that woman.'

'Why did you keep your relationship a secret then?'

'My wife is still alive. I didn't want to disrespect her by people finding out about us.'

Beth gawped at him. She would never have had him pegged for a cheater. Not in a million years. *Wait a minute, I've been to his place. There was no sign of a woman's presence there. It was all very muted and masculine. So where was his wife?*

'Are you separated, then?' she asked.

'You could say that. Separated by the cruellest disease. She's in a specialist facility down in Glasgow. I visit her once a fortnight, but she has no clue who I am. It's getting harder and harder to witness her decline. The reality is that I lost the very essence of her years ago. All that's left is an empty shell and even that is inexorably shutting down. Soon, it'll be as if she never existed at all.'

He dashed his hand across his eyes, his raw suffering revealed to her. Appalled, Beth wanted to turn away but of course she sat with him until he regained control of himself.

'I understand,' she said simply.

'I couldn't have it getting out about Darcie. It wouldn't have been right.'

'I'm so sorry, Lachlan. You've been grieving for Darcie on top of everything else. Would you like some time off? You can take as long as you like. We'll manage without you.'

'That's very kind,' he said with a forced smile. 'But honestly, I'm best off keeping busy. And I want to help catch the bastard who did this.'

She patted his hand across the table and left him in peace. The things she had learned about two members of her team today had shocked her. How could she not have realised they were struggling so much? If anything, it had only strengthened her resolve to bring the killer to justice so that Lachlan could at least gain some closure after losing someone he cared about in such a horrible manner.

NINETEEN

As Beth walked home, it was already dark. Despite her warm winter coat and fur-lined boots, the wind cut right through her. The trees huddled against the wind, fighting a losing battle to hold on to their remaining leaves. She could feel the frost crisping the leaves underfoot as she opened the small wooden gate and rushed up the path to her front door. As soon as she stepped inside, she heard the bang of the cat flap from the back door and Toby rushed forward to wind himself round her legs purring, his plump sides going in and out like a bellows. He'd disappeared from the shop sometime after lunch. She headed for the kitchen, trying not to trip as he seemed intent on doing some May dance in and out of her legs, as he insisted that she focus on the serious matter of delivering his dinner.

She'd just finished starting a fire in the wood burner when she heard the doorbell ring. Opening a curtain, she peered out and saw that it was Harris. She bid him enter and a draught of ice-cold wind swept in alongside him.

'Harris! What are you doing here? Not that it's not lovely to see you,' she added hastily. It was the first time he'd been to the cottage since she took ownership, and he cast an appreciative eye over what she'd done with it.

'A big change from before,' he said, having only the previous sales particulars to go on.

'For better or for worse?' she asked, watching him carefully.

'Oh, definitely for the better.' He grinned. 'You've got quite the flair for interior design.'

'I wouldn't go that far.' Beth laughed, then asked, 'Is this a business or a social call? Can I tempt you to join me for some supper? I have a homemade lasagna heating up in the oven.'

'That would be wonderful, if you're sure that I'm not putting you out?'

'Not at all. Sit,' she said, pulling out a chair at her antique pine table. A hand-painted jug filled with wild roses and ferns that she'd picked up from the local flower shop sat in the middle. She poured them both a glass of red wine and got the lasagna out of the oven, quickly slicing off two hefty wedges and throwing together a quick salad. Haris took a mouthful of the fragrant dish and his eyes lit up.

'This is divine,' he said.

'I thought everyone could throw together a lasagna?' She laughed.

'Only the ones in a plastic dish that go in the microwave.' He grimaced, taking a sip of wine before returning to his plate with pleasure. 'No comparison at all.'

'How come you never learned to cook?' she asked, curious now.

'Probably because I was sent away to boarding school at the age of seven and wasn't released until I was eighteen.'

'You make it sound like a kind of prison,' she said, saddened by the sudden bleakness that had commandeered his expression.

'It was a prison in everything but name,' he said. 'It was so regimented that there was absolutely no autonomy. Those who were sporty did all right but the bookish sorts like me hated it, forced out in all weathers to run around muddy fields. Even the holidays were strange. Your parents had this whole life that didn't involve you. It felt like you were a bit of an inconvenience interrupting that. All the local kids hung out in the summer – barbecues on the beach, camping out and stuff – but I didn't know them, and they weren't about to let a weird posh kid into their merry gang. It was lonely. It's still lonely. I find it hard to trust people even after all this time.'

'I'm not surprised,' she said. 'I was like that for a long time due to being bullied at school. Some of the kids who went along with it used to be my friends further down the school. When I was sentenced to secure accommodation, I was terrified that it would be even worse, but this older girl took me under her wing when she found out I'd been bullied. She said I reminded her of her kid sister. No one messed with me because that meant she'd mess with them.'

'What was she in for?' asked Harris.

'Murder,' replied Beth. 'She'd killed her stepfather for hurting her sister. She had her issues, but deep down she was a good person. One bad act doesn't always have to define you.'

'Are you still in touch?'

'We managed it for a while, but then she turned eighteen and got transferred to Barlinnie Prison. I got out not long after that. By then Mum was a lot sicker and my time was taken up with caring for her. I can't describe how wonderful it felt to have a home again. Mum was always a great cook. As her illness took hold, she didn't have the energy for it anymore, so she did her best to pass on her culinary skills to me, probably in the spirit of self-preservation.' She smiled.

They ate in companionable silence until both plates were cleared, and Beth made them coffee and carried it through to the cosy living room on a tray. She was amazed at how comfortable she felt with Harris. Due to what had happened when she was younger and her caring responsibilities for her mum, she had never dated anyone. Her mum had urged her to go out in the evenings, or to book her in for respite care, but Beth had always refused. It had suited her to stay in night after night where it was safe and predictable. A small life was a safe life, and she never wanted to feel unsafe again.

Suddenly, she remembered that Harris must have come here for a reason.

'Sorry, you wanted to talk to me about something? I didn't give you a chance to tell me before force feeding you lasagna,' she said, a little embarrassed now.

'You hardly had to twist my arm.' He laughed. 'But yes, I did have some information for you. I did a public search at the sheriff court against all the people who were at the book group meeting the night Darcie was murdered.'

'And?'

'I'm afraid that they're all squeaky clean in terms of convictions.'

'Oh,' Beth said, deflated.

'However,' he went on, 'as you know, there are very few legal firms in Oban. It occurred to me that there may have been civil disputes handled by my firm involving one or more of the participants. I searched against their names and discovered something rather interesting.'

'What?' she asked, agog.

'I'm afraid I can't tell you,' he said, looking conflicted. 'If I even gave you the tiniest clue, I could be disbarred, and rightly so.'

'You mean you came out here to tell me that you know something but can't tell me?' She groaned. 'I think I would rather not have known.'

'I take my responsibility to clients of the firm seriously,' he said. 'However, I would point out that all the local newspapers are contained on microfiche at the library. I'd recommend having a dig around in there. You never know what might spring to light.'

'That's it?' she asked, horrified. 'You're not going to tell me anything else? It'll take me forever to delve into those, especially if I don't even know what I'm looking for.'

'That's all I can say on the subject,' he said, getting up to leave.

Beth caught him looking at the remaining lasagna the way she wished someone might look at her one day. 'Would you like to take the leftovers home?' she asked. 'I've no intention of having any more. I've eaten too much already.'

'Well, if you're sure?' he said, his eyes lighting up.

'Of course.' She smiled to show there were no hard feelings. The man clearly had hollow legs!

After Harris had left, she made some tea and curled up on the sofa with a warm throw to ponder recent events. The cottage was silent apart from the crackle of logs on the wood burning stove. Toby joined her, turning round and round until he felt he had the ideal spot before flopping down beside her, purring.

Sighing at the thought of tackling the stacks of papers at the library, she wished for a moment that her lawyer could be a tad less ethical but then he wouldn't be Harris, would he? And she was becoming rather fond of him just the way he was.

TWENTY

The following morning, Beth strolled into work, with the clouds scudding across the bay on her left and the golden leaves fluttering down from the trees on her right. She had a home, a cat and a job that she loved. She would even go so far as to say that she had friends, people who cared for her. It was all a far cry from the chronic stress of the children's unit and the isolation of caring for her mum. Not that she would change a minute of that special time she had with her lovely mum. The isolation had come not because of her mum, who had constantly urged her to go out and do things for herself. No, it had come from the fear and shame that had penetrated so deep she felt that she reeked of it. If her mum hadn't arranged things in such a manner as to give her no choice on her death, she would no doubt have hidden in their house for the remainder of her life, ordering everything online and keeping her interactions with the outside world to an absolute minimum. She only wished that her mother had lived to enjoy it with her. Not a day went by where she didn't feel a stab of loss, a sudden immobilising pinch of pain that would catch her unawares.

Walking past the pier, her spirits lifted seeing the ferry departing for the islands. She hoped to visit them all one day but had been too busy starting up her new business to take any time off. Maybe when all this was behind her. To her, the sight of that ferry represented freedom. A freedom that would be abruptly curtailed if Detective Sergeant Hunter had anything to do with it, she thought, her mood darkening once more.

She paused outside the bookshop, taking in the autumnal window display to which Chloe had added a bed of crisp russet and yellow leaves as well as a huge glass bowl filled with twigs on which hung mini jewelled lanterns that lit up at night. She was so artistic, marvelled Beth. Pushing open the door and hearing the bell tinkle, she was pleased to see her staff already assembled. Lachlan appeared from the door to the kitchen bearing a tray with a large teapot and four mugs.

'I'm afraid we're out of biscuits,' he said, setting it down on the table as they all took their usual seats.

'Just as well I made these, then, isn't it?' Beth said, producing a plastic tub from her canvas tote bag and opening it to reveal still-warm chocolate chip cookies.

Chloe patted her non-existent tummy. 'If you keep bringing in these delicious treats I'm going to need to buy a whole new wardrobe. My skinny jeans are getting tighter,' she said, helping herself to one, nevertheless.

Morna glared at her and shook her head. 'Will you stop moaning about your imaginary fat? It's... insensitive,' she muttered. 'Crikey, if you swapped bodies with me for the day, you'd probably have a nervous breakdown.' She grabbed a cookie and took a large bite.

'Pardon me for breathing,' snapped Chloe.

Beth and Lachlan exchanged glances. Time to change the subject. They had a few minutes still before the shop opened.

'Harris came round last night,' she said. 'He mentioned that I should search back in the local papers for a dispute involving someone from the book group.'

'Who?' asked Morna.

'He couldn't say. Reading between the lines, a client of his firm was involved. I'm going to go into the library at some point to view back editions of *The Oban Times*,' sighed Beth, not relishing the prospect. 'Not today, though. I'll need to work up to it.'

'Sounds deadly boring.' Chloe winced. 'I've been digging into the book group's socials. I found some stuff that was interesting. Darcie's Facebook page, Insta and X accounts are still live. I started with hers in case a family member got in and took them down.'

'Anything helpful?' asked Beth, hopefully.

'Some interesting stuff. I went right back to the beginning of all her accounts. Took me forever scrolling back. She was a typical oldie.'

'What do you mean?' asked Lachlan.

'Well, she didn't really manage her pages to put a carefully curated image out there like everyone knows how to do these days. She would do drunk posts and not delete them. If she was going through stuff, it was out there for everyone to see. The good, the bad and the downright ugly. She got into some full-on spats with other users, public hissy fits about any number of topics. She was also very political, which in itself invites a lot of trolls.'

'She was tempestuous, to be sure,' said Lachlan with a sigh.

Beth shot him a glance. So far as she knew, no one else was aware of his relationship with Darcie. It must be hard on him hearing her life dissected like this, but it had to be done if they were to have any chance of identifying her killer.

'Any interactions with any of our book group?' asked Beth.

'This is where it gets interesting,' Chloe said. 'All of them, apart from Harriet, my old headteacher. They followed her on social media and she followed them back. She was quite flirty with Mike Carter for a bit. They're both lefties so seemed to bond over the latest political rant.'

'Do you think she was involved with him?' asked Lachlan, tight-lipped.

'It seemed to me that they might have been for a while, but then it was clearly over by last year, because he started having a bit of a go at her, sounding all bitter and twisted.'

'I wouldn't have thought he was her type,' snapped Lachlan, causing Chloe to shoot him a curious look.

'Anyway,' said Beth, rushing in, 'that could give him motive to kill her. A spurned lover?'

'Maybe,' said Morna. 'I still think it's more likely to be related to this secret she was going to splash across the nationals. If we work out what that was, then we find our killer.'

'You make it sound so easy,' sighed Beth, morosely helping herself to another gooey cookie. 'We know that Mike is a teacher and frustrated writer, consumed by jealousy for those writers who make it into the big time. What could he have been up to that she found out about?'

'Now I think about it,' said Lachlan, 'he certainly doesn't come across as broken up about her death.'

No, but neither do you, thought Beth. It set her thinking, though. Lachlan had been at pains to remove his toothbrush from Darcie's bathroom. Not exactly the action of someone who had nothing to hide. Oh, she hated this wretched investigation. She was starting to suspect everyone now, including a member of her own staff.

'Beth? Are you listening?' demanded Morna. She snapped her attention back to see her staff all staring at her.

'Sorry, Morna, can you repeat what you just said?'

'There's an underground teaching blog doing the rounds. It's called "A Teacher's Call to Arms". It's a no-holds-barred account from an anonymous Scottish teacher that has been running for around fifteen years.'

'And you think Mike Carter's behind it?' asked Chloe, looking startled.

'Well, Harriet Brown's also a teacher but I doubt very much that it's her,' said Morna. 'It's pretty vicious and inappropriate, but funny with it. The Department for Education has been on the warpath trying to find out who's behind it and shut it down, but to no avail. Whoever it is, must be tech savvy and reroutes the IP address around servers across the world.'

'What would happen to the teacher if they were outed?' asked Beth.

'They'd be drummed out of the profession,' said Morna. 'I've printed off a number of posts so you can see for yourselves. It's hilarious but pretty toxic, and clearly written by a male teacher.' She handed them round and they all started reading.

'The anger and scorn leaps off the page,' murmured Beth, after a few minutes. 'It's funny, but very caustic. Those kids and parents that he eviscerates would be humiliated to read what he's written about them, assuming it's true, of course, and not complete fiction.'

Beth glanced over at Chloe and noticed with alarm that her cheeks were flushed and she was struggling not to cry. Suddenly, she threw down what she was reading and ran out of the room. Beth looked over at Morna who was looking elated.

'Morna!' she snapped, in her most authoritative voice. 'What the hell is going on?' She snatched up the sheets of paper Chloe had been reading from and scanned them anxiously, her heart sinking as she read further. It was sarcastic and scathing and, judging by Chloe's reaction, it was all about her.

'Don't you get it, Beth? This proves that Mike Carter is behind the blog. I'm sorry that Chloe's upset but I couldn't warn her or put any ideas in her head. I had to see her unfiltered reaction to know for sure.'

Beth shook her head in disgust. 'That's wrong on so many levels, Morna. I'm disappointed that you could have so little compassion for someone you work with.'

'Look, I'm sorry, okay?' said Morna. 'But we're dealing with a little more than hurt feelings here. Surely finding a murderer trumps Chloe being upset?'

'It's the way you went about things,' said Beth, struggling to hold on to her temper. 'Now, I suggest you go and apologize to Chloe and make things right with her.'

Morna stormed off to the toilets just as the door to the shop opened and the first of the morning customers trickled in. Lachlan cleared away their mugs as Beth greeted the customers, moving behind the front desk to field any questions about their stock.

After a few minutes both girls returned and busied themselves in their sections. Chloe had repaired the damage her tears had caused and Morna avoided eye contact with her. Beth looked over at Lachlan and gave a slight shrug which he returned. She forgot sometimes just how young the girls were. She would need to be more mindful of that.

After a fairly quiet morning, Beth was just starting to think about lunch when the door swung back on its hinges and in trooped around thirty excited tourists led by a likeable guide with a ginger beard, wearing a Tam o' Shanter hat just like the one on the bookshop sign.

'Hi there, bus tour,' he said, grinning round at his flock who were pouncing on her stock with exclamations of pleasure. 'Ruaridh McLean, pleased to meet you.' He extended his hand.

'Welcome! Beth Cunningham.' She smiled back at him, shaking his hand.

'I love what you've done with the place,' he said, glancing round and nodding in approval. 'We came here last year and the place was a bit dull and old-fashioned. I wasn't even sure whether to stop off here today. Nice to see it's been given a whole new lease of life.'

'Thank you,' she said. Her smile dropped as she caught sight of Lachlan, frozen in place by the stockroom, his expression bleak.

The tourists kept them run off their feet for thirty minutes then departed as suddenly as they had arrived. The staff surveyed the chaotic shop in horror.

'It looks like there's been a party in here,' ventured Chloe. Everyone laughed, pleased to see she looked brighter again. Beth ordered in sandwiches and coffee from the deli on George Street and, when it arrived twenty minutes later, she turned the sign to 'Closed' and they all sank gratefully into their seats at the table.

'Have you thought about contacting all the tour operators that run tours through here?' asked Morna. 'You could send them some catalogues, and their tour bus could order by click and collect so they can just turn up here and get their preferred books easily instead of the mass snap and grab panic as usual. We could serve coffee and cakes while they wait.'

'That's a great idea, Morna.' Beth smiled, pleased things were back on an even keel again. 'Why don't you action that, since it was your idea?'

'Great!' said Morna, her face lighting up in a way that they didn't often see.

'I had an idea of my own,' said Lachlan, determined to contribute. 'Books have often helped me through challenging times. I thought we could maybe get a local journalist involved to write an article and ask people to write in anonymously with their feel good/inspirational books that helped them through a crisis or low time in their lives, then we can compose a list of twenty of these and put them on special offer in the window perhaps?'

'If people tick a box to say they agree, we could also put anonymous snippets of their experience up on postcards, too. And people can add to them, by posting them in a box in the shop,' said Chloe, excitedly.

'But it would have to be done via a booth with a ballot type box so people could do it privately,' said Beth, thrilled by the idea.

'Those who take part could be entered into a raffle to win a complete set of all the books,' said Morna.

'We could go even further than that,' said Lachlan, looking more animated than Beth had ever seen him. 'Maybe this could catch on as a national movement of sorts if the idea gains traction.'

'Wouldn't that be wonderful?' said Beth, energy racing through her at the thought. 'Perhaps you could lead with that initiative, Lachlan? Maybe even chat to the local doctors' surgery? They're open to all kinds of social prescribing now. They might be willing to buy all the books on our eventual list and lend them out to patients.'

It was so heartening to see her team's enthusiasm after what had been a gruelling few weeks for them that she decided not to return to Morna's discovery about Mike Carter for now. She would have to find a way to speak to both Chloe and Morna separately to see what exactly was going on. For now, she was going to take the win, she thought, munching contentedly on her sandwich as the others excitedly discussed their new initiatives. It was gratifying to feel that after a life living on the periphery of society, she was now becoming a fully paid-up member. But only if DS Hunter didn't succeed in ripping the rug out from underneath her feet.

TWENTY-ONE

'Not so fast, you two,' said Beth, as Morna and Chloe reached for their coats. 'I want to talk about what happened earlier.'

'But it's time to go home,' said Chloe, looking longingly towards the door.

'It's been a long day,' sighed Morna, looking mutinous.

'Look, I do know that, but I don't want whatever this is to fester. If you talk about it now, you can both have a long lie-in tomorrow and come in at eleven, instead. Deal?'

'Deal,' they both muttered, sliding into their seats at the table.

'Tea, coffee?' asked Beth brightly.

Both of them shook their heads. *Tough crowd.*

Morna cleared her throat. 'Look, Chloe, I really *am* sorry for what I did. I got a bit carried away with trying to prove Mike Carter was behind that blog. If he'd thought Darcie was about to go public and expose him, he might well have snapped. His whole career would've been at risk.'

Chloe looked up and gave her a small smile. 'It's okay, I probably overreacted. It was a bit of a shock. I always got on with him at school. I liked him and thought he liked me. He had a sarky humour, but I thought he was mostly funny. I never realised he was a bitter and twisted monster.'

'Can I see the other blog entries you have there?' Beth asked.

Morna slid them across the table to her. 'The one on top that you've already read is clearly inspired by Chloe. There are hundreds of the things. He publishes a new one every month and they go back around fifteen years or so. Weirdly, he's a really good writer, it's just so...'

'Brutal,' burst out Chloe. 'I wonder why he teaches at all if he hates us all so much? At least he didn't put the boot into my parents. That's something, I suppose.'

'You should see what he wrote about mine,' said Morna, passing copies across to both Chloe and Beth.

Chloe looked up after they had both stopped reading, her eyes questioning as she looked across the table. 'I didn't even know that you had a sister?'

Morna simply nodded. 'Yes, Cassandra Abercrombie. Someone worthy of carrying on the family name.'

'I've heard of her, she's often in the glossies for her modelling or dating some lord with connections to the royal family,' said Chloe, looking as though she couldn't believe what she was hearing. 'But... why is your name different from your family's?' she then asked.

'Because I changed it on my sixteenth birthday,' Morna said, her voice determinedly measured. 'They'd made it clear that they regarded me as a lumpen throwback, not worthy of the Abercrombie name because I was ugly, clumsy and bad at sports. They sent me away to boarding school at the age of seven and made me stay there in the holidays even though my sister was always allowed home. Eventually, when I was sixteen, I left there without their consent, got into Oban High School and went on benefits so I wouldn't be homeless. Where I live now is the only true home I've ever had. Nobody else knows and that's how I want to keep it. You can tell Lachlan, but only him. Agreed?'

'Agreed,' Beth and Chloe chorused.

'Why didn't you move far away?' asked Chloe.

'I rather fancied being a thorn in their side,' she replied with a sly grin, making them laugh.

Beth had caught up with both blog posts now and looked at them aghast. Chloe had been described as a popular bubblehead with an unmerited sense of entitlement who mistakenly thought she was desirable and laboured under the erroneous impression that her friends actually liked her.

'But how did you know this one was about you, Chloe?' asked Beth.

'He mentioned a Highland dancing medal I'd won. It was discontinued the following year,' Chloe said quietly, clearly still hurting.

'I remembered her banging on about it during tea break one day,' said Morna. 'She even showed me a pic and it stuck in my mind. That's how I knew, too.'

'I never knew you did Highland dancing,' said Beth.

'There's a lot you don't know about us,' said Morna.

Beth felt the rebuke. They were right. She'd become so invested in her fresh start and new life that she'd been selfish. She'd fallen into the trap of thinking that she was the only one who'd had problems. Feeling truly ashamed, she reached out a hand to each of them.

'I'm so sorry, girls. I've been so caught up in everything going on with Darcie's murder that I've been a rubbish boss and a worse friend.'

'Don't worry,' said Chloe. 'We've been just as bad.'

'Maybe it would be better if we just stopped digging into the murder and left it to the police?' said Beth. 'It's putting a huge strain on all of us. I'm sure they'll get to the truth of the matter and, if not, well, I'll have to take what's coming.' Her words came with a determination she didn't quite feel.

The two girls gave each other a searching look then nodded and turned back to her.

'No way, we're in this together. Darcie died in our shop,' said Chloe. 'She deserves to have her killer caught.'

'And the police seem to have tunnel vision on this case,' added

Morna. 'I don't know that we can trust them to get to the truth without our help.'

Beth's heart swelled as she looked at them. For the first time, she truly felt part of something.

'Okay,' she said, 'if you're sure. However, if things take a turn for the worse and I feel that any of you are in *actual danger*, we might have to think again.'

She glanced down at the blog posts once more; something was nagging at her. What was it? There, she had it. He'd spelled the word "grateful" wrong, writing "greatful" instead. Her heart quickening, she called up the suspicious one-star reviews for Dan's new book online and scanned them hurriedly. Chloe and Morna looked at each other, puzzled.

'What is it?' asked Morna. 'What have you seen?'

Exhaling in relief, Beth turned to them, triumphant. 'We can prove it's Mike behind the sock puppet accounts burying Dan's book in one-star reviews. He spells the word "grateful" wrong. It's in both the blogs and in two of the reviews.'

Morna groaned. 'I should have spotted that.'

'We'll pick our moment and get him to take them down,' said Beth, wishing everything else could be solved as easily. 'Right, time you both got out of here. See you tomorrow.'

As she watched them walking down the road as the sun was setting across the bay, she noticed Chloe tuck her arm inside Morna's and was glad that the girls seemed to have forged a new understanding.

TWENTY-TWO

After the girls had gone, Beth caught up on some paperwork, then did a mental inventory of the contents of her fridge and winced. She would have to do a proper shop tomorrow but for now fish and chips would have to do. Locking up the shop, she shivered. It was freezing cold. Turning up her collar she headed along George Street towards the chippie, its windows fogged up and people inside queuing, shoulders hunched about their ears to ward off the chill. Pulling back the door, a welcome blast of hot air warmed her. After she had placed her order, the door opened once more and she jumped as a familiar voice whispered in her ear.

'Fancy meeting you here.'

Beth swung round and gave a nervous laugh. 'Mike! You made me jump. How are you?'

'I've been up and down,' he said, narrowing his eyes as he looked at her. 'I'm guessing you've been the same. I still can't believe she's gone.'

'No, me neither,' she replied. 'I heard that you and she were... close.' She lowered her voice.

He grabbed her roughly by the arm and pulled her to one side.

'Ow! You're hurting me,' she hissed, shaking him off. The man behind the counter looked over towards them.

'Sorry,' Mike said, putting his hands up in surrender. 'I just didn't want you running off your mouth in public about how "close" I was to a recent murder victim.'

'Okay, fair enough,' she said.

His face was white and anxious. Was there more he wanted to share? Beth did some quick thinking.

'Look, how about we get our chips and go somewhere where we won't be overheard?' she whispered.

Ten minutes later they were sitting huddled on a bench by the seafront, the freshly fried chips warming her lap and the tang of vinegar making her mouth water. Smelling the fish, some seagulls perched on the metal railings, eyeing them hungrily. A pub door opened, discharging some locals on to the street, sounds of merriment following them until the door closed behind them. Mike seemed jumpy, his eyes flicking around them as if to reassure himself they were alone.

'What's this about, Mike?' she asked, after she had eaten some of her fish and chips.

He gave a hollow laugh. 'I don't even know where to begin. I really liked Darcie. It was no grand love affair, but we got along. She'd a wicked sense of humour – sarcastic, like mine. Also like me, she'd had hopes of a better life than stuck up here grinding away in the back of beyond.'

'Did you know anything about this secret that was her golden ticket back to Glasgow?' Beth asked.

'No, your guess is as good as mine. That wasn't the first time I'd heard her mention it. She'd been dropping heavy hints about a story she'd been working on that would propel her back onto a staff job at the nationals. Never mind Glasgow, she had her sights set on London.'

'How did that make you feel?' asked Beth.

'What are you, my therapist?' he snorted. 'I was happy for her. If I was in her shoes, I'd be off in a heartbeat.'

Beth paused, her heart racing. *Should I take a chance and tell him I know about his poisonous blog? But if he has murdered Darcie to stop it getting out, that might make me his next target.* Given the way he'd been trying to sabotage Dan's new book, he clearly had a mean streak. No, it was safer to leave it. For now. She didn't dare antagonise him further.

'I can hear the cogs turning from here,' he said, turning to stare at her curiously, a chip suspended in mid-air. 'What aren't you telling me?'

'I might ask you the same thing?' she fired back, meeting his stare.

He shook his head and got to his feet, screwing up his chip paper and depositing it in a nearby bin. 'I know that the police think you did it,' he said shortly. 'You need all the friends you can get. So, if I were you, I wouldn't be pissing people off by spreading malicious gossip about town. People stick together up here. Being an incomer, you'd better watch your back.'

'Is that a threat?' asked Beth, also rising to her feet.

'Hardly.' His lips twisted in a sneer. 'If I was threatening you, you'd know about it. No, more like a piece of friendly advice. You stay safe now, Beth.' He turned to walk away leaving her fuming.

Turning the opposite way, she walked home along the bay. The sound of the waves slapping against the sea wall punctuated her thoughts as she puzzled over the case. Pulling up her coat collar, she braced herself against the chill of the wind whipping up the tops of the waves. Tasting the salt of the spray on her lips she wondered how long she would be at liberty to enjoy the beauty of her chosen home. Not long, if DS Hunter had anything to do with it.

As she turned right to walk up Albany Street, the Calmac Ferry's horn sounded in the darkness, startling her. Turning right down into Gallanach Road, her footsteps quickened. As she moved out of the town centre and into the countryside, she felt more exposed and vulnerable as she left the streetlights and the potential to seek help behind. Nervously she glanced behind her as she groped inside her shoulder bag for the small powerful torch that she needed to illuminate her way. As she switched it on, she caught a movement out of the corner of her eye and swung the torch round, her heart hammering in the darkness. Nothing. Most likely a fox. Unless, of course, Mike had doubled back on himself and followed her out here? Carefully, she swept the road behind her once more before continuing. She was being ridiculous. It had been a long day. As she rounded the bend and saw her cottage perched high up off the road, she exhaled in relief. Hurrying through the small painted gate she ran lightly up the irregular stone stairs and let herself into the house.

TWENTY-THREE

The next morning, despite reading until the wee small hours, Beth was up bright and early. She'd vowed to herself that no matter how bad things looked, she was not going down without a fight. It had taken her years to stitch her shattered life together the last time. She didn't think she had it in her to do it again. At first, she'd assumed that it was her story that Darcie was about to divulge. Now, she realised that wasn't necessarily the case. Several people had secrets they were desperate wouldn't be made public. As far as those people were concerned, Darcie could have presented a clear danger that had to be responded to with immediate lethal force.

She already knew about Mike Carter's secrets. She had to pin down the others' secrets and expose them all to the police as potential murderers. What the girls had said about the former head, Harriet Brown, needed to be looked into further. Was it possible that such a pillar of the community had executed the perfect murder in relation to her husband? The police clearly hadn't suspected foul play but if the girls were right, she'd had ample motive to get rid of a cruel and controlling partner who took all her money and left her rummaging about in charity shops for work clothes. She couldn't ask her about it directly. Harriet would shut her down with just one glare from those icy blue eyes. She still had the whole headteacher vibe going on even though she was retired. She had no idea as to whether Dan or Ronnie had any secrets of their own but needed to look into them for the sake of completeness. Maybe it was time she indulged herself in a few beauty treatments, she mused. There's a first time for everything, she thought with a grin. She picked up the phone to Ronnie; fortunately, someone had cancelled an appointment and she was booked in for a pedicure that afternoon.

As she left the cottage, her thoughts turned to Dan. Unlikely though it seemed that someone so apparently open and congenial could be a killer, she had to be thorough and look into him as well. What possible secret could he be hiding? Well, for a start he wasn't married so he couldn't be cheating on his wife. Given the huge advance he was being paid, his book was set to be a runaway success; fame and prosperity seemed to be on the horizon. All the more to lose perhaps? Could he have done something so politically incorrect and heinous that, should it get out, he was at risk of being cancelled, his contract ripped up and his agent dumping him? Maybe she should speak to Mike Carter again. If anything was remotely dodgy about their literary golden boy, he wouldn't hesitate to divulge it.

As she walked alongside the ferry terminal, the Calmac Ferry blasted its horn, making her jump as usual. It sounded like a very deep vibrant burp. Continuing along, she passed The Corryvrechan pub on her right and got her usual whiff of fish from the fishing boat moored alongside. Out of the corner of her eye she thought she saw a black cat slink behind some lobster pots waiting to be loaded. Clearly, Toby was on the prowl. She didn't call out to him as she knew he would completely disown her. Glancing back at the pub, she paused to read a poster on the window. That night there was going to be an open mic night for new and emerging writers. What better way to get them all captive in one place again, away from the more formal book club setting? Hopefully, a few drinks might loosen some tongues. Continuing with a spring in her step, she arrived at the bookshop full of good cheer.

Morna and Lachlan were standing behind the cash desk nursing cups of coffee.

'Morning,' Beth chirped. 'Isn't it a glorious day?'

'Is it? I hadn't noticed,' muttered Morna. 'You're such a morning person. Lachlan and I are more night owls. We need to acclimatise gently to the morning.'

'Hi, Beth.' Chloe beamed, arriving from the stockroom with an armful of books.

'And there goes the other one,' groaned Morna.

'Do you have to be such a misery guts?' exclaimed Chloe, exasperated.

'Why are you so tired, Morna?' asked Beth. Her employee had purple shadows under her eyes and looked drawn and pale.

'I was up most of the night looking into the background of our various suspects,' Morna replied, stifling a yawn. 'All of them are incomers for a start.'

'Incomers?' queried Beth. 'But some of them have surely been here for decades?'

Morna gave a twisted grin. 'Doesn't matter. Anyone who wasn't born and brought up here counts as an incomer. You're accepted, but only so far.'

'But that's ridiculous,' said Beth, her heart sinking. *Am I never going to fit in here then?*

'Don't blame me.' Morna shrugged. 'I don't make the rules. Anyway, Mike came here as a newly qualified teacher and stayed. In his early twenties he joined a local writing group, Kilted Scribblers. They produced some writing anthologies, and he seems to have edited a few and contributed a story and poem to each. The group was very active and applied for Council and Creative Scotland funding for speakers, workshops and the like, but five years ago he left it abruptly.'

'Do you know what happened?' asked Chloe.

'No, but guess who joined the writing group the year before he left and has continued to be involved?' Morna said.

'Spit it out, lass, the suspense is killing me,' said Lachlan drily.

'Dan,' she replied. 'So, that might be the origin of the apparent grudge fest Mike has against him.'

A tinkling sound announced the first customer of the day, who Beth greeted with a warm smile.

'I wonder if you can help me?' said a well-groomed middle-aged woman. 'I'm looking for a present for my son. He's into gaming and I believe there's such a thing as a companion guide to some of the latest games?'

'Yes, indeed,' Beth said. 'That happens to be Morna's speciality. I'll leave you in her capable hands.'

'Follow me,' said Morna, walking over, her face lighting up with enthusiasm. 'We have a really good selection of those at the back of the shop. What games is he into?' Their voices faded as they rounded the corner.

'It never even occurred to me to stock anything like that,' said Lachlan.

'They're incredibly popular,' said Chloe. 'All the lads I know buy them even if they wouldn't be caught dead reading an actual novel.'

'Graphic novels have also become huge,' said Beth. 'Some of them have exquisite artwork.'

'I think Manga is pretty cool,' said Chloe.

'Things have changed so much since I started out in the book trade,' said Lachlan. 'It makes me feel old, past it, irrelevant.'

Beth and Chloe looked at him, taken aback by his bleak expression.

'You're anything but that!' exclaimed Beth. 'All that knowledge and experience is invaluable to the rest of us. Plus, you've years of experience in running a bookshop. We all completely depend on you, Lachlan.'

'What she said,' Chloe piped up, nodding vigorously, her blue eyes wide and earnest. 'All of this is completely new to me. When it comes to books, you're a rockstar, Lachlan.'

'Books will never go out of fashion, no matter how many

different ways there are to consume stories,' said Beth. 'So, I'm afraid you're stuck with us.'

'I suppose there are worse things,' he said, with a small frown, but looking pleased, nonetheless.

'There's an open mic night at The Corryvreckan at 7pm tonight,' said Beth. 'I figured some of our book group might put in an appearance, if encouraged. Chloe, maybe you could ring round and say there's a few of us going if they fancy tagging along?'

Morna overheard as she re-emerged with the woman and walked behind the till to ring up her purchase of two companion guides.

'I can ring Dan,' she said offhandedly. 'I was planning to see him later anyway.' She smiled at the woman who was clutching her card. 'That'll be £29.98, please.'

The woman leaned over and tapped her card. 'Thanks, you've been really helpful. He's such a nightmare to buy for.' She turned to leave and Morna went red as she looked up to find them all staring at her.

'What?' she demanded, grumpily.

'Are you kidding?' asked Chloe, her eyes like saucers. 'When were you going to tell us that you're dating lover boy?'

'We're NOT dating,' snapped Morna. 'We just happen to enjoy each other's company. What's wrong with that?'

'Nothing!' said Chloe, backing away with her hands up, though Beth could hear a faint refrain of 'Morna and Dan, sitting in a tree. K-I-S-S-I-N-G.'

'OMG!' exclaimed Morna to her departing back. 'What AGE are you?'

Beth reached across and patted her hand. 'Just ignore her, she's only teasing,' she soothed.

'Well, she needs to grow up,' fumed Morna.

'So, do you think Dan will be up for going tonight?' Beth asked, still feeling very conflicted about Morna's fledgling romance with a potential murder suspect.

'Probably, I'll drop him a message,' muttered Morna.

'Great! I've booked into the beauty salon later, so hopefully, I'll be able to get some more information after speaking to Ronnie,' said Beth.

'Look, I know you're desperate to clear your name, but I would feel a bit weird pumping Dan for information,' Morna blurted out.

'Relax.' Beth smiled. 'I completely understand. You can leave Dan out of the equation though I reserve the right to do some digging myself, just in case.'

'Fair enough,' said Morna. 'It probably won't come to anything anyway, knowing my luck.' She ambled back off to her section. Beth fervently hoped Dan had nothing to do with the murder or Morna was going to get badly hurt. A horrible thought crossed her mind. Could he have started something up with Morna to keep tabs on their investigation? Sighing heavily, and with her previous good cheer evaporated, she headed for her small office to catch up on some errant paperwork. It was hard to focus on the business when she knew that the police could arrive to arrest her at any moment. Just when was this nightmare going to end?

TWENTY-FOUR

Beth felt a thrill of anticipation as she stood in front of Glow, admiring the walled courtyard with its carefully chosen stone statues and charming water feature trickling under a tiny wooden bridge. Opening the door, she took a deep breath and entered. Everything smelt wonderful with a heady concoction of oils and fragrances blending into an exotic compound. Smooth jazz played softly in the background. The interior was black marble with brilliant white walls. Warm touches in coral and gold made it feel welcoming. She'd never set foot in such an establishment before and hadn't known what to expect. It was as if she had entered another world. A secret space for women. Belatedly, she wondered if she should have dressed up as she beheld the other two well-groomed women in the waiting area.

A stunning young woman glided up to her with a tray of drinks. She accepted a glass of prosecco and sank back onto a comfortable white leather sofa. Just as well it wasn't red wine she was drinking. She spent the next few minutes people watching and listening to snatches of conversation.

'Beth! How lovely to see you! Please, step this way,' said Ronnie, standing at the entrance to one of the treatment rooms. 'Just bring your drink with you.'

Beth lurched to her feet, a little lightheaded. As she walked away, she noticed the other two women whispering to each other and laughing behind their hands. Her back stiffened and her shoulders went back. She wouldn't let it bother her. She was used to not fitting in. Except at the bookshop, she thought with a glow of warmth. They accepted her for who she was there.

'Don't mind that pair,' said Ronnie, closing the door behind her, her shrewd brown eyes having taken in the situation at a glance. 'Empty vessels that aren't half as delightful as they think they are. You can relax now. It's just you and me.'

Not super relaxing to be trapped in a small room with you if you turn out to be the killer, thought Beth, coughing to hide a nervous laugh bubbling up inside her. In no time at all she found herself sitting in a comfortable chair with her feet in a massage bubble bath.

'That feels so good,' she sighed, wiggling her toes and taking a sip of her drink. 'My feet have taken a bit of a pounding since I started working at the shop.'

'Yes, I can see that,' Ronnie said. 'They're definitely in need of some TLC.'

'I've been a bit run down recently. I can't get poor Darcie out of my mind. The fact that it happened in my bookstore makes me feel somehow responsible.'

'You mustn't feel that way,' Ronnie soothed, taking a foot out and placing it on a towel on her knee before starting to scrape away the dead skin with a scalpel.

'I barely even knew her,' sighed Beth, though some of the others did. 'She certainly didn't deserve to die in such a brutal way. How well did *you* know her?' Was it her imagination or did Ronnie stiffen slightly, increasing the pressure on her foot?

'I'd seen her out and about, but I can't say that I knew her well,' Ronnie said, after a pause. 'Enough to exchange the time of day with. A casual acquaintance, if you like.'

'I would've thought she'd be a regular in here,' said Beth. 'She struck me as being more on the high maintenance side.' She laughed. 'Isn't this the only beauty salon in town?'

'I'm not saying that she wasn't a client,' Ronnie conceded. 'But I have two other beauty therapists as well as a couple of hairdressers and nail beauticians working for me here. She wasn't one of my personal clients.'

'She was certainly glamourous,' said Beth. 'The night she died I remember her implying she was desperate to get back to the bright lights of Glasgow with a job on the nationals. I heard that she'd screwed up big time in her last job and that's how she wound up here in the first place.'

'Everyone makes mistakes.' Ronnie shrugged. 'Mind you, I can't quite imagine her being content to cover council meetings and school sports days. She always had a hunger about her, as though she was waiting for something big to dig her teeth into, like a tiger on the prowl. Sorry, a bit fanciful, I suppose.'

'No, I know exactly what you mean,' said Beth thoughtfully. 'That night at the book group, it was like she was toying with us. I felt it, too.'

'No offence, but I wish I'd never come along that night. I still can't quite believe what happened. It was surreal.'

'The police think that it was her talk of revealing a secret and making a big splash with it in the papers that got her killed,' said Beth.

'Yes,' said Ronnie, staring up at her. 'In case you don't know, I feel I should tell you that it's all around town that you've been hauled in front of the police and that you're their chief suspect.'

'But it wasn't me,' Beth said quietly, staring back at her.

Ronnie looked away first. 'Don't worry, I believe you. As a small business owner myself, the very last thing I'd do is murder someone on the premises I make my livelihood from. As for the other stuff, from when you were young...'

'You know about that, too?' asked Beth, colour rushing to her cheeks.

'Yes. Let's just say that one of my other clients wasn't very discreet. We've all got stuff in our past that we aren't proud of. You paid for what you did. No one will hear about it from me.'

'Thank you,' said Beth meekly. 'One thing I'm glad about is that the killer didn't use one of my books to bash poor Darcie. Apparently, the police lifted every one of them off the shelves to check for blood.'

'I hope they put them all back again,' Ronnie said with a twitch of her lips.

'They did,' said Beth. 'But not necessarily in the correct order. Can you believe they're still no further forward in finding the murder weapon?'

'What are they even looking for?' asked Ronnie, patting her feet dry with a white fluffy towel, one at a time.

'All I know is that they're searching for a hard blunt object. Doesn't exactly narrow it down, does it?'

'Hardly,' Ronnie said with a frown. 'Like searching for a particular pebble on a beach. They might never find it. At least that must help your case a bit, surely?'

'You would think so,' said Beth with a sigh. 'But from their point of view, I've got motive and opportunity, so it wouldn't take much more for them to charge me. Anyway, let's switch to a more cheerful topic. Your salon has been a real eye opener. It's absolutely gorgeous! Have you always been a beauty therapist?'

'Yes, I grew up in foster care. I became obsessed with hair and makeup. It made me feel like I could do anything, become anyone. I could alter people's perception of me simply by changing the products I put on my face or the way I styled my hair.'

'That must have been really hard,' said Beth.

'No harder than you've had it, by the sounds of things,' Ronnie said, turning her shrewd gaze upon her.

'And look at us both now.' Beth smiled. 'Both running successful businesses that we love.'

'Women like us have to stick together,' said Ronnie, squeezing her arm.

'Is this the first salon you've owned?' asked Beth. 'Did you own one before you came up here?'

'Yes, I did, but nothing on this scale. I took a big leap of faith opening this place. I was mortgaged to the hilt. It was terrifying, I don't mind admitting.'

'I'm from Glasgow, too,' said Beth. 'Bit of a culture shock arriving up here where everyone has an opinion on how you should be living your life.'

'Tell me about it.' Ronnie grimaced. 'How did you work out I came from Glasgow?'

'Your accent is barely discernible,' replied Beth. 'Just the odd word here and there gave you away.'

'I did my best to get rid of it,' Ronnie said. 'I used to be as broad as you get. Like I said, I didn't want to be defined by my past. Onwards and upwards, right?'

'Onwards and upwards,' replied Beth, feeling that, to some extent, she had met a kindred spirit in this woman.

Ronnie was now massaging some fragrant lotion into her feet. Beth started to relax and even enjoy the experience, closing her eyes.

'What colour nail polish would you like?' Ronnie's voice made her jump, and she realised she'd dozed off. 'Are you going somewhere special tonight?' She smiled.

'Nowhere special, but I am going out,' Beth said. 'A few of us from the shop and book club are going to try the open mic night at The Corryvrechan,' she said. 'You'd be very welcome to come along with us. I meant to ask you earlier, but my mind went blank I was so relaxed.'

'That's what I like to hear.' Ronnie laughed. 'I'm sure I got a text from young Chloe earlier about that. Sure, why not? It'll be fun. Something a bit different. How about midnight blue with silver sparkles? I can do your hands to match as well if you like?'

'I like the sound of that,' Beth said, accepting a glass of lemon water with ice. She was a bit disappointed not to have learned more but at least she'd got sparkly toes out of it and rescued her feet from their life of drudgery for a while. Though Ronnie seemed so bubbly and nice, she clearly had had to fight to survive and prosper. Looking at her life now, she obviously had a lot to lose. Just how far she would be willing to go to protect it?

TWENTY-FIVE

Beth looked longingly at her cosy couch, the burgundy velvet curtains pulled snug against the night. It had been a long day and she was exhausted. If only she could relax there with a book instead of dragging herself out in the cold. Toby was perched on top of a cushion, glaring at her having realised she was going out. She scratched him behind the ears which triggered some resentful purring. *Sorry, boy, needs must. I'll see you when I get back.* He turned his back on her, tail flicking in annoyance.

Moving into the hall she checked her makeup and admired her nails which now matched her feet. With her long curly hair set loose she looked years younger than when she had first moved here eight months ago, dowdy and hopeless. Now her new life continued to open out like the petals of a flower, lit with seemingly endless possibilities. A life that she had longed to live for so long but scarcely dared dream that it could ever happen for her. Yet if she didn't find out who really murdered Darcie it could all be snatched away from her any day now. She couldn't be locked up again. It would finish her. For good. Throwing on her heavy wool coat, with a last lingering look around her precious home, she opened the door and stepped out into the night.

Pushing open the door into The Corryvrechan just before

seven, she noticed all her team, together with the remaining members of the book club, sat at a big table towards the rear of the pub. It was busy and already loud with people blowing off steam before the event got started. Hurrying over she took a seat between Mike and Dan.

'You owe us twenty quid for the kitty,' Chloe shouted over, handing her a glass of white wine from one of the bottles on the table. Beth passed across the money and took a grateful sip before turning to Mike who was looking deathly pale and glassy-eyed as he finished off his pint of beer.

'Are you okay? You look... stressed.'

'No kidding, Sherlock,' he snapped.

The penny dropped. 'Oh! You're one of the readers, aren't you?'

Mutely, exuding misery from every pore, he nodded. Despite his rather hostile personality, Beth felt for him, she really did. Drama or any kind of performance art had always been torture to her at school.

'You'll smash it,' she said softly in his ear. 'A little bird told me you're an amazing writer. You've nothing to worry about. Head up, shoulders back and look into the audience at times, even if you're not really seeing them. We've got your back!'

He looked at her as though really seeing her for the first time. Squeezing her arm, he muttered, 'Thanks,' and rose to his feet on hearing his name called, making his way through the tables to a smattering of applause.

Beth turned to the others. 'Poor Mike is really nervous, let's give him our support,' she said, clapping vigorously and whistling.

'What? Like he does to everyone else?' said Dan, slow clapping with an unpleasant smirk on his face.

'Hey, cut it out,' said Morna, poking him in the ribs. 'Give him a chance. He came, didn't he?'

'Only because he's desperate.' He laughed, knocking back his beer.

They all stared at him. Just how much had he had to drink

before they all arrived? As if sensing their collective disapproval, Dan looked defensive.

'Look, I'm only saying what everyone else thinks. Mike is a total jerk. Instead of being pleased for me he's eaten up with jealousy and does me down at every turn. How am I supposed to react?'

Beth looked into his eyes. Part of her understood what he was trying to get across. Mike *was* bitter and consumed with jealousy about Dan's success. But Dan's lack of generosity to a vanquished enemy was also troublesome. He was young and he had the world at his feet. Fame and prosperity beckoned, yet he couldn't find it in him to forgive Mike for his sour grapes. Morna was looking troubled as well. The chatter died down and Mike began to speak into the microphone, reading a short story he'd recently written. Beth cringed for him, worrying that it wouldn't be up to much but, to her surprise, she was soon hanging on his every word. It was a chilling tale of a psychopath getting ready for a killing spree with an unexpected twist that turned everything on its head. Enthusiastic applause and whistles broke out as he made his way back to their table looking endearingly pink about the ears.

With the notable exception of Dan, they all congratulated him, then Beth turned to Dan. 'Are you reading from your new book tonight?'

'No,' he muttered. 'My publicist wouldn't like it. This is strictly an amateur night.' He shot a barbed glance at Mike.

'Well, I thought Mike nailed it,' said Morna. 'Well done, mate!' She raised her glass and toasted him across the table.

Dan's eyes narrowed. What on earth has got into him tonight? Beth wondered. Everyone fell quiet as the next person started to read but after the fourth reader, a twenty-minute break was announced. Beth glanced at her staff. Time to mingle. But before she could make a move, Lachlan slid into the now-vacant seat beside her.

'What Dan said,' he whispered. 'I don't buy it. Any publicist would say the more events you can do the better. He obviously can't stand Mike so what better chance to crush him by reading here and having the whole pub desperate to buy it? Something doesn't add up.'

'I agree,' said Beth quietly. 'Maybe Morna will be able to shed some light on his behaviour later.' With that, she wandered over to Ronnie, who was chatting away to a beaming Mike. When he drops his world-weary, snarky façade, he is really quite attractive, she was surprised to catch herself thinking.

'Didn't he do great?' Ronnie exclaimed, her vivacious face lit with joy. 'I'd no idea you were a writer before tonight, Mike.'

'I dabble,' he said, with a self-conscious smile.

'It's clearly more than that,' said Beth, as Ronnie excused herself to go and get them another two bottles of wine. She checked no one was listening and lowered her voice. 'I hear that you also have a blog that documents your life as a teacher, the good, the bad and the downright ugly.'

The smile slipped from his face and his eyes hardened. 'I don't know what you mean. Who have you been talking to?'

'One of my staff came across it and showed it to us.' She pulled up a screenshot on her phone. 'Chloe was very hurt.'

He groaned, wiping a hand across his face. 'I never meant to hurt anyone. It was just a way to blow off steam after a bad day. I also used it to hone my writing skills. It's not how I really felt about Chloe or any of them. It was more satirical and as a means of helping other teachers feel less alone in this mad world we live and teach in. I'm a weary old cynic. It was an outlet. It stopped me lashing out verbally at students and parents because I knew I could come home and mercilessly lampoon them for my audience.'

'Did Darcie threaten to expose you?' asked Beth, giving him a hard stare.

'Wait... are you saying Darcie knew? I'm pretty sure she didn't. Why would anyone care, anyway? It's hardly earth-shattering news. Teacher writes snarky blog, so what? Are you telling me that's what her big secret was? God help her then. Look, you won't tell anyone, will you? It might not be newsworthy, but it could have some pretty serious consequences for me on a personal level. I'd lose my job, for sure.'

Ronnie came back to the table as the bell rang to signify that they were getting going again. Beth returned to her seat, but she could feel Mike's eyes burning into her like hot coals. He'd seemed genuine about not knowing that Darcie was interested in exposing him, but he could still be lying to try and put her off the scent. She didn't know him well enough to judge.

At the next break, Morna nipped off to the loo so Beth took her chance and drifted over to sit in her vacant seat beside Dan. 'Are you enjoying it so far?' she asked with a smile.

'Sure, I love open mic nights.'

'I'm surprised you didn't want to take part,' Beth said. 'After all, you'll be doing lots of promo events when your book comes out, so I thought you'd welcome the practise?'

'I would if it was anywhere but here,' he said, grim-faced.

'Why's that?' she asked, startled.

'Too many people who want me to fall flat on my face,' he replied with a twisted grin, '*him* among them.' He inclined his head towards Mike. 'I've been in local writing groups for years. Everyone in them wants to be sitting where I am today with a top literary agent and a massive publishing deal. They pretend to be happy for me to my face but most of them are secretly spitting nails, all twisted up with jealousy. The sooner I leave here the better.'

'How do you know that?' asked Beth, somewhat taken aback. 'You might be wrong about them.'

'I know because I would be just like them if it had happened to someone else. That honest enough for you? This may come as a surprise to you, Beth, but life isn't all kittens and rainbows.'

'You don't know me,' she said quietly, rage building within her. 'I hope you're a better judge of character in your writing.' With that, she rose to her feet and returned to her chair, continuing to seethe. Morna stared from one to the other as she arrived back at the table, but Beth didn't meet her gaze. She hoped Morna wasn't getting too involved with the handsome young author as it seemed that his beauty and charm were only skin deep.

She glanced round the table as the bell rang for the final segment. Everyone was happily chatting, but she knew that dangerous currents were boiling up between the cracks. They had all been thrown together by a love of crime fiction or their paths might never have crossed. If only Darcie hadn't said anything that night about a secret she was going to expose, she might still be alive today. Her indiscretion had cost her life and plunged the rest of them headlong into chaos.

TWENTY-SIX

Beth inhaled deeply, breathing in the cool, crisp Highland air as she walked home. It was only 10pm but she was desperate to be on her own and away from the others. She was starting to see something bad in everyone and she hated that she'd been forced into this way of thinking by recent events. It wasn't who she aspired to be. Normally she didn't think twice about walking home alone here but tonight's events had made her a little jumpy. In particular, she'd glimpsed a rather unpleasant side to Dan that she hadn't known was there. Why couldn't people be more straightforward? As for Mike, he had disclosed a vulnerability and charm tonight that had quite disarmed her until the shutters had come crashing back down. He'd tried to minimise it but they both knew his secret blog could result in him being hounded from the teaching profession. He was clearly a talented writer over and above all that, yet he was consumed by jealousy in relation to Dan's burgeoning success. If he really was behind those one-star reviews, then that could also have been the secret Darcie was going to expose.

So far, he appeared to have the strongest motive for wishing secrets to remain buried, but she still hadn't winkled out enough information about the others. Ronnie hid a forceful personality and drive to succeed beneath her good-time vibe. She ran a hugely successful business and there was talk about her expanding to another salon in Fort William. Where was all that money coming from? Times were hard yet Ronnie was undoubtedly flourishing. Beneath all the glamour and glitz, Beth had sensed a hardness in her that day. She was someone who would take action to protect herself or her assets. But to what degree? The moon drifted behind the clouds and the darkness seemed to press in on her, stoking her fevered thoughts.

She froze. Were those footsteps she heard walking behind her, matching their stride to hers? She spun round but saw no one. The wind was whipping up now, blowing an empty Coke can across the road. 'You're being ridiculous,' she muttered, crossing Albany Street and turning down onto Gallanach Road. She hurried along, the sea slapping against the walls on her right, her torch pointing the way in front of her. She was desperate to get home and curl up on the sofa with Toby.

Suddenly, she cried out in pain, dropping to her knees and clutching her head. What on earth...? Had she banged into something in the dark? She felt sick and woozy. Tentatively she put her hand up to the back of her head. The moon came out from the clouds in time for her to examine the viscous liquid on her fingers. Blood? She tried to stagger to her feet, but they went out from under her, leaving her collapsed on the narrow pavement. The footsteps earlier. Had someone attacked her? Blearily, she looked around. No one was in sight but there were myriad ways they could have escaped while she was on the ground. There were houses on both sides set back from the road with gardens, but their curtains were drawn to shut out the night. A wave of nausea swept over her and she vomited into the road.

'Beth! Beth! Are you alright? What happened?'

Blearily, she turned her head to see Harriet Brown running down the stairs of a handsome terraced property. There seemed to be two of her which was odd. Maybe she had a twin sister?

'I don't know,' she managed. 'I had a bang to my head and fell down.'

Harriet looked puzzled. 'There's nothing you could have banged your head on. Anyway, can you stand?'

Beth tried to struggle to her feet, but her body wouldn't cooperate.

'Here, let me help you,' said Harriet, managing to hoist her upwards with much huffing and puffing.

The world swam and her legs felt like overcooked spaghetti but with Harriet's help Beth stayed upright.

'I need to get home,' she murmured. 'I live along here, just ten minutes away.'

Harriet looked worried. 'I don't see you making it that far, even with my help. Best if you come inside with me. Then we can assess the situation from there.'

Beth nodded her acquiescence as Harriet was now in full head-teacher mode and resistance was futile.

'We missed you tonight at the open mic night,' she said, as Harriet lowered her onto a chintzy couch in an elegant living room.

'I would've come but I was meeting an old friend for dinner,' Harriet replied. She rushed off to the kitchen and a few minutes later reappeared with a cup of sweet milky tea. She examined Beth's head, probing gently. 'It's still bleeding,' she said, sounding worried. 'After you've had your tea, I'm going to take you to the hospital. You can't be too careful with head wounds. I still can't quite see how you did it.'

'Unless I didn't,' said Beth quietly, her heart pounding as the unpalatable truth finally sank in. 'I think someone hit me on the head. I thought I heard footsteps following me at one point but when I turned round there was no one there.'

'That's quite a big leap,' said Harriet, moving away to sit in one of the cosy armchairs. 'Maybe they were just coming back from town and disappeared into another house? There are loads up the top end of Albany Street.'

'How did you know that's where I walked?' asked Beth, turning to look at her and causing her head to throb even more.

'Well, what other way would you have come? You surely didn't walk alongside the harbour at this time of night?'

'No,' admitted Beth. 'I only go that way when it's light.'

'Well then.' Harriet tutted, as though Beth had been accusing her of something.

Beth dutifully sipped her tea. She could feel strength seeping back into her limbs now that the shock was wearing off.

'You have a lovely home,' she said, glancing round the sumptuous room with its expensive swagged curtains and works of art adorning the walls. 'Have you lived here long?'

'I bought it after my husband died,' she said. 'Too many memories in the old house. It seemed easier to make a fresh start.'

'Yes, I know exactly what you mean,' Beth said. She pulled out her phone and called a taxi to take her to the hospital and was assured it would be with her in less than ten minutes.

'I would've gladly taken you,' said Harriet, looking slightly offended.

'You've been more than kind but I'm feeling so much better now. It's just a precaution really.' Beth smiled. 'By the way, I had no idea that Mike was such a talented writer. The short story he read out tonight was amazing.'

'He's talented alright,' Harriet said. 'He's been in various writing groups over the years, but his abrasive personality usually leads to him stomping off in a huff. He's his own worst enemy.'

'Maybe that's why he struggles so much with Dan?' offered Beth. 'It can't be easy seeing a younger man succeed where he's not amounted to much.'

'Did you know that Mike and I both taught Dan over the years? He demonstrated no writing talent whatsoever. We're mystified as to how he's transformed his clichéd unimaginative prose into work that triggered a bidding war,' said Harriet.

'People can change,' said Beth. 'Maybe he took some great writing courses and was a late bloomer?'

'Maybe, though I would've expected to see evidence of some

seeds of talent. Anyway, that aside, it's always gratifying when a former pupil does well.'

The doorbell rang and Beth managed to get to her feet without assistance, even if the room did spin like a kaleidoscope for a few seconds. As she was borne away in the taxi something was niggling her. Harriet's curtains had been closed. So how had she even spotted her falling down on the pavement?

TWENTY-SEVEN

Despite Beth's polite protests, a very nice but persistent doctor insisted she remain overnight for monitoring due to exhibiting symptoms of concussion. She'd ticked them off on her long fingers.

'You lost consciousness, albeit briefly. You vomited. I noted nystagmus in your eyes which isn't fully resolved yet. Also, when you move your head quickly, the room spins. I would be derelict in my duty if I didn't admit you as a patient.' She produced a blue and white hospital gown with a flourish.

Beth reluctantly accepted the gown. 'Okay, you win,' she said wearily, a tidal wave of fatigue threatening to carry her off into its depths.

'I usually do,' Dr Jones informed her, smiling to remove the sting. 'I'll leave you in Nurse Gordon's capable hands. I'll check back with you in the morning.' With that, she departed, a woman on a mission.

Once she was tied into the gown and settled beneath the starched sheet and blanket, Nurse Gordon looked at her as she smoothed the covers, as if gauging her likely reaction to what she had to say next.

'The police are here,' she said, tentatively.

Beth pulled herself upright, her head swimming and acid flooding into her mouth.

'Are they here to arrest me?' she gasped, heart pounding.

'What? No, of course not,' Nurse Gordon soothed, looking confused. 'They're here because you've been a victim of an assault.'

'Oh! Is that what they think happened?' asked Beth, tears springing to her eyes.

'Yes, I'm afraid so,' the nurse said, patting her hand. 'Can I send him in?' she asked. 'If you don't feel up to it, I can ask him to return tomorrow.' She adjusted the pillows so Beth could sit up more comfortably.

'No, it's fine. Best get it over with,' Beth replied with a grimace.

A couple of minutes later, DS Hunter entered. His bulk seemed to fill the tiny space and for once he looked somewhat at a loss. His suit was rumpled and there were dark shadows under his eyes.

'You look worse than I do.' Beth grimaced. 'Please, sit down.'

A smile twitched on and off. 'It's been a long day,' he admitted, doing as she asked. 'How are you feeling?'

'A bit sore and sorry for myself. In all the years I lived in Glasgow, I was never assaulted just out walking about.'

'The wound in your head has debris in it consistent with having been hit with a brick or large stone. Plus, an elderly lady looking out of her window saw you crumple on the pavement and someone wearing dark clothing run off down by the harbour. She phoned it in, that's how I got to hear about it. I went to your address then figured you must have come here.'

'So, someone definitely tried to hurt me...' Beth said.

'It appears to have been a targeted attack. Random assaults like this don't really happen up here,' he admitted, scratching his head and leaning his long body back in the chair. 'The odd crime of passion, an attempted bag snatch, a drunken punch-up maybe, but nothing like this. I take it your bag or phone weren't taken?'

'No. To be honest, I didn't even realise I'd been assaulted at first. I felt a bang on my head and my legs went from under me. I thought maybe I'd walked into something but there was nothing there. You really didn't have to come out. There's no chance of catching whoever it was. And given that you think I murdered Darcie Baxter you probably think it's poetic justice anyway.' Her lip wobbled as she said the last part and she strived to keep it under control. She was not going to break down in front of this man. She wouldn't give him the satisfaction.

'Look, Beth, I understand how you feel but I'm really not the enemy here. I admit it felt like a crime match made in heaven when I first learned about your background, but I've dug deeper since then. I even spoke to a couple of officers who worked the case that landed you in jail. Your former lawyer has been disbarred, did you know that?'

'No, I didn't. What for?' asked Beth.

'A long litany of professional incompetence.'

Beth was shocked. 'Incompetent? But... I put my trust in him,' she said.

'Anyway, I want you to know that while you remain a suspect, for obvious reasons, I'll follow any and all avenues that reveal themselves to me with equal determination.'

'Thank you,' Beth said, meaning it. 'I can't ask for any fairer than that, I suppose.'

'So, you were completely unaware of being approached before you were hit on the head?'

'Yes. I did hear footsteps behind me a short while before I was attacked but when I turned round no one was there.'

'The light's not the best out along that road,' the detective said. 'It'd be fairly easy to duck in a doorway or blend into the shadows. When you say footsteps, was there anything distinctive about them?'

'You mean did they have a wooden leg?' asked Beth, raising her eyebrows.

He laughed, which made him look a whole lot more friendly...

and handsome. Crikey, I really must have concussion, she thought in consternation.

'No, I meant, did it sound like they were high heels or flat, for example?'

'Sorry, I really couldn't say. All I know is that they seemed to match mine. They stopped when I stopped and continued once I started up again. Probably completely unrelated.'

'Unfortunately, there's no CCTV coverage there. If you'd been closer to the harbour, we might have had a shot at picking up something.'

'It's fine, really,' she said. 'Hopefully it was a one off.' She glanced down. 'Either that or someone was trying to send me a message.'

He narrowed his eyes. 'Tell me you haven't been trying to investigate the murder?' he growled.

'How could I possibly be doing that, when according to you lot, I did it myself?' she replied, lifting her chin and glaring at him defiantly.

'If you didn't, you do realise that poking this particular bear could result in the same thing happening to *you*? Why can't you just take a telling and leave it to us?'

'Maybe because that worked out so well for me before,' she snapped right back.

'What's going on in here?' demanded an angry male voice, as Harris entered the room.

'Nothing,' they chorused, looking guiltily at each other for reasons they didn't quite understand.

'What on earth do you think you're doing interviewing her when she's suffered a significant concussion?' Harris flung at the sergeant.

'Harris!' Beth interjected. 'How did you know I was here?'

'Taking ambulance chasing to a whole new level,' muttered DS Hunter, jumping to his feet as if embarrassed by being caught sitting down on the job.

'Harriet called me. She thought I'd want to know. Just as well I came, by the look of things. I picked you up a few things from the house.'

'How did you get in?' she asked.

'Yes, tell us, Harris, how did you get in?' said DS Hunter, folding his arms and looking from one to the other. 'Unless you and she...?'

'No! That's not it. I know where she keeps her key. I thought she'd need some stuff, that's all. It was a quick in and out. I don't know why you're making such a fuss. I'd do the same for anyone.'

The two men glared at each other, fizzing with mutual antipathy. Beth looked from one to the other. Why did they hate each other so much? She didn't want to be piggy in the middle of whatever beef they had with each other. The thought of Harris marching into her cottage and rifling through her drawers and toiletries felt just a bit invasive somehow. She could feel a wave of fatigue sweeping over her body as the adrenalin from before dissipated. Her eyes flickered, desperate to close as sleep beckoned.

Nurse Gordon bustled in, the light of battle in her eyes.

'Now, gentlemen, Beth needs to rest so I'm going to have to ask both of you to leave.' She stood by the open door, arms folded in a manner that brooked no argument.

Beth was asleep before the door closed behind them.

TWENTY-EIGHT

Beth was woken by the lights brightening and the arrival of Nurse Gordon. There was a swish of curtains being pulled and tea trolleys rattling as the ward slowly came to life. She had a banging headache but felt fine apart from that.

'What time is it?' she asked blearily, as a blood pressure cuff was wrapped round her arm.

'7.30am,' said Nurse Gordon. 'That's come down nicely. Follow my finger with your eyes without turning your head.'

Beth did as she asked.

The nurse nodded and smiled. 'The nystagmus has gone.' She changed the dressing on Beth's head wound next. 'Your wound is healing nicely. You'll likely be discharged when the doctor does her rounds.'

The tea trolley arrived at her door and Beth was surprised to discover she was hungry.

'Tea and toast, love?' asked the cheery woman, who was about her mother's age.

'Yes, please.' Beth smiled, beginning to feel slightly embarrassed about all the fuss being made over her.

The nurse hurried off and Beth settled back on her freshly plumped pillows, sipping tea and eating warm buttered toast. She frowned as she remembered last night's visit from DS Hunter and also from Harris. She'd seen a different side to the policeman. He had been kinder. She remembered his laugh and felt a pang of... what? Hurriedly she pushed that thought away. His visit last night didn't change anything. She was still his main suspect in a murder enquiry. Her mind drifted to Harris. It had troubled her that he'd let himself into her house and gone through her things, but it had come from a good place, she supposed.

To her relief she was discharged just after ten. As she got out of the taxi, the wind whipped her hair and she struggled up to her front door, braced against the cold. She'd phoned her staff from hospital and told them what had happened, so they knew she was going to be late. Toby rushed forward to greet her, meowing plaintively and winding in and out of her legs. As she walked through to the kitchen, she noticed that Harris had thought to put out a full bowl of dried food so Toby wouldn't be hungry and she was grateful. After feeding her cat a sachet of his favourite chicken feast and replenishing his dried food, she made a cafetiere of strong coffee and grabbed a Tunnock's tea cake from the tin as she pondered the events of the previous night. Did someone feel she was getting too close to the truth and wanted to warn her off? Could it have been the same person who murdered Darcie or someone else entirely? Her gut feeling was that it had to be connected.

Everyone who had been at the book group apart from Harriet had also been at the open mic night. She remembered her confusion as to how Harriet had even seen her through her closed curtains. What if she hadn't been in her house at all but lying in wait for her, rock in hand? Too slow to run away without being seen, so appearing to be her rescuer instead. But that would appear to be contradicted by the elderly witness, assuming she hadn't just seen someone out for a run rather than her attacker. Her head was starting to pound again so she took a couple of painkillers and drained her cup. If she sat ruminating here all day, she'd drive herself mad. She needed to be busy. Hurriedly she washed up her dishes and got showered and changed. As she picked up her keys, she glanced at the draining board with her dishes dripping dry. It looked so lonely somehow, a place setting for one. Surprised by unbidden tears, she gave herself a strict talking to. 'Don't be such a baby, Beth. Get your arse in gear and get on with some work.'

Head held high and shoulders back, she strode out of the house, pausing to consider whether to leave a spare key under the plant pot and deciding not to. She'd no intention of letting anyone rifle through her drawers again! Her face reddening at the thought of it, she rushed off down the road.

As she pushed open the door into the shop, she was pleased to see that it was busy and concentrated on helping her slightly harassed staff. Another tour bus. Morna's initiative of sending details and a catalogue ahead of time to the tour companies seemed to be paying off handsomely. The tourists got to choose and pay for their books in advance so had more time to explore the town on their stopover. It had caused a welcome spike in their projected turnover. Although it was Morna's idea, Chloe had promoted it across all their social media channels, proving that she was very much a team player.

Once the rush had abated, leaving a handful of regulars browsing in their wake, Beth paused. Her head was throbbing. She needed a rest. 'Time to stick the kettle on,' she announced.

'I'll make it,' said Lachlan. 'You need to sit and take it easy. You shouldn't have even been in today. I don't know what you were thinking.' He stalked off and Chloe made a gentle clucking sound as he went.

'Don't be mean.' Morna scowled. 'He's only worried about her. And he's not wrong,' she said, turning to scrutinise Beth. 'You're as white as a sheet. How's your head?'

'Still pounding,' Beth admitted, popping a couple of pills from her bag.

'I can't believe someone thumped you,' said Chloe. 'Oban is usually such a safe place. They could've killed you.'

'I don't think they intended to kill me, more just to stop me asking questions,' said Beth.

Lachlan overheard as he walked back through bearing a loaded tray. 'More like Russian roulette,' he said, as he placed it on the table for people to help themselves. 'A rock isn't exactly a finely tuned instrument. They were prepared to kill, in my humble opinion. Especially as whoever it was has most likely killed already.'

They all sipped their tea in worried silence for a few minutes.

'I didn't realise Harriet lived out that way,' said Beth. 'She came rushing out to help me. I just remember seeing her running down her garden steps to the pavement. But the thing is...'

'What?' they chorused.

'I can't see how she could've been aware of what happened. Her curtains were completely closed as it was dark. I didn't scream or make a sound. I was too shocked initially. My legs just went from under me.'

'Surely you're not suggesting that it was Harriet who hit you?' said Lachlan, sounding shocked.

'I'm not saying that exactly,' said Beth. 'But isn't it odd that I didn't see anyone run away?'

'It would've been easy for someone to dive over a garden wall and lie low until you'd gone inside Harriet's house before slipping away,' said Morna. 'Maybe Harriet looked out of her window for some reason and just happened to see you?'

'Maybe she was taking a fag break at the front door?' offered Chloe. 'Lots of people don't like to smoke in their house.'

'That would certainly explain it,' said Beth, feeling relieved.

'Did she suggest you call the police?' asked Morna.

'No, I don't recall that she did,' said Beth, struggling to remember. 'But I'd have said no anyway.'

'That's not the point,' said Morna. 'If someone was assaulted, it'd be the first thing you'd think of.'

'Normally,' said Chloe. 'But I suppose it all depends on whether her secret is that she murdered her husband in a scarily similar way.'

'Yes, she might want to fly under the radar,' said Morna. 'The last thing she would want is to involve the police. But it could just be that she thought getting you to a hospital was the most important thing.'

'I doubt she's even been considered as a suspect in Darcie's death,' said Beth with a sigh. She brightened. 'Talking of police,' she said, 'you'll never guess who paid me a visit in hospital!'

'Not the intrepid DS Hunter,' said Lachlan drily.

'The very same,' Beth replied. 'The weird thing was that he was actually pretty decent this time. At one point he even laughed... Imagine!' She played it up for dramatic effect.

'Nonetheless, I wouldn't let your guard down,' cautioned Lachlan. 'The longer this murder goes unsolved, the more pressure will be brought to bear on him by his superiors. If he doesn't charge someone soon then I reckon they'll send up a crack team of investigators from Glasgow to knock it on the head.'

Beth shivered. 'I don't know what's worse. Harris brought me some stuff from the house. I need to be more careful about where I hide my key. He just took it upon himself to enter my house. It was well intentioned, but it made me feel a bit...'

'Creeped out?' supplied Chloe.

'Well, yes, I suppose so.' Beth laughed.

Lachlan shook his head. 'With all that's going on you need to stop doing that. I suggest you leave a spare key here in the shop inside the safe. That way it might be a bit of a hassle coming back in but no one else can access your home.'

'How did you get on with lover boy last night?' asked Chloe.

'Stop calling him that!' Morna snapped. 'I don't know how many times I need to say that we're not together.'

'Well, that's good, because I did think he was a bit off last night,' said Beth. 'It's a side of him I haven't seen before. He was quite unpleasant to Mike.'

'Yeah, there was the poor bloke putting himself out there with his writing and Dan was so mean and sarcastic,' said Chloe. 'What was all that about? I mean, Mike was so lit up with pride he was positively glowing, yet Dan couldn't wait to tear him down.'

Morna shrugged, looking troubled. 'I've no idea. He was in a foul mood for sure. It didn't sit well with me considering how he's going to be this big shot author himself soon.'

'It's not all that long till his book launch,' said Lachlan.

'He's heading down to the central belt after Christmas then launching in all the major cities, culminating in some splashy affair in London, Piccadilly,' said Morna.

'I did ask him to do a launch event here, just before Christmas, but he said his publisher wouldn't allow it,' said Beth. 'It would've been quite the feather in our cap launching the career of a top tier author.'

'A bit of a shame,' said Lachlan, 'given the amount of support he has locally. The local press have been bigging him up and pre-orders for his book in the shop are the highest I've ever seen. They aren't even doing an event in Inverness. I can't understand it.'

'That said, it's one less thing for me to worry about,' said Beth, draining her cup and starting to load up the tray. 'Maybe it's for the best given everything else that has been going on.'

TWENTY-NINE

Beth hunched against the cold as she walked into the library from town, having picked up some more cat food. The wind was whipping up the golden leaves into a frenzy and white horses were galloping up the bay and crashing onto the pebble beach with a bang. Normally, she had a lie-in on a Monday but she felt time was running out for her so she was headed there to do the research that Harris had hinted might bear some fruit.

Fortunately, in this weather, she didn't have far to go as the library was in Albany Street past the police station. As she passed the window of the station, something compelled her to look in. Her eyes met those of Detective Sergeant Hunter. He was standing there, strong and rugged, coffee in hand, looking out. Beth's mouth opened in surprise and her steps slowed as though his gaze had pinned her in place like a butterfly on a board. Startled, he looked right back at her until she gave an awkward wave and moved on, her cheeks flaming. Why couldn't she behave like a regular person around him? It was infuriating. He must think she was a total weirdo. She had to extricate herself from this mess by finding the real murderer. Then she would never have to be glared at by him again. In fact, he might even have to apologise. The thought of that abject apology from the mighty detective kept her warm until she reached the library.

The heat hit her as she blew in the door along with several leaves.

'Hi, Sarah.' She grinned at the middle-aged librarian seated behind the desk.

'Beth! You're up and about early. I've only just opened up. Why don't you hang up your coat there?' she said, pointing to the mahogany coat stand. 'Are you here to tackle those microfiches you phoned about?'

'Yes, for my sins,' Beth replied, with a sigh.

Sarah led her through the back into a small room where the microfiche was located. She explained how the system worked and how to find back copies of *The Oban Times*.

'How far are you looking to go back?' she asked.

Beth thought about it. The last thing she wanted to do was to miss the needle in the haystack. Mentally she waved goodbye to her whole day off.

'Ten years or so.'

'Okay, so if you start over here. I'll load the first one for you. It won't take you long to get into the swing of things.'

'Thanks,' said Beth.

Sarah glanced around and whispered conspiratorially, 'Fancy a coffee? I shouldn't really but there's no one else in here and you're going to have your work cut out.'

'You're an angel.' Beth smiled. 'Milk and one sugar, please.'

She gathered up fiches for the first year and was already slowly moving through them when Sarah returned with a hot milky coffee and a plate of biscuits. Smiling her thanks, Beth continued. It would help if she knew what she was looking for, she thought.

Two hours passed. Beth groaned and massaged her stiff neck. This was hopeless. Bending to her work again she peered more closely, looking at a school photo from Oban Academy. That looked like... Mike. It had been taken in 2015. He was standing to the left of a mousey looking woman. She glanced at the names below the photo... Harriet? She was the deputy head here, and far more dowdy than the vibrant woman with impeccable taste that she knew now. Beth glanced at the date. It was only a few months before her husband died... or was murdered. She zoomed in on the image. Everyone else in the photograph was smiling but she was expressionless, with dark shadows under her eyes. Mike looked much younger and less cynical, like he hadn't given up on his dreams yet. The school had won a regional debating competition, and the winning team were holding a giant cup aloft. She didn't recognise any other names.

More vigilant now, she continued to plough through them all. It brought home to her the whole cycle of life. Births, deaths and marriages, the stuff of living. In one edition she discovered a twelve-year-old Chloe holding a huge cup for Highland dancing at the Fort William Highland games. She looked very cute but would probably die of shame should such a photo surface these days. There was a picture of Harris standing next to his father on the steps of their office on the day he was assumed as partner. He looked pale, tense and very young. His father was smiling expansively, but his eyes were hard as flint. The grip he had on Harris's shoulder didn't look entirely friendly.

Two hours later, her eyes felt dry and gritty, and she hadn't found anything else of major interest. Sighing, she stood up and stretched then sat back down again. There must be something in here. Harris wouldn't have sent her on a fool's errand. Whatever it was probably postdated Harris's arrival at the firm which she understood to be two years prior to being made partner. She scoured all the court reports as well as the news sections. It gave her a jolt to see a less weathered Lachlan standing proudly outside the bookshop beside an older man who was clearly the owner. He looked so happy, Beth thought.

She peered at the photo again. There was a woman standing to one side, wreathed in smiles. She looked familiar. With a jolt she realised that it was a softer, younger-looking Darcie Baxter. The way she was looking at him... it seemed intense. Just how long had they been intimately involved? Her death had probably caused him even more pain than she had realised. Giving herself a shake, she continued. She couldn't keep going down the rabbit hole or her research would never be done. As the years advanced, she noticed more and more of the local court cases seemed to have DS Hunter as a witness for the prosecution. No wonder there was bad blood between him and Harris. They must have enacted numerous court battles over the years. She hoped that was all that it was. Maybe it wasn't the best idea having a defence lawyer who had an enormous beef with the local police.

Another couple of hours passed and she was on the verge of calling it a day when she spotted something. It was a small paragraph at the end of the news section about the death of Harriet's husband. It said that he'd left The Fisherman's Arms pub down by the harbour late at night and suffered a fatal blow to the head on falling. Witnesses in the pub indicated that he had been inebriated and unsteady on his feet when he left. It was found to be an accidental death. He was survived by his wife. Beth's pulse quickened as she read the next paragraph. Local fisherman, Murray Jones, who was drinking in the pub that night said that Arthur Brown had been drinking steadily all night and had become aggressive and argumentative. His wife had been there earlier that night but had left after an argument. As far as Beth was concerned, that gave her means and opportunity for murder. She sat back in her seat to ponder the significance of her find. She had to track down this witness and persuade him to tell her exactly what happened that night without alerting Harriet that she was digging into her past. Was this what Harris had meant her to find? With a sinking heart she realised it couldn't be. There appeared to have been no Fatal Accident Inquiry and no criminal trial, therefore his firm would have had no reason to be involved. There must be something else. Glancing up at the clock on the wall she saw that it was already nearly 3pm. Her eyes were dry and gritty and her stomach was rumbling with hunger. She'd have to come back another time. Noting the issue that she was up to in her notebook, she slammed it shut and left. At least she had one solid lead to pursue in the meantime.

THIRTY

Beth presented herself at the bookshop half an hour before closing. A warm fug of heat and coffee hit her as she opened the door. 'I need someone to come to the pub with me tonight,' she said. Her startled staff looked at her then at each other. She had never made such a request of them before.

'Er, I have this thing ...' said Chloe, twisting a strand of hair between her fingers and avoiding eye contact.

'Sorry, no can do,' said Morna. 'There's a new expansion pack on my game released today. All my guild will be there tonight.'

Chloe burst out laughing. 'It would've been better if you'd said you were washing your hair!'

'What? Like you clearly need to do?' fired back Morna.

'I do NOT!' said Chloe, fishing out a mirror from her bag.

'Gotcha!' said Morna, with a contented smile.

'What's this really about?' asked Lachlan.

Wow, thought Beth, a little hurt. So she was Billy No-Mates. 'Relax,' she said. 'I'm not proposing it as a social event as such. It's just that I learned the name of someone today who was in the pub the night Harriet's husband died. He'd said they had an argument and Harriet left early. I thought if I went to The Fisherman's Arms, I could maybe get into conversation with him and ask about it.'

'What's his name?' asked Lachlan.

'Murray Jones?'

Lachlan nodded. 'I know who he is. Been a fisherman all his life and his dad before him. All but ruined with the drink, I hear.'

'Well, hopefully not too much to remember what happened to Harriet's husband,' Beth replied.

'You don't want to go in there on your own,' cautioned Lachlan. 'It's a bit of a spit and sawdust place, popular with the men on the boats. Not your kind of place at all.'

Beth drew herself up to her full height. 'I'm not as feeble as you seem to think I am,' she said. 'I can handle a bit of swearing and the like. Fine, if no one will come with me, I'll go on my own. I'm sure it'll be perfectly fine.' She turned to go.

'Wait!' called Lachlan. 'I'll come with you. It'll be safer if I'm there, albeit marginally. I'm no Mohammed Ali if things turn ugly.'

'Thanks, Lachlan. It really shouldn't come to that.' Beth smiled.

'I can come, too, if you like,' muttered Chloe, looking like she'd rather pull out her own fingernails.

'No need,' Beth said. 'I'm sure we'll be okay. Meet you outside the pub at seven?'

'Fine,' said Lachlan. 'I've never been the muscle before.' He smirked.

She walked home as fast as she could, taking care to be vigilant and glance all around her as she went. She wasn't going to be caught napping a second time. Once home, she drew the curtains and put on some music as she first fed Toby then cast about for something to make for her own supper. She certainly wasn't going to drink on an empty stomach. Settling for macaroni with tomatoes and broccoli, she flopped onto the couch to eat it. If she could only get to the bottom of who killed Darcie and remove herself from suspicion, her life here would be quite perfect, she decided. Her eyes flew to the picture of her mum which took pride of place on the mantelpiece with a beautiful candle beside it. Losing her beloved mum to the ravages of MS had left her heartbroken.

She put her empty plate in the kitchen then moved to light the candle, closing her eyes as the lime and bergamot scent drifted into the air, her mother's favourite. 'I hope you're happy wherever you are,' she murmured, planting a kiss on the photo frame. 'I'm living my big life just as you wanted for me, or I will be, once I'm not in the frame for murder, but you don't need to worry about that,' she added hurriedly. 'It's being handled.'

Putting the photo frame down, she glanced at her watch and hurried through to her bedroom. What to wear? Toby jumped up on her bed and made himself at home, as if to offer a critique on her fashion choices. It was apparently a bit of a dive so she needed to look like she belonged. Somewhat at a loss she looked at her wardrobe which mainly consisted of floral or tweed skirts and cardigans with pearl buttons. Her one pair of skinny jeans were in the wash. Wait a minute, didn't she have some old gardening jeans? She pulled them out from the back of the wardrobe and viewed them with distaste. They were clean but faded. Next, she cast around for a top. Pussy bow blouses weren't going to cut it. She managed to find a plain navy t-shirt she could tuck in to the jeans and tucked those in turn into her boots. An eighties fringed scarf she'd pinched from her mother completed the look. She messed and scrunched her hair and threw on a denim jacket. After that it was time to attempt some makeup. Instead of her usual barely-there look she outlined her eyes in kohl and applied smoky eye shadow as well as choosing a bolder lip colour. 'What do you think, Tobes?' she asked, giving her cat a twirl.

He looked at her as though she had taken leave of her senses, which perhaps she had. Dropping a kiss on his grumpy head she slipped out of the house into the crisp night air.

THIRTY-ONE

The smell of fish grew stronger as Beth rounded a corner, heading for the harbour. It was darker here than elsewhere, as though the sparse lighting favoured dodgy deals in the shadows. It didn't seem like the type of place a prim and proper headmistress would choose to drink but her husband must have been cut from coarser cloth. A man stepped from the shadows and she did a double take. Lachlan, too, had modified his usual wardrobe and was wearing faded jeans and a blue fisherman's sweater underneath a battered brown leather jacket. He'd even mussed up his hair, bless him.

'Will I do?' She grinned, batting her heavily coated eyelids at him.

'I'm getting a student Beth vibe,' he said.

The smile slipped off her face. 'If only,' she said. 'I never even sat my exams, let alone went on to university.'

'I'm sorry, I'd no idea,' said Lachlan, looking thoughtful. 'You've always come across to me as well educated, the stuff you know...'

'All courtesy of my local library.' She shrugged. 'I suppose you could say I'm self-educated.' She took a deep breath and squared her shoulders. 'Right, let's do this.'

Determinedly, she led the way and pushed through the heavy

wooden door with stained glass panels into the pub beyond. Despite the early hour, the pub was heaving and a warm fug of beer, whisky and food engulfed her. Lachlan fought his way to the bar as she looked round for a space to sit. Some of the fishermen were still in their oilskins getting wired into heaped plates of food that smelled homemade, making her mouth water. Observing Lachlan as he weaved through the crowd, drinks held aloft, she was surprised to see that he didn't look at all out of place. He was a bit of a chameleon. Fortunately, an old couple got up to leave their table before he joined her so she shimmied into the vacated space as quick as a flash. Her heart sank as she glanced at the animated faces around her. A few of them were several sheets to the wind already. How on earth was she going to find out if this guy was even here without getting a knuckle sandwich?

Lachlan squeezed in beside her, handing her a glass of white wine and taking a slug from his pint of lager. 'He's over there,' he said, jerking his head over to the left. Beth craned her neck and saw a wiry old man in oilskins sitting on his own, nursing a pint and a whisky chaser.

'How well do you know him?' Beth asked.

'Barely at all. My mother was friendly with his wife. They were in a knitting circle together before she died a few years ago. He's been a bit of a lost soul since then by all accounts. I didn't even recognise him at first. I had to get the bar man to point him out to me.'

'That's so sad,' said Beth.

'You know who else is here?'

'Who?' Beth asked, looking swiftly around the busy bar. Suddenly her heart almost stopped as she locked eyes with Detective Sergeant Hunter who was sitting at the side of the bar staring at her. Ironically, he raised his pint to her then proceeded to approach them. He was clearly off duty so what the hell was he doing in here? she wondered wildly as he materialised in front of her.

She craned her neck to stare up at him and was mortified to see that he looked amused. She could withstand his hostility but being mocked was another thing all together.

'Mind if I join you?' he asked, his brown eyes daring her to say no.

Rather desperately, she glanced over at Lachlan before turning back to her nemesis.

'Sure,' she said weakly, shifting along to let him in. She could feel the heat emanating from him as he squashed in beside her. He turned those appraising, all-seeing eyes on her. Defiantly she stared right back at him, her colour rising. His jeans hugged the curve of his thighs and she had the strangest impulse to brush his hair with her fingers. Her mind snapped back to the present and she realised she'd been caught staring. *Great*. Now he'd think she was a proper bunny boiler.

'What on earth are you doing here?' she blurted out.

'It's the closest boozer to my home. Love the new look, by the way.' His eyes crinkled as his mouth twitched. 'Very retro. It suits you,' he said, reflectively. 'Makes you look less... well, never mind.'

'No DC Quinn tonight?' she asked, striving to keep things on a professional footing. Lachlan was no help because a woman he appeared to know had now engaged him in conversation. No doubt another customer. She longed to be as accepted in the community as he clearly seemed to be. All those years of managing the bookshop had sewn him into the fabric of the town. Was she always destined to be an outsider?

'We're work colleagues, not friends,' he said. 'She's more of a wine bar type.'

'I don't know what type I am,' she mused. 'I'd never been out socially until I arrived here, due to caring for my mum.'

He looked at her, his eyes warmer than usual. 'That must have been tough.'

'Not at all!' she replied defensively. 'I was glad to do it. My mum was my best friend. She stuck by me when everyone else melted away. So, how long have you known Harris?' she asked, desperate to change the subject.

'We were both born here but he was sent off to some posh boarding school while I grew up here and went to the local comprehensive.'

Gosh, it was hot in here tonight. Although she'd only had one glass of wine, it had quite gone to her head. Awkward as this was, she decided it was a golden opportunity to pump him for information from his local knowledge. If she was careful, he might not work out what she was up to.

'You must know one of my customers, Harriet Brown?' she ventured. 'I gather she used to be headmistress of the local school. What was she like back in the day?'

He grimaced. 'Tough as old boots, if I recall. She hauled me over the coals many a time. Not saying I didn't deserve it, mind,' he said with a twinkle in his eye. 'I was a bit of a bad boy back then, if you can believe it.'

'Bad how?' she asked, laughing. She was certainly seeing a different side of him tonight and she liked it.

'Let me see? There was the time me and my mate set off a joke tear gas capsule in the class. Everyone's eyes were streaming and we'd to evacuate the class. It got me out of maths at least. The science teacher thought it was a chemical spill from a local plant. Harriet, however, saw right through it and marked my card good and proper. Then there were the days I bunked off to go fishing and drinking. Poor woman thought I was heading for a life of crime. Back then, I admit, it could've gone either way. She did her best to straighten me out.'

Beth wondered if his gratitude and loyalty to his former teacher had blinded him to the possibility that she might have murdered her husband.

'Such a shame that she lost her husband the way she did. It must've been hard on her,' Beth said, trying to insert the right amount of sympathy into her voice. 'The girls in the shop mentioned it.'

'Yes and no,' he said, his face sombre. 'Arthur was a real piece of work. It's no secret around here that he kept her on a tight leash.

Nowadays, you'd call it coercive control. He was a mean drunk and not shy about lashing out with his fists. I remember going to the house to tell her he was gone. She collapsed in my arms. Still had feelings for him despite everything.'

'My father was one of those. It put me off men for life,' she said, aiming for light-hearted. It didn't come out that way. She cringed as he gave her one of his long considering stares.

'Is that why you've never married?' he asked softly.

'Married? I've never even been on a date,' she blurted out, then immediately wanted to stuff the words back into her mouth. She didn't want his pity. 'After what I went through when I was young, all I wanted was to feel safe again. I suppose you could say I became risk averse. I was... am... perfectly content.'

'You're hiding,' he said, bluntly. 'I get that but it's no way to live.'

Beth felt her hackles go up. How dare he presume to give her relationship advice on the one hand whilst doing his best to put her in the frame for murder with the other? It was time she put *him* on the spot.

She stared right at him and smiled sweetly. 'So, what about you? Married? Divorced? Kids?'

He looked evasive but she wasn't going to let him off the hook. He shifted in his seat so that a space opened up between them. Part of her irrationally wanted to shuffle after him and close it again.

'Married to the job,' he deflected with a grin.

'And?'

He sighed as though he wished he'd never started this conversation. 'Widowed, one child, a little girl aged six.'

Beth's hand flew to her mouth in shock. 'I'm so sorry, we can absolutely change the subject.'

'It's fine.' He grimaced. 'It's not as though it's a secret. I married Ailsa in my mid-twenties. We were very happy. After a couple of years, we had Poppy. Life was good. And then it wasn't. Cancer. She fought it with everything she had. It wasn't enough.' His voice cracked on the last word and he looked away. Beth squeezed his arm then changed the subject so he could recover himself.

'We were talking about Harriet earlier,' she said. 'I know it's probably a crazy coincidence but coming into the town as a complete outsider with no context, it occurred to me that there were similarities in both cases.'

'How so?' he asked, back in sceptical copper mode.

'Well, Harriet's husband, Arthur, died from a blow to the head which was put down to him being so drunk that he fell and banged his head on the pavement. Darcie suffered a blow to the head as well, most likely from a brick or rock of some kind.'

'Where are you going with this?' he asked, impatient now, the fire back in his eyes.

'Have you considered the possibility that Harriet might have murdered her husband then killed Darcie to avoid her secret getting out? Don't you see? She had means, motive and opportunity.'

His jaw tightened and he narrowed his eyes. Their previous tentative rapport had vaporised, and Beth felt its loss but knew she had no other choice but to make him see that there could be additional suspects he hadn't considered.

'Did it ever occur to you that she might have had an alibi?' he said, his voice dripping sarcasm.

'Well, did she?' Beth snapped.

'I have no idea. I wasn't the investigating officer,' he admitted reluctantly. 'The woman I know, it's unthinkable,' he then muttered.

'But it's not unthinkable that it was me,' she said flatly, turning away from him and sending a desperate look across to Lachlan who was still chatting to the person he knew.

'I'm sorry, this was a mistake,' he murmured, downing his remaining pint in one swig and getting up to leave. She felt a pang seeing him go, just when she felt she'd been getting through to him. Making him see that she was a person and not just a mugshot in his gallery of rogues.

THIRTY-TWO

Lachlan's friend got up to leave and he leaned across to Beth. 'Right, if we're going to do this, we'd best get on with it,' he said, inclining his head towards the local fishermen. 'I'll get him a round in first to sweeten the deal. I'll go in first then I'll wave you across if he's amenable.'

Beth nodded her agreement and sat back to wait. She was impressed by Lachlan's quiet confidence as he first visited the bar then slid onto a stool at the old man's table. A couple of minutes later he waved her across and she got up to join them. 'Beth,' she said with a smile, sticking out her hand. He roared with laughter, ignoring it. 'Right city lass, this one,' he said to Lachlan, who nodded in agreement. 'Sit yourself down, lass, we don't stand on ceremony up here.'

Beth perched on a stool, her cheeks flaming red in embarrassment. How to begin?

'Lachlan here tells me you're interested in an argument I overheard ten years ago?'

'Yes, between the man who died, Arthur, and his wife, Harriet.'

'I'm not one for the tittle-tattle,' he said, the mischievous gleam in his eyes suggesting otherwise. 'Maybe another drink might help me polish up the old grey cells. It gets harder to remember at my age.'

The years of boozing won't help either, thought Beth, as she jumped up to order yet another round of drinks and carried them back to the table.

'Arthur was a hard man,' he said, downing his last pint and chasing it down with the whisky. 'He'd pound you to a pulp just for looking at him the wrong way. Don't get me wrong, when he was a young man, he was quite the charmer. He'd never have snared a fine lass like Harriet otherwise. When they first got wed, he was the one in the driving seat, everyone thought he was going places. He'd money to burn then. Never set foot in this boozer. Back then he fancied himself a pillar of the community, thought he was more upmarket like, better than the likes of us in here.' He started coughing, hacking away till he was gasping for air, his chest rattling.

'I'll get you some water,' said Beth, jumping to her feet.

A bony hand grasped her wrist. 'Another beer and a wee dram will do the job,' he said, peering up at her through rheumy eyes.

With some reservations she acquiesced and got another round for him. There was no way she and Lachlan could match him drink for drink so they didn't even try.

'Thank ye kindly,' he said, eagerly supping.

Beth felt guilty that they were enabling someone who clearly had a drinking problem but felt she had no choice but to continue.

'Well, that young lass Harriet, it wasn't long before she lost her bloom. There were more and more so-called accidents where she'd supposedly walked into doors and the like. My sister, Nancy, was a nurse at the hospital at the time. Harriet was down as a frequent flyer. Nancy tried her best to get her to accept help, but she was having none of it. It made her rage with frustration but there was nothing she could do with her tight-lipped as a clam.'

'Do you remember the night he died outside here?' asked Beth, eager to cut to the chase as he was already slurring his words.

'Clear as a bell.' He snuffled. 'By then, he'd become a sour drunk and got barred from the more upmarket places round here.

Reduced to slumming it in here, he was, dragging the missus everywhere with him like a whipped dog on a chain. It was hard to watch.'

'I heard they'd a row that night,' said Lachlan. 'Could you hear what it was about?'

'I was sat at the table next to them. He started cosying up to some random woman, you know the type, makeup pasted on with a trowel. False eyelashes batting away like a bloody Tarantula. I remember that much.'

'Poor Harriet,' said Beth.

'Harriet was a classy woman, despite what he put her through, but that night was a humiliation too far. She upended his pint over him and stormed out. Course, he was up and at her like a raging bull but a few good men in here held him back, knowing if he caught up with her, she'd get a pasting. Eventually, he sat back down, nursing a pint the landlord bought him, and stayed until nearly closing time. He was staggering by then. He'd had a gutful. It was only when the rest of us turned out onto the street at closing time that we clocked him lying in the gutter, the back of his head bashed in from where he'd banged it on the edge of the pavement. And good riddance,' he added.

'When you all spilled out, did you notice anyone else hanging around who hadn't been inside?' Beth asked. 'What about Harriet?'

The old man snorted. 'There was no sign of her. I expect she'd got out of there sharpish. She'd not have dared to go home, the mood he was in.'

But she had, thought Beth, feeling a flutter of excitement. The police had notified her at home. A place she would only have gone if she'd known she was free of her abuser. She was as sure as could be that Harriet had murdered her husband that night. But whether she would have it in her to murder Darcie to protect herself, she still didn't know...

THIRTY-THREE

The following morning, Beth woke early after a restless night of feverish dreams. To clear her head, she sat outside in her small back garden, muffled up in her winter coat watching Toby chasing the autumn leaves. As night gave way to day, the sun streaked the sky with red and gold. Cupping her mug of hot tea in her fingerless gloves, she munched on a slice of hot buttered toast. A robin hopped over and perched on the wooden trellis beside her, its beady eyes beseeching her for crumbs. She threw a corner of her toast for him, mindful of Toby but he was distracted and didn't notice. The robin dropped down and took it in his beak before flying off to a place of safety to enjoy his spoils.

She thought back to that fateful meeting of the book group and fervently wished she had never started it. It had clearly acted as a catalyst. The moment Darcie had mentioned exposing a secret she had effectively signed her own death warrant. At first, she had been sure it was herself who was the target and she remembered her heart beating faster and her hands feeling clammy as she wondered whether she was about to be exposed. Had it occurred to her for even one second to commit murder to ensure her new life wasn't put in jeopardy? Of course not. Legally she had paid for her crime already. She was no stranger to starting over if needs be. No, it made far more sense for the secret that had triggered the murder to be something for which no debt had yet been paid.

Ronnie had no obvious secret that she'd been able to discover but that didn't mean that she didn't have one. Beneath the glamour beat the heart of a hard-nosed businesswoman. How else could she have succeeded to the extent that she had, coming from such a troubled background? But what could her secret be? Was it something to do with her finances? Could she have been bankrolled by organised crime or drug money? No, that was completely insane. Or was it? How on earth could she find out without putting herself in the firing line once more?

They'd uncovered two of Mike's secrets but were they sufficiently heinous that he'd kill to avoid them coming to light? Could there be something else of which she was still unaware? Until the open mic night, she'd have sworn Dan was a regular boy scout, but he'd shown a rather unpleasant side to him then. It seemed that the antipathy between him and Mike was not a one-way street. Dan was on the cusp of literary fame and fortune. Could Darcie have uncovered something unsavoury about his past that would lead to him being cancelled and dropped by his publisher? He certainly had a lot to lose.

The cold was starting to bite and her whole body was trembling, whether from nerves or the cold, she couldn't say. She had a feeling that time was running out for her to solve the mystery before the police decided to arrest her. If she was remanded into custody, she would have no means to discover the truth. This had to be her top priority, or she could very well have her freedom taken from her for the foreseeable future. Shivering with dread she rose to her feet and Toby followed her into the house where he snuggled down on his favourite chair and commenced grooming before settling down for his morning nap. She made a fuss of him then grabbed her keys. It occurred to her that she hadn't heard from Harris in a while. He was meant to be her defence lawyer. Shouldn't he be agitating for more disclosure of evidence from the police? Perhaps it was time to pay him another visit and check that he was well and truly on her side. She wasn't going to face another serious charge with lukewarm representation, that was for sure.

The moment the heavy wooden door swung back, Beth stepped forward, a bright smile on her face.

'Good morning, Miss Pringle,' she said.

The older woman sighed. 'Miss Cunningham. I suppose you'd better come in.' As they walked up the stairs to reception, she added, 'I really don't know how to convince you to make an appointment like everyone else.'

'I'm sorry,' Beth said, genuinely contrite. 'The trouble is I never really seem to know in advance when I'm going to have a pressing need for Mr Kincaid's services. I'll try to do better. You really are a dear not to turn me away. I appreciate it. Really, I do.'

Miss Pringle sighed but looked mollified. 'Tea? Milk and one sugar?'

'Thank you, I'm flattered that you remembered.' Beth smiled.

'Some clients have a way of sticking in one's mind,' was the dry reply, though accompanied by a slight twitch of the lips.

She was ushered to the waiting room where she sat in her regular chair. There were two other clients in the room this morning. A lean angular farmer and a young woman with reddened eyes as though she'd been crying. Everyone studiously avoided everyone else's gaze as though they were embarrassed at being caught out with a legal problem. The other two were claimed by two other lawyers in turn. Miss Pringle turned up with her cup and saucer on a tray. She'd even put a piece of shortbread on the side.

'Thank you.' Beth smiled up at her. 'That's really very kind.'

'All part of the service,' the older woman said, but with a warning glint in her eye, as if to say, don't get too used to it. Beth suspected that her mother and Miss Pringle would have got along famously.

'I don't suppose you remember my mother, Rosemary Cunningham?' she asked diffidently. Miss Pringle stiffened, as if unsure how to respond at first, but her voice when she spoke was warm.

'I do indeed, a lovely woman,' she said. 'We even acted for your grandmother as well. Your grandmother had the very first Mr Kincaid then your mother dealt with Harris's father when she began planning for her... untimely... demise. And now, you have young Mr Harris. It's the way things used to be done. Your relationship with your doctor or lawyer was from cradle to grave.'

'I like that idea,' said Beth. 'It's rather comforting, that kind of continuity.'

'Not for much longer,' Miss Pringle sighed. 'Nowadays everyone is fickle, running here, there and everywhere for the lowest quote, the bottom line. Sadly, that doesn't mean a better service, but no one seems to care about that anymore.'

'I care,' said Beth softly, which resulted in a proper smile this time.

'Drink your tea before it gets cold,' she said. 'He won't be long now.' With that, she left to impose order elsewhere.

It was strange to think of her mother and grandmother before her sitting in these very chairs waiting for their lawyers just as she was now. She really hoped that Harris was on the level. It would hurt in so many ways if he was not acting in her best interest.

Suddenly, her teacup froze halfway to her mouth as she heard raised voices coming from the corridor. It was Harris and Detective Sergeant Hunter. They were clearly arguing... about her, she realised, the colour rising in her cheeks.

'You do realise I'm going to have to charge her soon, don't you? I mean, I've got the Chief Constable breathing down my neck on this one. This kind of murder never happens here. It's a total anomaly. The Procurator Fiscal is on my case. The press is all over us like a rash. My hand is being forced.'

'I don't know what you expect from me,' Harris argued back. 'I can't pluck another suspect for you out of thin air.'

'Just do your job, man, and mount her a bloody good defence.'

'I fully intend to,' snapped Harris.

'She's going to need it,' the sergeant said.

Beth heard brisk footsteps marching away and the door at the end of the corridor being opened and shut none too gently. She felt Harris's presence outside the door, but he didn't march in and claim her immediately. Her stomach churned and she felt clammy. What had just happened? It sounded like she was going to be charged but DS Hunter seemed to feel that while the evidence pointed to her culpability his gut was telling him otherwise. It could also be interpreted as him feeling that Harris wasn't working hard enough on her behalf to mount a strong defence. If not, then why not? He'd gone from being very proactive to her not hearing from him at all.

Quiet footsteps approached. 'Miss Cunningham's in the waiting room for you, Harris.'

'She is? But she doesn't have an appointment,' he snapped back at her.

'No, but you were free, so I thought...' she said, clearly taken aback at his tone.

The door opened abruptly. Beth jumped to her feet in time to see Miss Pringle hurrying away, her head down as though she was upset.

'I can come back another time,' she said quietly. 'Make an appointment...'

She went to move past him, but he grabbed her arm. Surprised, she just looked at him and he released his grip.

'Sorry,' he muttered. 'Look, don't go. We need to talk. I haven't been entirely honest with you.'

Shocked, she followed him along the corridor and perched on the edge of the chair opposite his desk. He looked pale and drawn, with dark shadows under his eyes and a twitch at the side of his mouth. What on earth was going on?

'Someone has been blackmailing me,' he said.

'What?' Beth gasped. 'Who?'

'I've no idea.'

'When did it start?'

'Around a week after the police detained you that first time.'

'So, that's why you haven't been working on my defence,' Beth said quietly. Although she understood, she still felt let down. She had put her trust in him.

'No, I have been working on it,' he said. 'I've just been giving the appearance of not doing it. I paid a friend in one of the other firms to dig around and obtain witness statements whilst staying under the radar and keeping my name out of it.'

'Oh!' said Beth, brightening. Maybe all wasn't lost after all. 'So that's why Logan... I mean, Detective Sergeant Hunter, was in earlier, trying to chivvy you along?'

His face darkened. 'Yes. Although what gives him the right to barge in here shouting the odds when he's meant to be working for the prosecution, I have no idea.'

Beth blushed, remembering that night in the pub. Maybe the attraction hadn't been as one-sided as she thought.

'Are you alright?' He frowned across the desk at her. 'You look a bit flushed.'

'Just a bit of a bug coming on,' she said hastily. Time to change the subject. 'So how much money is the blackmailer asking for?' she asked, pushing the focus back onto him.

'Nothing,' he replied. 'It's not that kind of blackmail.'

'What do you mean?' she asked, confused. 'What other kind is there?'

'Whoever it is wants me to mount a shoddy defence for you and basically do everything I can to get you convicted. Once that happens, they've said I'm off the hook.'

Beth jumped to her feet and began to pace up and down as she tried to absorb what he was telling her. Harris slumped back in his chair and waited, his eyes tracking her movements. Finally, she spun back round to face him.

'But that's crazy? What on earth have I done to them that they want me put away for a murder that I didn't commit?'

'Don't you see?' he said, his voice wooden. 'You're just the fall guy. The person blackmailing me is the person who DID commit the murder.'

'So, who is it? Tell me!' she demanded.

'Honestly, I have no idea,' he said, sinking his head in his hands. 'All communication has been by text from a burner phone.'

Flopping back down in her chair she realised that there was something else he was keeping from her. Something that might be big enough to change her regard for him for ever.

'What on earth did you do?' she asked.

'Look, I can't tell you why I'm being blackmailed. But I can tell you that it's got nothing to do with your case.'

'And I'm supposed to trust you because...?'

'Look, I get why you're angry, but I'd never do anything to hurt your case, Beth. I just need whoever it is to think they've nobbled me for a bit longer until I can work out exactly who they are and how best to proceed. This is someone else's mess but it's down to me to clear it up.'

'Why don't you just go to the police?' she asked, bewildered. 'I'm sure you can trust DS Hunter. You might not be best mates, but you said yourself he's got integrity. You could come by my house and I could arrange for him to be there to hear what you've got to say.'

'Oh, he'd love that,' he said, his voice bitter. 'I can't bring this to the police, Beth. Don't you see? That's the whole point. Lives and reputations will be ruined.'

'Including yours?' she asked quietly.

'Yes, including mine,' he said, unable to meet her eyes.

'So, should I get another lawyer?'

'That is your right,' he said wearily. 'I won't stand in your way.'

'I'll think about it and let you know,' she said formally. Without further ado, she gathered up her bag and left the room without looking back. She could feel the net closing in on her. Time was running out. She had to discover the truth before it was too late.

THIRTY-FOUR

Beth bought herself a hot chocolate and sat on a wooden bench overlooking the bay. The cup warded off the chill in her frozen fingers as she stared out at the small island of Kerrera and tried to organise her whirling thoughts into a plan of action. The black storm clouds looming over the dark frothy waves mirrored how she felt.

Despite what he had said, she felt that her relationship with Harris had been irretrievably compromised. But the thought of starting from scratch with a new lawyer who knew nothing about her past made her feel sick with dread. Without knowing what whoever it was had on him, how could she trust that he wouldn't cave and hang her out to dry just like her first lawyer had done all those years ago? She had to get him to talk. But how? Her options were limited. She would worry about that later, she decided. Her immediate priority had to be unmasking the murderer before she was arrested herself which, judging by what she had heard, was likely to be imminent.

Even though DS Hunter now appeared to be open to the fact that she might be innocent, it would still count for nothing if he was leaned on from above without a plausible alternative suspect to hand. After what had happened to her as a child, she had always strived to play by the rules as though doing so could inoculate her from ever falling foul of the law again. Now, though, it looked like she no longer had a choice. She was fighting for her survival. If ever there was a time for taking risks, it was now. Decisively, she drained her cup and stowed it in her satchel before jumping to her feet and heading to the shop.

A welcome blast of heat warmed her as she stepped over the threshold to find a large number of kids in fancy dress sitting listening to Chloe who was finishing off a ghostly Halloween story. She was amused to see that Chloe had positioned Toby's basket beside her and was encouraging him to stay there for the children by drip feeding him fish-flavoured Dreamies. She was an absolute natural with kids, thought Beth, feeling a bit of a pang as she took in how cute they all looked. A bunch of parents sat conversing quietly around the large table drinking tea as Chloe weaved her magic spell over their offspring. As the story ended, they all started clapping and the noise shot from zero to high-pitched mayhem in an instant as they all ran across to their parents for juice and orange cupcakes with witches' hats etched on them, chattering nineteen to the dozen. Toby shot up to the top of a bookcase, viewing the mayhem with a furrowed brow. She was shocked to come face to face with Detective Sergeant Hunter, as he emerged from the children's section, clutching the hand of a little girl dressed as a witch with black and red stripy tights and a purple silk tunic with a sparkly belt. She was clutching a book about witches and looked up at Beth with solemn dark eyes and a shy smile.

There was an embarrassed silence then he cleared his throat. 'This is Poppy. I hope you don't mind... there was a leaflet in her schoolbag and she really wanted to come...'

'Of course not! Delighted to meet you, Poppy. My name's Beth. I hope you've had fun today. Halloween is one of my favourite times of the year. Are you going guising tonight?'

Poppy looked confused. 'No, we're going trick or treating,' she said, looking up at her dad for confirmation.

'In my day, it was called guising and all the children used to perform a party piece before they got given their sweeties.'

'And what was yours?' he asked drily.

'I played the recorder.' She grinned up at him. 'They gave me sweeties to make me stop.'

'I can imagine,' he laughed, his eyes crinkling.

'Anyway, Poppy, thank you for coming to storytime this morning and have a lovely time tonight. Don't eat all those sweeties at once!'

'I won't.' The little girl smiled sweetly, and they went off to the till to pay for their book.

Beth circulated amongst the remaining parents and their children, but her eyes followed DS Hunter and his daughter until they left the shop. She felt an irrational sense of loss. Seeing him with his daughter had somehow made him whole in her eyes rather than the disjointed fragments of interrogator and disturbingly attractive beer drinker that she had assembled to date. Frustratingly, she wanted nothing more than to become closer to the one person who was most likely to destroy her. What kind of twisted logic was that? Giving herself a mental shake she resolved to put the elusive police detective out of her mind and focus on extricating herself from the huge mess she was in.

As Morna closed the door behind the last sugar-fuelled kid and turned the sign to 'Closed' they all heaved a sigh of relief.

'Great job, Chloe.' Beth beamed at Chloe, whose idea it had been. Despite some misgivings she'd allowed her to organise and run the whole thing.

'That was utter torture,' moaned Morna, 'but also pretty cool.' She treated Chloe to one of her rare smiles.

'Thanks, guys,' said Chloe. 'I was terrified it'd be a huge flop, but loads came. The kids seemed to really enjoy it.'

'And the adults got a bit of a break, too,' said Morna. 'God knows, they must need it.'

'Don't you want kids of your own one day?' asked Chloe.

'No, thank you.' Morna laughed. 'I'm not that much of a masochist.'

Beth noticed that no one sought her views on the subject. They probably thought that she was too old, but she wasn't, was she? Not quite. But, on the other hand, if she was thrown in prison? That would definitely slam the door on her hopes of having a child of her own one day. She turned away from them as she dashed away the tears that had suddenly filled her eyes. It was time for action, not feeling sorry for herself.

They cleared away the plates and cups and brought out their packed lunches as Beth walked through with the tea tray and pulled out her own sandwiches from her satchel. She quickly updated them on what she had overheard at her lawyer's office. She paused as she considered whether to reveal what Harris had told her about blackmail. Despite everything, she was reluctant to blacken his name.

'What aren't you telling us?' demanded Chloe, perceptive as ever.

Beth grimaced as she repeated their earlier conversation.

'Beth, you've to get another lawyer,' said Lachlan emphatically. 'Where do you draw the line between the appearance of not working hard on your behalf and actual negligent representation? If Detective Sergeant Hunter thought he needed to fire a warning shot across his bows, then he's clearly not doing enough of what is expected of him.'

Morna nodded decisively. 'I agree with Lachlan. It sounds to me as though he's more worried about saving himself than saving you. He must've been up to some really dodgy stuff if someone's able to blackmail him over it.'

'I got the impression it related to the firm, which has been owned by his family for several generations. It may not be something he's done but something related to his father or grandfather,' said Beth, knowing they were right but still looking for a way to fix things without her having to leave and start over.

'That would be an explanation but not an excuse,' said Lachlan firmly.

'Fine,' Beth capitulated. 'I'll give myself one week to get to the bottom of it, failing which, I'll get myself another lawyer. In fairness to him, he did say that he's paid a friend in another firm to take statements from the crown witnesses and is still actively assembling a defence.'

'But what can you do in a week?' asked Chloe.

'All ideas gratefully received,' said Beth, taking a sip of her tea. For a couple of minutes, they all chewed in silence, brows furrowed in concentration.

'He has a mother who's still alive, doesn't he?' said Lachlan, the first to break the silence.

'Yes, I think so,' Beth replied. 'I should go and see her, see what she knows. If Harris won't tell me maybe she will.' She blanched at the thought, but Lachlan was right. Desperate times called for desperate measures.

'I've a vague idea where she lives,' said Lachlan. 'She ordered some coffee table books on photography from me about five years ago. I'll look up the electoral roll and text you her address when I find it.'

'Thanks.' Beth smiled across the table. 'Anyone else?'

'If he's been getting texts off a burner, we need to get hold of his phone,' said Morna. 'Maybe we could set a trap if we text who is blackmailing him?'

'That's a great idea but how on earth could I get it off him?' asked Beth. 'He's not just going to give it to me.'

'It's possible to clone a phone, including text messages,' said Morna. 'But both devices need a particular app installed to enable that. If you could get it off him long enough, you could install the app. He probably wouldn't even notice an extra app as we've so many these days.'

'Yes, there's no point in just getting the phone number as whoever it is will spot it's a different number and go quiet,' said Chloe.

'Most men carry their phones close to them,' said Lachlan, frowning.

'Unless they're charging,' said Morna. 'Most people have a charging port beside their bed.'

'I think he might still live with his mother,' said Beth.

'What? At his age?' scoffed Morna.

'Some of us actually get on with our parents,' snapped Chloe, then clapped her hand over her mouth as she saw Morna's stricken expression. 'Sorry, I shouldn't have—'

Morna shrugged off her apology. 'It's fine. Maybe, if you get in to see his mother, you can grab a key, leave a window open or something and come back later at night, grab his phone, install the app then put it back on the charger and leave with him being none the wiser,' she said.

'Morna, what you're suggesting is breaking and entering,' Lachlan said, sending a severe look her way. 'Don't you think that Beth is in enough trouble with the law already?'

'That's true,' said Beth. 'But I'm trying to solve a crime more than I'm committing one. It's worth thinking about. The way I see it, the perpetrator has to be someone who was there that night. The murder was, therefore, in the eyes of the killer, driven by necessity and therefore unplanned and spontaneous. If we find that burner phone in the possession of Ronnie, Mike, Dan or Harriet then we'll also know who the killer is.'

'I can look through Dan's stuff,' said Morna, reddening. 'Although I don't, for one minute, think he's the killer. But if it'll put your minds at rest...'

'You're still seeing him then?' asked Chloe, looking worried.

'Sort of.' Morna shrugged, clearly unwilling to talk about it.

'I could go and visit Mike,' said Lachlan. 'I could be asking for the lowdown on the various local writing groups and ask for his advice on my writing.'

'On your writing?' they all chorused in unison.

Lachlan looked down at the table and fidgeted with his pen. 'I may have dabbled a bit more than I let on over the years,' he admitted.

'It's nothing to be ashamed of,' said Chloe, wide-eyed. 'Good on you, Lachlan! I suppose I could go and see Harriet. I could ask her advice about applying to teacher training and ask if she'd be willing to give me a reference?'

'You're thinking of leaving us?' asked Beth, with a pang.

'It wouldn't be for ages yet,' said Chloe. 'I'm still thinking about it, but I do love when the little kids come in for storytime. Anyway, that should get me over the doorstep.'

Beth looked at her employees – or should she now say her friends? The way they were prepared to go out on a limb like this really touched her.

'Look, I appreciate all the support,' she said, 'but I'm not encouraging any of you to break the law or get into trouble on my behalf. That would make me feel even worse than being arrested myself.'

'I reiterate what Beth said,' chimed in Lachlan. 'We can legitimately visit the suspects and have these conversations legally but conducting a search of their personal belongings to look for a phone should only be done if there's no risk involved. No matter how innocent we consider some or all of these people to be, it should always be at the front of our minds that each and any one of us could be interacting with a cold-blooded killer. One who will almost certainly have no scruples about killing again to protect their secret.'

On that sobering note they started clearing away their lunch and Beth turned the sign to 'Open' once more. Things were becoming serious. Very serious indeed, thought Beth, as she approached a regular customer with her smile nailed firmly in place. A few minutes later her phone pinged with a text from Lachlan. It was the address for Harris's mother. She resolved to visit her that afternoon so that, hopefully, her son would still be working at the office.

THIRTY-FIVE

Mrs Kincaid lived in a handsome three-storey town house with an immaculately tended garden, not far from McCaig's Tower, therefore enjoying panoramic views of the bay and town below. The walk up to the street she lived on was so vertiginous it made Beth feel dizzy. Of course, that might have been nerves, she thought, unsure of what her reception would be from Harris's mother. Her calf muscles aching, she pushed open the bespoke wrought iron gate and walked up the drive to the beautiful yet imposing stone house. It even had a couple of turrets. So, this is where Harris grew up, she thought, looking around her at the velvety lawn and mature shrubs and trees waving in the breeze. Except, he hadn't, had he? she thought, standing in front of the smart navy door with its brass letterbox. He'd been sent off to boarding school at the age of seven. Gathering up her courage, she pressed the bell and heard its loud ring echo throughout the house followed by the sound of brisk footsteps. The door was flung open and there stood a tall slender blonde woman in a tweed skirt and baby blue cashmere twin set. Icy blue eyes swept her from head to toe then the woman paled and held on to the door jamb for support.

'Are you alright?' asked Beth, somewhat alarmed.

'I knew this day would come,' the woman said, trying for a

smile. 'You'd better come in.' She turned and walked away from Beth, her back ramrod straight.

Beth was puzzled as to what she might be referring to and followed her along the parquet flooring into an elegant sitting room. The woman gestured to her to sit down on a soft brown leather sofa and sat opposite her in a chequered wingback chair.

'Shall we have tea?' Mrs Kincaid asked.

'Yes, please,' said Beth, still baffled by the woman's reaction to seeing her. 'Would you like me to get it?'

'Certainly not!' the woman replied with asperity. 'And I suppose you should call me Susan.' She rose to her feet.

'My name's Beth Cunningham,' she offered.

'I know who you are.' the woman said, then left the room for the kitchen. 'I won't be long.' She left the door to the hallway ajar.

Beth sprang to her feet and looked wildly around her, searching for something useful. Needless to say, there were no phones on chargers. That would have been too easy. She opened the door and crept into the hall. She could always say that she was looking for the loo. She could hear the sound of a kettle boiling further down the hall on the right. She didn't have long. Hurriedly, she rushed to the front door looking for a key she could pocket in order to come back later under cover of darkness. In a dish on a table, she found a yale key, which on closer inspection, she discovered should unlock the chub on the front door. It was on its own and not in a keyring, so she hoped it was a spare that wouldn't be missed for a while. Pocketing it, she hurriedly ran back to the lounge and threw herself on the couch just as she heard Susan's measured footsteps returning.

Beth accepted a cup and saucer. 'The reason I'm here is—'

'He didn't know, you know. My husband, that is...' Susan said, leaning forward, her shaking hand causing her cup to rattle in its saucer. Hastily, she put it down on the table.

Beth was confused. She was trying to explain why she was here, but Susan had gone off at a tangent. 'He didn't...?' she asked, trying to bluff her way forward.

'No, neither of us knew a thing, until your mother pitched up on our doorstep a year before she died.'

'Wait... my mother?' said Beth, with a strangled gasp, her mind racing. This conversation was taking on a surreal edge all of a sudden.

'Yes, didn't you know she'd been to see us?'

Beth shook her head mutely.

'Well, of course, it was a dreadful shock. For both of us, my husband in particular. He'd had no idea that their relationship had resulted in a child.'

As the full implications of what she was being told started to sink in, Beth suddenly felt a heat spread within her and the room fade from her eyes. Everything went black.

She came to with Susan's worried face looming over her as she slumped back on the couch.

'You really didn't know? Here, take this.' She cupped Beth's hand around a glass of water and helped her to sit upright once more.

'No, I had no idea,' said Beth bleakly. It all made sense now. No wonder her mother had married the man she had come to know as her father. Beth had done the math and realised that she had been conceived out of wedlock but now realised that the father who she always felt had abandoned her hadn't even been her father at all. Her mother had truly married in haste and repented at leisure. She wondered if he had known? If he had, it would explain so much over the years. Part of her felt lighter to loosen a filial bond that had always chafed so much. But a tiny voice whispered in her heart that all it meant was that she had been abandoned by two fathers now rather than just one. What was wrong with her?

'When I saw you standing there, I knew who you were right away. You look so like your mother. I was sorry to learn that she had passed away,' she added graciously. 'Don't think badly of her,' she said, with a kind smile. 'She and my husband were friends long before I became involved with him. We didn't meet and get married until much later. They met when they were both students at Glasgow University. Strange, really, given that they each grew up in Oban, but they'd never crossed paths before. William was sent off to boarding school at the age of seven, but your mother was schooled locally. My husband told me that they were just becoming serious when, without any warning, she dropped out and moved away, leaving no contact address. When he managed to track her down again, a couple of years later, she was married to someone else with a young child. She sent him away with a flea in his ear and it quite broke his heart, I think.'

'My mother left university when she was diagnosed with MS,' Beth said, quietly. 'If she truly loved your husband, she wouldn't have wanted to lay all that on him and a pregnancy to boot. I think she most likely sacrificed herself out of love for him. Wait... does that mean that Harris is my half-brother?' she asked, her eyebrows shooting up. 'Does he even know?'

'He found out a week ago,' Susan said. 'Until then, he thought you were just a client who had been passed to him by his father. I thought it necessary to tell him once I realised that he was going to be representing you in relation to a potential murder charge. Once your mother had visited and explained her situation to us and also that unfortunate business in your past, we offered to help you financially, but your mother said she'd been able to leave you sufficiently well provided for. She wanted your father to use his legal skills to ensure that everything she had planned for you came to pass as she wished. She wouldn't accept anything else.'

'Now that sounds like my mother,' Beth said with pride. Her face fell. 'When did my... your husband die?' she asked.

Susan's eyes filled with compassion. 'I'm afraid that he died a couple of months before you arrived in Oban, my dear. Not long after the death of your poor mother, in fact. A heart attack.'

Beth scarcely knew how to feel after this revelation. How could she mourn a man that she'd never known and yet was a part of her? 'I'm sorry I didn't get to meet him. What was he like?'

'Gosh! How to answer that?' Susan said, with a tremulous smile. 'I think the young man your mother knew was probably very different to the man he ended up becoming. But I imagine that's true for most of us.' She gave a wistful smile, as if recalling her own girlhood. 'His father, your grandfather, was a very harsh man and came down hard on him once he graduated. Your father was an idealist, but his father forced him into practising law at the family firm using a combination of threats about disinheriting him and emotional manipulation. He didn't allow him to be the kind of lawyer he wanted to be and eventually that flame of idealism was extinguished and he lived the life that was expected of him. In most respects it was a good life.'

Something was worrying Beth. 'You said that your husband died not long after he found out about my existence. It wasn't the shock that killed him, was it?' she said, her voice breaking.

'Good heavens, no, my dear. You mustn't think that. He was already suffering from heart disease and had a coronary bypass five years ago. He was a large man who enjoyed life. A penchant for port and cheese was the more likely culprit. Learning about your existence brought him great joy. He wanted to meet you, but your mother asked him to watch over you from a distance, at least until she was gone. We hoped that he would have time to get to know you but sadly it wasn't to be.'

They sat in silence for a few moments as Beth tried to absorb this new information which had knocked her clean off her stride.

'When I saw you standing there, I assumed you were here to talk about your father,' said Susan, placing her cup back on her saucer and leaning forward, her expression curious. 'But if it wasn't about that, then why did you come here today?'

Beth froze, her head still reeling. All her plans for subterfuge went out of the window. She owed this gracious woman nothing but the truth. 'I don't know where to start,' she said.

'Then start at the beginning,' Susan said, settling back in her seat, as if she had all day.

Beth took a deep breath. 'I think your son's in trouble, but before I get to that you're going to need to understand the background. You alluded to the fact that I'd been in trouble as a child. Did my mother tell you that I'd been detained in a secure unit for causing the death of someone who was bullying me?'

'Yes, she did,' Susan replied. 'It sounded like a travesty of justice, one that I imagine you've worked hard to distance yourself from.'

'Exactly,' said Beth. She told her all about the bookshop and what had happened to Darcie after she had boasted about the secret that was going to be her ticket back to a national newspaper and the rebirth of her career. 'So,' she concluded, 'you can see why that made me chief suspect in the eyes of the police.'

'And that is where Harris comes in, I assume?' Susan said.

'Yes, it never occurred to me to go anywhere else. At first, he was really proactive in my case then it slowly dawned on me that it had been a while since I'd heard from him.'

'You want me to speak to him?' asked Susan. 'I'm not sure that he would...'

'No, that's not it,' interrupted Beth. 'There's more.' She mentioned her visit to the firm that morning and the conversation she had overheard between Harris and Detective Sergeant Hunter.

'I don't understand,' said Susan, looking troubled. 'Harris has always been so conscientious. There's been no complaints about his work whatsoever.'

Beth winced. 'I'm afraid there's yet more,' she said. 'He admitted to me that he'd given the appearance of backing off my representation, because he's being blackmailed.'

'What!' exclaimed his mother, going white. 'Over what?'

'He wouldn't tell me. Whoever's doing it hasn't asked for money, they just want him to sabotage my defence and if he does that, he's off the hook. I've no idea what they've got on him. All he would tell me is that lives and reputations would be ruined.'

Susan wrung her hands in distress. 'He must go to the police. That's the only proper course of action to take. I'll speak to him and you must arrange alternative representation right away.'

'I need to gain access to his phone,' Beth pressed. 'If I can clone it, I'll be able to see what the killer's texts involve and have access to their burner phone.'

'Their... er... burner phone?'

'A cheap pay as you go phone that has no contract and can't be traced,' Beth supplied. 'It's possible that Harris has purchased one, too, in case the police later gain a warrant to obtain his main phone.' She hesitated. 'Look, I know that this is a lot to lay on you all at once but, if I'm to prove my innocence, I need access to that information. The police could arrest me at any moment.'

'Leave it with me,' Susan said, her voice steely. 'I'll confront him and demand that he comes clean and shows you that phone. Whoever committed this murder isn't going to get away with it.'

'Did you know Darcie at all?' asked Beth.

'No, we didn't move in the same circles, but I'd seen her byline in the local paper. She was clearly a talented journalist. A terrible shame she was cut off in her prime.'

'What she hadn't banked on was that everyone at the table that night was harbouring a secret of their own,' said Beth. She stood up to go, conscious that her world had tilted on its axis after this new information about the true identity of her father. She knew that in time she would feel a kind of grief for this shadowy figure she had never known. But, for now, she had more pressing things to deal with.

'You're welcome to visit here any time,' said Susan, rising to her feet and clasping Beth's hand between both of her own. 'Once things have settled down and the immediate danger has passed, perhaps you might care to join us for Sunday lunch?'

'I'd like that very much,' said Beth warmly, as she took her leave after exchanging contact details. As she walked back down the driveway, she felt she had even more to lose now that she had found this new family to embrace her.

THIRTY-SIX
LACHLAN

Lachlan felt his stomach burn and acid flood his mouth as he walked towards Mike's unassuming terraced house. He was so stressed these days he wouldn't be surprised if he developed an ulcer. It was all getting too much for him. At first when the owner sold the bookshop, he was glad to be out of it, but it hadn't taken long for boredom to settle in. When Beth had offered to take him on to manage the shop he'd had mixed feelings. It had been hard at first but lately he'd come to appreciate that the business was now thriving on the fresh blood and innovation. Beth was a fair and compassionate boss, and the young ones had brightened him up no end. It was good to feel part of something again. He even had a modest social life now after years of sterility. It felt good to reclaim that part of himself.

It had been difficult but necessary, keeping his relationship with Darcie a secret. He'd hoped that in time she would consider marriage but when she'd revealed that she was intent on moving back to Glasgow to work for the national press it had been a body blow he wasn't expecting. The fact that she destroyed his hopes and dreams so casually had made him feel disrespected and angry. His hurt pride, coupled with a private grief, had prevented him revealing the extent of his attachment to the team.

Walking up the small well-tended garden, he rang the bell, hoping he could be sufficiently convincing.

The door was flung open and Mike stood there, a tea towel flung over his shoulder. Cooking smells wafted out behind him, condensing on the frosty air.

'Hi, Mike, I can come back if this is an inconvenient time?' he offered. 'I was just after some advice, but it can wait.' He turned to leave.

'Hey, not so fast,' said Mike, sounding amused. 'It's fine. I was just knocking up some pasta. Have you eaten?'

'No, not yet,' Lachlan admitted.

'In you come then, we can eat in the kitchen. I could use the company.' Mike grinned, making Lachlan feel like a heel for being there under false pretences. He sat at the mahogany table in the comfortable kitchen where a steaming bowl of spaghetti carbonara was put in front of him. It was delicious. Once they were finished, Lachlan sat back in his seat.

'I've started writing again, after a long hiatus,' he said. 'Up until now I've written mainly poetry and quite frankly it wasn't very good. I've also written a number of short stories and I'm embarking on a longer work, specifically a crime novel.'

'That's great!' said Mike, clapping him on the back as they took their dirty dishes to the counter. 'Coffee?'

'Please,' said Lachlan, praying Mike wouldn't ask for plot and character details. 'I'm looking to join a writing group again. For accountability, you know? I've heard some of them can be pretty toxic, so I thought I'd come and ask you which, if any, you'd recommend locally?'

'You're not wrong there,' said Mike, as he led them through to the comfortable sitting room. 'I've been round them all over the years. It only takes one corrosive person to ruin it for everyone. There are the ones who hog the conversation and don't let anyone get a word in edgeways. Then there's the one where a retired colonel spews absolute vitriol towards everyone else's work but won't tolerate any constructive criticism of his own. Some of them are complete snake pits.'

'Crikey, maybe I should quit while I'm ahead!' laughed Lachlan.

'The one I'm in at the moment, Highland Scribes, is pretty cool,' Mike said. 'A good bunch of people with a few really talented writers as well as some aspiring newbies, eager to learn.'

'What about the boy wonder? Is he in it?' asked Lachlan, hoping to get Mike onside with the slightly negative tone.

Mike laughed. 'You mean Dan? No, thank God. Can't take any more of his humble bragging. He's in Kilted Scribblers with all his female acolytes.'

'Bit of a ladies' man, is he?' asked Lachlan.

'The worst,' replied Lachlan. 'A total user. He picks them up then goes all tortured artist and drops them with a "it's not you, it's me" schtick that leaves them begging for more. Glad I don't need to witness that anymore. You'd better watch out for that young lass in the shop. She's not his usual type, granted, but he's bad news. And they call ME unreconstructed!'

Lachlan's heart sank at hearing this as he worried about how deeply Morna was in thrall to the rising literary star. She put up a tough front, but he suspected she wasn't half as hard as she liked to make out.

'I really enjoyed your short story at the open mic night,' Lachlan was able to say in all honesty. 'Have you thought about embarking on a longer work yourself?'

'I did write a novel a few years back,' Mike admitted. 'Never showed it to a soul. I learned the hard way about backing up your work. I lost my laptop along with a host of other stuff in a burglary. I knew about the Cloud but I'm not hugely techie and just assumed it wouldn't happen to me. It bloody did. I'd poured blood, sweat, and tears into that novel and, basically, I just couldn't stomach starting again. Then I channelled all that frustration into my blog. Maybe one day... I do have a few ideas brewing. I lost my mojo for a while, but that open mic night got me going again. I guess I've got Beth to thank for that.'

'Well, thanks for the advice. I'll give the writing group a try.'

'It's every Wednesday at 7pm,' said Mike. 'You'd be very welcome.'

Lachlan stood up to leave. 'Mind if I nip to the loo before heading off?'

'Sure,' said Mike. 'Up the stairs and second on the left. I've got some marking to do, so just let yourself out when you're done.'

'Cheers,' said Lachlan, 'and thanks for the food.'

'Any time,' said his host with a cheery wave.

Lachlan ran lightly up the stairs feeling like the biggest jerk in the world for abusing Mike's hospitality in this way. Pushing such thoughts away he went past the bathroom before entering the master bedroom. A quick look round the room revealed no phone anywhere. A worn leather briefcase was sitting open and he rifled hurriedly through the contents. No phone there either. He heard the door to the lounge open and hurriedly raced next door to flush the toilet and turn on the tap. He also opened the window and sprayed some air freshener on his way out. Hurrying downstairs he saw Mike waiting for him, a quizzical look on his face.

'Thought you might have got lost up there,' he said.

Lachlan grimaced and clutched his stomach. 'Bit of a dodgy tummy. No reflection on the great food.'

'Probably stress,' said Mike. 'Goes for me every time.'

Not wrong there, thought Lachlan, as he rushed out the front door with a sickly grin, hoping to God he had left no trace of his snooping. He was definitely not cut out for this. From now on he would stick to selling books.

THIRTY-SEVEN
BETH

Beth paced up and down inside her warm cottage, the wind howling around the bay outside. Toby watched her, his tail flicking in annoyance that she wouldn't sit down in front of the wood burning stove and provide him with a comfortable lap to sit on. Absently, she scratched his ears on the way past his vantage point on the back of the couch.

'Sorry, Toby. I can't sit right now, I need to think.' She continued pacing and Toby jumped down in annoyance and stalked from the room. Why hadn't her mother told her all this before she died? Did the man she had previously thought was her father know about her existence before he married her mother? Her gut told her that he did and he'd used her mother's vulnerability and need for security, having recently been diagnosed, to latch on to her. She'd always thought he was punching well above his weight and now she'd realised why. Despite the death of her father, Susan was clearly inviting her to become a member of their family. The thought was comforting. She really liked Susan, but she had no idea how Harris felt about the prospect of a new sister parachuting into his life right now, let alone one fighting the prospect of criminal charges for murder no less. What an absolute mess!

'Way to go, Mum,' she muttered, then felt guilty. Her mum had done her best for her. Clearly Harris's dad had been the love of her life and she had loved him enough to set him free. But what if he'd wanted to stay? Their lives could have been totally different. Angrily, she shook that idea from her brain. What did it matter now? It was what it was. Now they all had to learn to deal with it.

Finally, she dropped on to the couch and Toby came at a run and jumped up onto her knee, purring, going round in circles and kneading her with his sharp little claws until he found the perfect spot. Absentmindedly, Beth stroked his head, while watching some reruns of *Friends*, which never failed to lift her out of despondency.

Eventually she switched off the TV, stretching as she yawned. It had been a long day. The silence of the house wrapped around her, as she walked through the hall to offer Toby the chance to go outside. Just as she put her hand on the doorknob, the bell rang, scaring her half to death. Who on earth could be calling on her at this time of night? It was after ten. Putting her eye to the spyhole she noticed a familiar figure. It was Harris. She had absolutely no idea what to say to him. Reluctantly, she swung open the door and he stepped across the threshold. He looked even worse than her. An unhealthy pallor greyed his face and his eyes were bloodshot, as though he'd been drinking. His lips were pressed tight together, white and bloodless.

'I gather you've been to see my mother,' he snapped.

So, this was how it was going to go. She sighed internally.

'Yes,' she said, stiffening her spine. 'If you can't sit down and air our differences civilly over a cup of tea then I suggest you leave the way you came in.' She held the door open in a manner that brooked no argument. She wasn't going to be pushed around by *him* when he had deceived her at every turn. She watched the internal struggle play out across his face, then relaxed and closed the door once she saw the anger leave his body.

Once they were sitting facing each other across the kitchen

table with a pot of tea between them, he lifted his head and stared into her eyes.

'What were you thinking? Going to see my mother? Don't you think she's been through enough? Finding out that my father had a secret love child she knew nothing about?'

Beth felt a rush of anger. 'What *she's* been through? Are you kidding me? I've just discovered that my father isn't my father, and my real father died before I even got here, without me ever getting the chance to meet him. Not to mention the fact that my idiot lawyer, who has apparently given up on defending me, is my half-brother. You couldn't even make it up! What's more, for the record, your mother was gracious and lovely, which is more than can be said for her offspring.'

'Look, this isn't really about that. I'm stoked about the fact that I have a sister. Or I will be one day, but this is about the danger we're both in. It was a reckless act that could have had serious consequences.'

'You left me no choice,' said Beth quietly. 'I had no one else to turn to. I had to figure out what was going on. Don't you see? We have to work together on this.'

Harris got up and went over to the window, lifting a corner of the blind to peer out.

'What are you looking for?' Beth asked.

'I'm looking to see if I'm being followed,' he said, returning to the table.

'Harris, are you sure you're quite well?' she asked, gently.

'What? Of course I am. Can we focus on the matter at hand?'

'Okay, I'm afraid you're going to have to show me these texts you claim to have received.' She held out her hand for his phone.

'Can't I simply tell you what it's all about?' he asked, clearly still reluctant to trust her.

'No, I'm afraid that's not going to work for me,' she said, injecting an edge of steel into her voice now.

'Fine,' he grumbled, rummaging around in his jacket pocket

and producing a slim phone she'd never seen him use before. 'Here you are.' He slapped it down into her hand.

Beth looked at it like it was a ticking bomb as she wondered what fresh mayhem was going to explode in her life. 'I take it this is a complete record of the texts and that you haven't deleted any?' she checked.

'I'm not a complete moron,' he snapped. 'I knew that this could likely end up in court one day.'

Beth scrolled back right to the beginning of the texts, her heart in her mouth as she commenced reading.

> I know what your grandfather did. I have proof.
>
> Your father covered it up.
>
> Now you are following in their dishonourable footsteps.
>
> Only one thing can stop me serving you up to the press and the Law Society and outing you as thieving criminals.
>
> You must ensure that Beth Cunningham is convicted of murdering Darcie Baxter. On her conviction your secrets will remain safe and your family's reputation untarnished.
>
> I will be watching you…

Beth wordlessly handed the phone back to him, her heart sinking. What did he expect from her? If he thought she was going to serve herself up as a sacrificial lamb for his family then he was very much mistaken. Even if that family was technically hers now as well. The silence between them stretched out on a silken thread until her nerves were at screaming point before he spoke.

'My grandfather, it turns out, had a gambling problem, one that he went to great lengths to conceal from his family. He started fiddling the books, embezzling from the estates of wealthy deceased clients, fully intending to repay the sums taken after his next big win. He even started an affair with his legal cashier to enlist her help with it all. Back then it was relatively easy to get away with things like that. My grandmother went to her grave never knowing what he'd done, having died eight years before him.'

Beth's blood ran cold as she realised that every time that he referred to his father or grandfather, he was referring to hers as well. This was going to take some getting used to. And she'd thought her life was complicated before!

'When did you find out about all this?' she asked.

'After my father died. He left a wax sealed letter with his lawyer to be passed to me unopened once his estate was wound up. These things take time. I was only given his letter a few days before the first text arrived. In it, he explained what his father had done and that he had managed to repay over half of the large sums of missing money. He then apologised for pressuring me to join the firm but said that to protect our family honour he had no choice but to enlist my help after he passed, in the same way his grandfather had done to him.'

'You could have simply gone to the police?'

'Honestly, I didn't know what to do. The whole thing threw me into a panic as I faced up to what this meant for us all. For you, for my mother, and for the whole reputation of our family firm, which had been trusted by everyone in this community for over a hundred years. I needed some time to investigate the firm's finances and work out the best course of action to take but it was too complicated for me to untangle on my own, being bound up in convoluted large estate trusts. For example, in one set of trust accounts, a wealthy landowner has a huge library. I discovered my grandfather had sold off the most valuable books but the asset value in the accounts continued to increase year on year. He had covered his tracks well.'

'I can't believe that your father did that to you,' said Beth.

'He clearly couldn't see any other way,' said Harris. 'I wouldn't be surprised if the stress of carrying that mental burden for all these years contributed to his premature death.'

'You can't allow the same thing to happen to you,' said Beth firmly.

'After your visit, my mother let me have it with both barrels when I got home. I had to tell her everything.'

'What did she say?' asked Beth.

Harris ran a hand over his face, his voice breaking. 'She said that protecting the family honour by doing something dishonourable is not the way to go. She offered to sell the family home to help balance the books.'

'Maybe you should listen to her,' Beth said gently. 'This burden your grandfather placed around your family's neck was his to carry, not yours and not hers. Maybe you should come clean and report the matter yourself. Your father died under a year ago. You've been struggling with grief and trying to sort out his affairs and have only very recently been made aware of the situation. I'm sure they would be as lenient as possible in the circumstances. Given the sums involved, I don't see how you can ever repay it.'

'I'm sorry to lay all this on you but given my mother's revelation a couple of weeks ago, that you're my half-sister, I didn't know where to turn or what to do for the best. It's all such a complicated mess. I can't see a way out, yet it's all I can think about.'

'I don't suppose you'd consider taking this to DS Hunter?' asked Beth. 'If I'm sure of anything, I'm sure that he's a fair man. Look at the way he was trying to scare you up into doing a better job representing me? Any other policeman would have rubbed his hands together in glee and said nothing.'

Harris scowled. 'I suspect his motives may not have been quite as pure as you imagine. He'd be the last person I'd take this to.'

'It's clear to me that the only way for us all to crawl out from under this is to find the killer. It doesn't even matter anymore what secret Darcie was going to expose. It only matters that someone in the book group felt it was theirs,' said Beth. 'We have to flush whoever it is out into the open and now, due to your text messages with the killer, we have the means to do that. Once the killer has been unmasked, we go to the police with the evidence and then hopefully, that's me out of the frame. At the same time, you can explain what your grandfather did and how your father tried incredibly hard to put it right. You can say that you've decided, after a short period of investigation and reflection, to bring it to the police and the Law Society to deal with it as they see fit.'

'I don't know...' Harris said. 'If we're dealing with a killer, it's someone who has killed before and may well be prepared to kill again. I can't let any of you take that risk. It's too dangerous and there's probably a whole host of variables we don't even know about, let alone can control.'

'You don't get to decide that for me, Harris,' Beth said firmly. 'I think we should sleep on this tonight then have a meeting at the shop tomorrow lunchtime. With your permission, I need to fill them in on the whole story.'

'What? All of it? But I don't see—'

'Yes, all of it,' replied Beth firmly. 'There's no other way. If we do this, we all need to be on the same page. My staff are a tight team. I trust in their discretion.'

'You're right. I know you're right,' Harris said, holding up his hands in defeat. 'It's just hard to let it go... to trust someone else with all of this.'

'You won't regret it,' said Beth, hoping with all her might that would prove to be true.

THIRTY-EIGHT
MORNA

Morna felt the frost crisp below her feet as she slipped out her front door onto the High Street. She'd been nerving herself to call on Dan all evening and it was now almost eleven. If she didn't go now, it would be too late and she'd have to confess to the others that she'd wimped out, which would not do her street cred any good. Best to go now and get it done. Her cheeks pinched red by the cold, she huddled down into her duffle coat and pulled her bobble hat further down on her head.

She hadn't been out with many men before Dan inexplicably took an interest in her. Years of put-downs by her parents had given her a very low opinion of her own attractiveness, which in turn made her prickly and defensive, even when someone did seem to want to spend time with her. She wondered what it might be like to live a charmed life like Chloe then pushed away the thought. To her surprise, she'd come to rather like her new colleague recently. It wasn't her fault that the world seemed to warm to Chloe whilst turning its back on her. When Dan had blown into their lives, she couldn't believe her luck when he singled her out to spend time with. At first, she'd thought that it was a prank, that he was setting her up to take a fall, but the punchline had yet to be delivered. However, since the open mic night she'd noticed flashes of behaviour that suggested he wasn't as genuine as she'd thought. The boorish way he'd reacted to Mike at the open mic night, for one. She remained sure of one thing though. However disagreeable a side he might be hiding, there was no way he could have murdered Darcie and then carry on like nothing had happened. For that matter, she couldn't see any of the book group as killers. It surely had to be someone else entirely. Given the stress her poor boss was under, though, she was eager to eliminate Dan from consideration so that she wasn't so conflicted about seeing him. When he was on good form, he made her laugh and also listened to her opinions on things, like what she said really mattered. She hadn't had a lot of that in her life. Her estrangement from her family was like a cancer gnawing at her insides every single day. She knew that it hurt her more than them but there was no going back. When she reached his building overlooking the bay she buzzed his number. No reply. Drat, she wanted to get this over with. A couple with a child in a buggy approached. She nodded a greeting, having seen them before in the shop.

'Hey, just waiting for my boyfriend.' She grinned, her teeth chattering with the cold.

'He lives here?' the woman asked, as she struggled through the door held open by her husband.

'Yes, number six, top floor,' Morna replied.

'Just come inside then,' the woman said. 'You'll be warmer if you wait for him inside rather than standing out here. It's not as if I don't know you, I've seen you in the bookshop.'

'Thanks,' Morna replied. 'I was losing the feeling in my feet.'

She continued through after them and headed up the stairs as they opted for the lift, welcoming the wall of heat that hit her inside, defrosting her numb extremities. Her own place wasn't much warmer than being outside if the ice inside the windows was anything to go by. Breathing hard as she arrived on the sixth floor, she then walked to the farthest of the four doors. Putting her ear to the door she listened hard. Not a sound, though he might have headphones on, of course. Gnawing her bottom lip, with worry she reached up and felt along the door frame. Bingo. He'd left a key there. She'd seen him do it once before when he thought she wasn't looking.

She inserted the key, her hands shaking, and with a sick lurch of her stomach, she was inside the flat, her heart hammering. The door quietly closed behind her. She had to get a wiggle on and get out of here. The thought of him catching her inside his place like some obsessed fan girl was completely mortifying. First, she ascertained that he really was out, then she went through all the pockets in his jackets in the hall before running through to the bedroom, where she had never ventured before. Sure enough, his phone charger was plugged into the wall, but she suspected that was for his iPhone as it was the same as hers. She ran to the other sockets but found no burner phone or mystery charger. Groaning, she headed back into the bedroom and opened the drawer of his bedside table. This was a total invasion of his privacy. She winced as her hands rustled through condoms, mints and breath spray as well as one or two questionable magazines. This was getting her nowhere fast. Slamming the drawer shut, she peered under the bed, pulling a heavy cardboard box towards her. Copies of his new book! She'd asked for an advance copy many times, but he'd always refused, citing the contract with his publisher. Hurriedly, she extracted one and stuck it in her shoulder bag, rearranging the rest so it looked as though it wasn't missing. Next, she ran over to the chest of drawers, sweating with discomfort and vowing she would never again do anything like this, no matter what the stakes. She plunged into his boxers drawer, raising an eyebrow at the designer names on the waistbands. Vain, much? She'd just reached the bottom drawer and closed her hand around a promising cardboard box when she heard a key turn in the lock.

She heard Dan's voice. He sounded a bit sloshed. Then she heard a tinkling laugh and froze. He wasn't alone. This could not be happening! What to do? She pulled out the box and saw that it was a cheap phone but the packet remained sealed so she knew it couldn't be that one. She noted the make and model then shoved it back and closed the drawer as quietly as she could. Now, how could she escape? Her mortification was so severe she looked longingly at the window but then gave herself a talking to. No man's opinion was THAT important! The voices drew closer. *Please God, don't let them be coming in here.* She cast about wildly for a hiding place. Then, she heard the woman's voice demanding champagne first and they headed into the kitchen. Champagne? Morna was more of a beer girl. His new squeeze had expensive tastes. Resisting the urge to close her eyes, she sneaked out of the bedroom towards the door at the end of the hall, her heart hammering so loudly she feared they might hear it. She opened the door and slid out. As she started to close it quietly behind her, she heard the sound of their laughter spilling into the hall, in no doubt where they were heading next.

'Who's that grungy girl I hear you've been hanging out with?' The voice was teasing, playful, confident that she wasn't a threat.

Against her better judgement, Morna froze in place, her hand still on the handle, the masochist in her needing to hear his reply.

'Morna? She's nobody. Just a useful contact I need to keep sweet for a bit. I'm going to cut her loose at the first opportunity. If I have to hear her bore on about *Lord of the Rings* one more time, I'll slit my own throat.'

Morna flinched as though he'd inflicted a physical blow, then quietly closed the door and let herself out. Placing the key back where she had found it, she hugged the pain inside of her as she hurried back down the stairs and out into the cold night.

THIRTY-NINE
BETH

The morning in the shop passed quickly as they were putting up Guy Fawkes decorations and helping Chloe with her fiery displays. The focal point was a huge bonfire built of sticks they'd all gone foraging for in Dunollie Wood. Beth felt that she'd be checking her car for spiders for evermore. Chloe had fashioned a hugely realistic Guy Fawkes with her mother sneakily donating some threadbare clothes of her father's that she'd been trying to get him to part with.

Morna stomped past carrying armfuls of orange, yellow and red crepe paper, looking like she was marching to the scaffold. At that moment, Lachlan emerged from the kitchen carrying a tray of hot chocolate and a plate of biscuits.

'Lachlan, you're a star!' exclaimed Chloe, dashing over with a wide grin, tossing her long blonde ponytail behind her. 'Let's get this party started.' She fiddled with her phone and a cheesy pop song came on. 'Look!' she exclaimed, pointing to the window. 'It's snowing!'

'It hardly needs to,' said Morna, scooping up a mug and a custard cream. 'There's enough fake snow in the stock room to create a snow drift.'

Chloe spun round to make a sassy retort but then as her eyes swept over Morna, she paused. 'What are you doing for Bonfire Night this year?' she asked instead.

'Nothing special,' Morna admitted grudgingly. 'In case you haven't noticed, I'm not big on holidays anyway. Just another day as far as I'm concerned. I'm treating myself to a new game, though.' She gave a forced smile.

'Come and spend it at ours!' exclaimed Chloe, warmly. 'Dad lights a big bonfire in the field behind our house with a huge Guy Fawkes to go in it for all the kids in the housing scheme. We have fireworks, a ton of food that will need to be eaten. Hot dogs, toffee apples, toasted marshmallows. Mum's been telling me to invite you over for ages, seeing as I talk about you all the time.'

'You do?' said Morna, startled and a bit overwhelmed.

'Course.' Chloe shrugged. 'I hope you'll decide to come.'

Beth was startled to see tears spring to Morna's eyes. 'Morna, be a love and grab those pretzels from the cupboard in the kitchen and stick them in a dish, will you?'

Morna nodded and rushed off to compose herself. Beth glanced around at them all, her heart full.

The door opened just as she was walking towards it to turn the sign to 'Closed'. Harris stamped the snow off his feet onto the mat and took in the scene before him with raised eyebrows.

'Seems like I've stumbled on a plot to blow up the government,' he said, taking in the huge bonfire and all the Guy Fawkes decorations.

'Very funny,' said Beth, hanging up his coat and leading him into the next room to join the others at the staff table where they had all assembled. 'Sorry to bring the tone down but I've asked Harris here to talk to us as he has some information relevant to Darcie's murder. He's prepared to share it with us on condition of absolute confidentiality. Not a word leaves this room. Is that agreed?'

Serious now, they all nodded and turned to look at him. Harris's skin looked bloodless, and a twitch jumped restlessly at the corner of his mouth. At first, he just stared at them all as if he was contemplating running back out of the door but when Beth gently cleared her throat he flinched and began to haltingly explain what he had told her last night at the cottage. When he was done, no one said anything at first, shooting nervous glances at each other.

Lachlan cleared his throat before speaking. He looked angry. 'So, basically what you're telling us is that you've been sitting in your office doing diddly squat to prepare a defence for Beth who has quite literally put her life in your hands? All to save some scandal leaking out in relation to your family?'

'Put like that, it does sound bad,' said Beth, rushing to Harris's defence. 'He did say he's been working on my case under the radar. Right?' She turned to Harris.

'How exactly?' asked Lachlan, folding his arms. 'Clearly if you had to be chased by the police you weren't going through the expected steps. How many witnesses have you interviewed? Have you logged any special defences? Have you looked into incriminating someone else? What about the murder of Harriet's first husband? Have you obtained copies of the pathology report? She, too, could have had motive, means and opportunity.'

'It's too early for most of that,' protested Harris. 'She hasn't even been charged yet. What you're talking about is pre-trial preparation and the trial is likely more than a year away, assuming that she gets bail on her first appearance in court. I've paid a colleague in another firm to get what witness statements he can in the meantime. At this stage of the proceedings, I simply don't have access to any of that information. I intend to explore all of these avenues and more once the case gets going.'

There was a deafening silence. Beth didn't know where to look.

'Like I thought,' Lachlan continued, his tone contemptuous. 'You've been too busy with your pity party for one to look after the needs of your client. Beth, you need to dump this guy and get another lawyer.'

In for a penny, in for a pound, thought Beth, stiffening her spine. 'When you made me waste a day in the library searching the local paper for a clue that was there which you said you couldn't spell out, was that simply to keep me out of your hair but make me feel I was doing something proactive?'

Harris nodded miserably.

'I think we've heard enough,' said Lachlan, standing up.

'Wait,' said Beth. 'There's more.' She hadn't run this past Harris, but he'd been calling the shots for far too long. It was time to take back control. 'It turns out that Harris and I are brother and sister. His father was my father as well.'

'Good heavens,' said Lachlan faintly, falling back into his chair with a thump.

'I'm starting to feel like I'm in a reality TV show,' said Chloe, staring wide-eyed about her as if she expected some media luvvie type to sashay from the wings with a clipboard.

'I've got some news as well,' offered Morna, clearly trying to take the temperature down a notch. 'I had a look round Dan's apartment. He did have a burner phone, but it was still sealed in its box.' She showed them a pic she had taken of the make and model. She wasn't about to enlighten them about her own personal humiliation, though. Instead, she drew out the paperback and placed it on the table with a flourish.

'Is that...?' asked Lachlan.

'Hot off the press. Time to see what all the fuss is about.'

'I must say,' said Lachlan, 'I think it's extraordinary that the publisher hasn't been sending out advance copies left, right and centre. It's a strange marketing strategy.'

'Yet it does seem to be generating demand,' pointed out Beth. 'We've got loads of pre-orders on file. It's a shame he wouldn't agree to do a launch here before heading down to the central belt to kick off his UK tour. I doubt we'll see much of him after that.'

'I see his flat's gone up for sale,' said Chloe.

'What? It can't be,' said Morna, going brick red. 'There's no For Sale sign.'

'You mean, you didn't know?' asked Chloe, shocked. 'That's

awful! I'm afraid it's true. I went into the estate agents and got a copy of the particulars, just to be nosy. They said it's already under offer for well above the asking price.' She fished about in her tote bag and flung a glossy brochure on the table. They all stared at it, stunned both at the asking price and the luxury disclosed in the glossy photos.

'No wonder he's traded me in for a superior model,' said Morna, too miserable to hold it in anymore.

'His loss,' said Chloe, rushing round to enfold her in a hug. 'He's a superficial prick. You're worth ten of him.'

'I'll make some tea,' muttered Lachlan, always a bit uncomfortable when the emotional stakes were raised high.

'I'm sorry, Morna, break-ups are never easy,' said Beth sympathetically, whilst feeling a bit of a fraud for never having even been in a relationship. It wouldn't do to let on about that though.

'He hasn't broken it off... not yet. I just saw them... together,' stumbled Morna.

Lachlan returned from the kitchen with the teapot refilled and another plate of biscuits. Sitting down, he pulled the book on the table towards him.

'Mind if I have a crack at this first?' he asked. 'I'm intrigued to see if it lives up to the hype.'

'Be my guest,' said Morna. 'Remember, he doesn't know I borrowed it. He's got this massive box of them under the bed. I can't believe he hasn't given me one before now. What does he reckon I'm going to do with it? Leak it to *The Times Literary Supplement?*'

They all laughed and reached for the biscuits as Lachlan poured the tea. 'I called on Mike last night,' he said. 'Saw a whole different side to him. He offered me dinner and we spent a pleasant couple of hours together. I did get a chance for a hasty sweep of his sockets, but didn't see any evidence of a second phone. He's not as cynical as he comes across. I must admit I rather enjoyed his company.'

'I popped round to Harriet's after work, but she wasn't in,' said Chloe. 'I tried again this morning, too, but no joy.'

'Probably been away for a long weekend,' offered Beth. 'Anyway, I can't thank you enough, guys, for all the help and support, but I want you all to tread carefully. I don't want anyone getting in trouble with the law over me.'

'So, Harris, are you here with a plan or simply to grovel?' asked Lachlan, an edge to his voice. 'You heard what DS Hunter said. She's about to be charged. What are you going to do about it?'

'I think we need to smoke this person or persons out into the open,' Harris said firmly.

'Persons? You think two of them might be working together?' asked Beth, startled.

'It's quite possible everyone at the table that night had a secret that they wouldn't like plastered over the press,' said Harris. 'It's also quite possible that when Darcie alluded to it, she was talking about someone else entirely and they got wind of the fact that she'd been digging into them.'

'Like you, for example,' Lachlan said, with a hard stare.

'Like me,' replied Harris evenly.

'So then, we need a two-pronged approach,' said Beth. She didn't like the developing undercurrent between the two men, which felt like it could flare up into naked aggression at any moment. 'In relation to the book group, we need to send each and every one of them a text on Harris's burner phone, telling them they have to attend the next meeting of the book group on Tuesday 4th November or their secret will be revealed in their absence. No exceptions. We can try to add a hint of ambiguity so that it could conceivably be a fun part of the evening or a threat depending on how guilty they're feeling.'

'I'll handle that,' said Morna, scribbling in her notebook. 'Harris, can I have the phone, please?'

He reluctantly handed it over.

'I'll help her,' piped up Chloe.

'Come round to mine after work?' asked Morna, offhandedly.

'Sure, let's get a takeaway then get to work after.' Chloe grinned.

'What about the person who's been blackmailing me? What if it isn't one of the book group, but someone different?' asked Harris.

'Are all of them clients?' asked Lachlan.

Harris looked down and remained silent.

'Come on, man, we're way beyond that. This could be a matter of life and death.'

'All of them, at one time or another,' Harris admitted. He looked at their agog faces. 'It's not as crazy as you think. There are only four full-service firms in Oban and, at one time, we were the biggest.'

'What about your staff?' asked Beth.

'My staff?' He looked puzzled.

'Think about it,' Beth urged. 'How else has someone managed to get private financial information about your firm with which to blackmail you? Someone on the inside is either behind it in its entirety or has been feeding information to a member of the book group.'

Harris blanched but nodded. 'You're right. We have to look at things from every angle. All of our staff members are on our website. I can't give you their addresses but in a place the size of Oban, and with the electoral roll, I'm sure you'll manage to locate them.'

'Morna and I will do a deep dive into their socials tonight, see if we can find any connections linking them to one of the book group,' said Chloe, her eyes lit with enthusiasm.

'I've a fair amount of local knowledge,' said Lachlan. 'I'll run the names against the data box in here.' He tapped the side of his head, making them laugh.

The growing mood of optimism was shattered by blue lights flashing outside the window and someone pounding on the door. Beth's heart thudded in her chest, and she knew with complete certainty that it was time. The police had come for her. Quietly, she gathered up her bag and rose to her feet. Her eyes locked on Harris. He was already standing.

'That's the police,' she said, her voice steady. 'I'll most likely be detained overnight and appear in private before the sheriff tomorrow. Harris has explained how it all works. Don't worry, I'll be fine,' she added, with a confidence she didn't feel. Taking a last look around her at the festive Guy Fawkes displays and the dear faces of her staff and friends, she walked to the door, her back ramrod straight as they all stared at her in shock. Opening the door, she came face to face with DS Hunter. His eyes were expressionless and his face might have been carved from granite.

'Beth Cunningham, you are under arrest for the murder of Darcie Baxter. Anything you say can and will be noted down in evidence against you and can be used in a court of law.'

She held out her wrists in front of her as DS Hunter snapped the handcuffs on her wrist and cautioned her. This was it then. The end of her life as she knew it. Her new life had never tasted so sweet.

Detective Sergeant Hunter settled her in the back of the police car beside DC Quinn, who was struggling to keep the triumphant grin off her face, and the car moved off. Already, a small crowd of festive shoppers had gathered at all the commotion and a few bright sparks had their mobile phones out filming. Heart sore, she turned her gaze away from them as the car's tyres hissed along the wet roads. It felt like a funeral. Hers.

FORTY

Beth sat in the interview room with Harris beside her and the two detectives opposite. Although her lawyer been allowed to sit in, he was powerless to intervene now she had been arrested and charged. At least they had removed her cuffs after getting to the station, she thought, rubbing her wrists where they had chafed. The whole atmosphere had changed since she was last here. She was in deep trouble now and she knew it. Something else must have happened. Heart sore, she waited for the axe to fall as they tested the recording equipment before commencing. Everyone formally identified themselves, the caution was repeated then Beth sat back and waited for the blow to come. It wasn't long in arriving.

DS Hunter suddenly dipped into a carrier bag down by his side and took out a plastic evidence bag which he placed in front of her with a thump.

'Recognise this?' he asked, his tone scornful.

Beth pulled it towards her, her heart beating wildly. It was a large blue glass paperweight. She examined it and mutely shook her head, thoroughly confused.

'For the recording please?' he said.

'No, I've never seen it before,' she said, with a hitch in her voice. 'I do sell paperweights but it's not one of ours.'

She now had a horrible feeling she knew where this was going.

'Well, that's rather surprising given that several of your fingerprints were found on it,' he shot back.

'What? But that's impossible,' said Beth indignantly. 'Not unless someone crept into my house when I was asleep and put my hand on it.'

'Is that your defence?' he asked, looking her right in the eye.

'No! How would I even know if that had happened? My defence is that I have no idea how my fingerprints got on it. Are you saying that's the murder weapon? Is there blood on it?' She gulped, her mouth suddenly dry. 'Is it Darcie's?'

For the first time his gaze slid away. 'We're the ones asking the questions here, not you.'

'How is that fair?' she challenged him.

'You weren't worried about fairness when you murdered Darcie Baxter to stop your terrible secret coming out, were you?' said DC Quinn, leaning forward with a vindictive gleam in her eyes.

Beth had had enough. 'For the last time, I did not murder Darcie Baxter!' she almost shouted, staring first at one and then the other. 'You can badger me all you like with questions, but that fact will never change. Stop being lazy and look for the real killer. Someone has done this to me. I don't know how, but they have.'

DC Quinn was clearly struggling to hold on to her temper with only the fact that the interview was being recorded stopping her from exploding. DS Hunter stared at her, looking troubled. Was she getting through to him?

'Where did you find it?' she asked, more quietly now. 'Can you at least tell me that? I've never seen it before.'

'We had a tip off from a member of the public who saw someone acting suspiciously and then placing a package in the bin you left out for collection,' said DS Hunter.

'Where was this?' demanded Beth. 'At my home or at the shop?'

DC Quinn was shaking her head as though she thought her colleague was revealing too much information.

'At the shop,' he continued. 'We obtained a warrant and seized it earlier this evening.'

'I assume that this person left their name and address?' said Beth.

The rather uncomfortable silence that followed told her all she needed to know.

Beth slumped down in her chair and refused to engage with the remaining questions. It was hopeless. They'd clearly made up their minds and, just like she had before as a child, she felt powerless to alter the outcome.

FORTY-ONE
MORNA

Chloe rang the buzzer up to Morna's place, the hot Chinese food she was carrying making her mouth water. The door clicked open and Chloe entered, curious to see where her colleague lived. The entryway was sparse but clean and smelled of disinfectant. Somone had made a brave attempt to cheer the place up by putting some plastic flowers in a vase on the window ledge. At the top of the second floor, Morna stood at an open door waiting for her.

'That smells good,' she said, with a small smile. She poured Chloe a glass of white wine and served the steaming food onto plain white plates from the tiny open-plan kitchen counter and brought it over to the coffee table in front of them.

The room was sparsely furnished but Morna had made it her own with framed artwork from her favourite games and faux velvet throws together with a couple of warm glowing lamps.

'Love your place,' said Chloe. 'It's very you. I need to get my act together and move out of my parents' house. It just seems SO hard. I don't know that I'm ready.'

'I didn't really have a choice,' said Morna. 'But, hey, I've no regrets. It feels good to have my own space.'

'I can't believe that poor Beth is spending the night in a police cell,' Chloe fretted. 'I know Harris said she should get out on bail tomorrow but still... just the thought of it.' She shuddered.

'She'll cope,' said Morna. 'Beth is tougher than she looks. She's had to be.'

They finished their meal in silence then washed the dishes before getting out their phones and notepads. Morna went through to her bedroom and emerged with a state-of-the-art laptop which she booted up once she was sitting down.

'Wow! That is one serious piece of kit,' said Chloe with a low whistle.

'Sure is,' said Morna. 'I have a rich uncle who's a lot cooler than my parents. He works for a tech company.'

Chloe took out her iPad and brought up the website for Harris's firm. 'There's not all that many staff but their names and pics are on here.' She turned it to face Morna. 'I'll do a dive into their socials, see if there's anything leaps out there, if you can find addresses, family trees, any points where they cross paths with our book group.'

They'd been working and taking notes for an hour when Chloe slapped her head to her forehead and groaned. 'I forgot to call round on Harriet after work. I knew there was something.'

'Probably won't make much difference,' said Morna. 'None of the rest of us turned up anything important. That's me got all their addresses. I've also got the maiden names of anyone who's married.'

'Any luck?' asked Chloe.

'Nothing's jumping out at me yet,' sighed Morna, cracking her knuckles and stretching before hitting the keys again. 'No one is related by marriage or blood to a member of our book group that I can see.'

'Can you find out how long they've been working for the firm?' asked Chloe. 'Maybe some of them overlapped with the father or even grandfather.'

'Most of them are fairly young,' said Morna. 'There's an office junior, three secretaries and a cashier. The cashier looks like she's not far off retirement. I suppose we can't rule out the young ones either. They could have been planted there to get to Harris and gain access to the firm's financial records.'

'Don't forget the receptionist, Miss Pringle,' said Chloe. 'She worked for his father back in the day, maybe even his grandfather, too. She's like a sort of legal nanny or something. Bet she knows more than she likes to let on about what went down back then.'

'It's probably a misguided loyalty to the family that's prevented her speaking out,' said Morna. 'With careful handling she might split open.'

'Eww, gross image,' muttered Chloe. 'I reckon the best person to have a crack at her is probably Beth. From what she said, the old dear sounds quite fond of her.'

'We'll have to wait and see what happens tomorrow,' said Morna. With that they both fell silent thinking of their beleaguered boss alone in a police cell just a few streets away.

'Wait, there's something we've missed,' said Morna.

'What?' urged Chloe.

'Well, the whole thing at Harris's firm came about because Harris's grandfather got in over his head with some scary gambling set up. We need to know more about that. It won't be some local bookies, that's for sure.'

'It won't be online either,' said Chloe excitedly. 'His grandfather must have been ancient. He was also a lawyer so he's not going to be hobnobbing with his clients down the bookies.'

'Poker?' ventured Morna.

Chloe shrugged. 'We can ask Lachlan tomorrow. He's old enough to have some idea, isn't he?'

'I'll get him to speak to Harris, too,' said Morna. 'He might have some old paperwork stuffed in a cupboard somewhere that might lead us in the right direction.' She yawned. 'Sorry, I'm absolutely shattered.' Her fingers continued to fly over the keyboard, as Chloe started to gather up her things.

'You know Ronnie, from the beauty salon? Well, I can't see much, if anything, about her before she moved up here,' said Morna.

'It's fine. I looked into her briefly before. She's active across all the main social media channels.' Chloe shrugged, winding her scarf round her neck and picking up her bag.

'Yes, she is, but she's forty-seven and I haven't yet managed to dig up anything about her prior to living in Oban.'

'Maybe she's been married a couple of times or something,' said Chloe. 'She's been up here for over ten years anyway.'

'True,' said Morna. 'If she's been married more than once, that would explain it. I think it really sucks the way women have to change their identity on marriage. It's almost like a complete erasure of their previous life. So, unless we find out her name changes, I can't do much more for now.'

'What about the stuff you did find?' asked Chloe. 'Anything of interest?'

'Nothing. All her social media is brand based. All she does is bang on about how she only uses the highest quality products, free from this... free from that... blah blah.'

'Well, that's good, isn't it? Means she's ethical at least,' said Chloe. 'I've certainly never had any problems after a treatment. Anything else?'

'Well, she's into all that manifesting stuff, vision boards and all that nonsense.'

'Don't mock it till you try it,' said Chloe, striking a pose. 'How else do you think I've become so fabulous?' She pouted and gave an exaggerated hair toss.

Both girls burst out laughing.

'See you tomorrow!' said Chloe, grabbing her bag and heading for the door.

Morna stood up, flushing bright red. 'Er, if the offer still stands, I'd like to come to yours for Bonfire Night...'

'That's great!' replied Chloe, her eyes shining. 'Mum will be stoked.'

With that, she headed out and clattered down the stairs.

Morna dropped onto the sofa and slowly exhaled before

composing a text to send out to all the members of the book group for the following evening.

> Dear Armchair Detective, come along to our explosive Guy Fawkes meeting, where a secret will be revealed that will blow your socks off. The fuse has been lit, and everything set in motion for an evening of fireworks. Dare you miss it?

FORTY-TWO
BETH

Beth shivered and drew her knees up to her chest, tucking the thin blanket tightly around her. There was only one barred window high in the wall and the sole thing to look at was the blue metal door in front of her. She shivered and closed her eyes, feeling the walls starting to close in on her. They'd taken her phone, so she had no means of contacting anyone. She'd been allowed a quick meeting with Harris on arrival. He had assured her that he'd be at court tomorrow to represent her and apply for bail. If bail wasn't granted, she'd be remanded in custody and most likely held in HMP Stirling, pending her trial. Fervently she hoped that Harris would come through for her.

She jumped as the blue metal door opened with a clang and DS Hunter stood awkwardly before her. He handed her a thick blanket and a small clear toilet bag with a bar of soap and deodorant as well as a toothbrush and toothpaste.

'Thank you,' she managed, her teeth chattering with the cold.

'You're freezing,' he said to her, looking worried. 'I'll be back in a minute with tea and toast.' As he was leaving, he paused and turned back to face her. 'I'm sorry, the matter was taken out of my hands with this latest discovery.'

'I know,' she said simply, trying to move her frozen lips into a smile.

Minutes later, he returned with a mug of hot sweetened tea and two slices of hot buttered toast which she fell upon ravenously.

'I have to go now,' he said, sounding torn. 'Hang tight until tomorrow. Hopefully you'll be released on bail pending trial.'

Her eyes welled up as she looked up at him.

'Thank you. You've been very kind… in the circumstances.'

With that, she was left to her own devices. It was going to be a long night. But as she snuggled into the non-regulation blanket, that she suspected had come from his car, and sipped her tea, she felt the detective sergeant's kindness warm her more than anything else as she readied herself for the battle ahead.

After a few hours of fitful sleep, Beth jolted awake with a crick in her neck as she heard the clang of the door opening once more. The smile slid off her face as she realised it was DC Quinn and not DS Hunter bringing in her breakfast.

'I see you've been enjoying some home comforts,' she said, her eyes narrowing.

'Hardly,' retorted Beth.

After the police officer left, banging the door harder than was necessary, Beth forced herself to eat her breakfast then hurriedly used the toilet and gave herself a brief wash, praying no one was watching. Having made herself as presentable as possible, she sat down on the concrete shelf running along the wall, the blankets folded and her dirty dishes stacked by the door. She clasped her hands in her lap and composed herself for the ordeal of her looming court appearance.

FORTY-THREE

Morna, Chloe and Lachlan stood behind the till, hands wrapped round their mugs of coffee, darting anxious glances at the clock on the opposite wall. A loud yowl penetrated from outside followed by a determined scratching at the door.

'That'll be Toby,' said Chloe, rushing to the door and letting him in. 'Poor boy is looking for Beth.'

'He does look rather forlorn,' said Lachlan, getting up to find a tin of cat food. 'Maybe a good feed will cheer him up.' He emptied half the tin into a clean bowl.

'I can't believe they wouldn't let me into the court,' grumbled Morna. 'No one should have to face that alone.'

'Solemn procedure always takes place in private at the first hearing,' said Lachlan. 'And it doesn't come much more solemn than a murder charge. I thought you knew that.'

'Why would I?' fired back Morna.

Abruptly the shop phone rang, startling them.

Lachlan reached over to answer it, his lips compressing into a straight line. 'We have no comment to make,' he snapped, replacing it in its cradle with a bang. 'That's all we need,' he said, wearily. 'The press has got wind that Beth has been charged with Darcie's murder. It was just the local paper but by the end of the day all the nationals will be onto it.'

'We can't let this derail our plans,' said Morna urgently. 'After today, all of our suspects will have heard that Beth's been charged. They'll be desperate to hear everything about it so there's no way any of them will want to miss our November book group meeting. There's no better way to flush them out. We already sent out the invitations for tomorrow night, so we need to be prepared.'

'You're right,' said Chloe. 'This nightmare could all be over by tomorrow if we play our cards right.' She pulled out a large notebook from her tote bag together with a sparkly pen. 'So, guys, what do we need to buy in for tomorrow?'

They'd just finished making their list and apportioning tasks when the bell rang above the door and in rushed Beth, turning to slam the door behind her and flipping the sign to 'Closed'. Immediately the reporters, who had followed her from the courthouse, started banging on the door and windows, a clamour of indistinct voices.

'Vultures,' hissed Morna. She turned off the lights so that only the twinkling fairy lights remained, and they gathered round the table in the other room, safe from prying eyes.

'I'm afraid this is how it's going to be from now on,' said Beth, lifting Toby onto her lap and making a fuss of him.

'Only until the real murderer is unmasked,' said Lachlan.

'At least you got bail,' said Chloe, always one to look on the bright side. 'That takes some of the pressure off.'

'True. The sheriff figured that I wasn't a flight risk,' said Beth, mustering up a small smile.

'We've been getting organised for tomorrow night,' said Lachlan. 'I'll do the shopping later as I've got a car. Beth, here's the list if you want to add anything to it?'

Beth perused it then added a couple of items. 'Just keep the receipt and take it out of petty cash in the morning, Lachlan. That's a big help. I don't want to show my face in public any more than I have to at the moment.'

The noise level outside was increasing as the journalists grew louder. Some additional members of the public had joined them to see what all the fuss was about. One of them banged on the door, making them all jump.

'It feels like we're under siege,' complained Lachlan, rubbing his forehead and looking strained.

'I know how frustrating all of this is, but all we can do is keep going until we know more.' Beth went over to the window and peeked out. A handful of journalists stood outside, stamping their feet to ward off the chill. 'How on earth can we open the shop with that lot out there ready to charge in the moment I flip the sign?' she fretted.

'I've had enough of this,' said Morna. She strode to the door and flung it open. 'Right, you lot, you're wasting your time. Beth has absolutely no comment to make to you or anyone else at the present time. Your presence here amounts to harassment and you're impeding our customers. If you don't leave right now, then I'm going to phone the police and get them out here to deal with you. Your choice.' She folded her arms and glared at them each in turn.

After a bit of bluster and shuffling around they all dispersed, glad of an excuse to get out of the cold. Morna watched them until they rounded the corner, hands on her hips, chin thrust forward, then headed back in flipping the sign to 'Open'.

'Crikey! How did you do that?' gasped Beth, impressed.

'One of my previous jobs was bouncer at a club in Glasgow.' Morna grinned.

A steady stream of customers subsequently entered and they were kept busy. There were a few covert stares towards Beth, but no one actually came out and said anything. *Probably worried I'll murder them where they stand*, she thought bitterly.

After an hour or so, she decided to leave her staff to it and pay a visit to the library. Something had occurred to her during the afternoon and she knew that she wouldn't be able to rest until she'd looked further into it.

FORTY-FOUR
LACHLAN

Lachlan stirred the risotto simmering on the stove and then cut some fresh crusty bread to go on the table. He'd almost cancelled his invitation to dinner with everything that had been happening, but figured that he still needed to eat. Besides, it was only fair to return Mike's hospitality. He rather enjoyed his caustic wit. In that regard he reminded him of Darcie. Mike entered, sniffing the air like a fox.

'Something smells good in here. Shall I open the wine?'

'Please do,' said Lachlan fervently. He didn't normally drink all that much, but tonight definitely warranted a stiff one.

Once they were seated and tucking in with gusto, some Puccini playing quietly in the background, conversation between them flowed easily enough. Lachlan was surprised to discover he was enjoying himself. By nature a fairly solitary man, who'd invited Mike out of a sense of obligation, he wondered whether he should perhaps open himself up to the possibility of more people in his life?

'That was incredible,' said Mike, putting down his fork and patting his stomach. 'You should go on that TV show, what is it? *Come Dine with Me*, that's it.'

Lachlan laughed and poured the last of the wine into their glasses. 'I hardly think so. Shall we go into the lounge?'

'Sure,' said Mike, following him through. 'I'm happy to take a crack at the dishes.'

'No, leave them,' said Lachlan. 'That's what the dishwasher's for.'

'I hope you don't mind me saying but I heard that Beth has been indicted for Darcie's murder,' Mike said quietly, yet staring directly at him.

Lachlan froze. What to say? 'Yes,' he said finally. 'She's been released on bail. The evidence, such as it is, is completely circumstantial. Wrong time, wrong place.'

'That's what I thought,' said Mike. 'For what it's worth, I don't have her pegged as a killer.'

'None of us do. But that doesn't seem to matter to the police,' sighed Lachlan, taking a sip of coffee. 'I hope you're still coming tomorrow night?'

'Wouldn't miss it,' Mike said, with a hint of his usual irreverence creeping in. 'What's this?' he asked, pulling the book lying on the coffee table towards him. 'Any good?'

Lachlan cursed himself for failing to hide it before Mike came.

'Wait a minute, is this the boy wonder's book?' said Mike, turning the book over so its cover was facing the front. 'How did you manage to get hold of this? I heard it's locked down tighter than the Harry Potter books were. I've been dying to get my hands on a copy.' His tone was gleeful. He looked at the back of the book again then flipped to reading the front page.

'What? No, this can't be right,' he said, his hands starting to tremble. He shook his head as though trying to dislodge a troublesome fly.

'What is it?' asked Lachlan, leaning forward, alarmed now.

'Lachlan, this is MY book. That bastard has stolen my book!'

'You can't be serious,' breathed Lachlan.

'I'm deadly serious,' Mike said, continuing to read. After a few pages he flipped to the end and read the ending. When he put it back down there were tears in his eyes. 'I can't believe this,' he said. 'How has this happened? I didn't show it to *anyone*.'

'Well... You mentioned a burglary a few years ago when your laptop was stolen,' said Lachlan, thinking aloud. 'It must have been him. Think, man, did you ever share even a *part* of your book with anyone else?'

'I did tell Dan I'd written a crime novel around a couple of years before the break-in, but I said it was probably no good and was likely to stay in a drawer. Back then, I suppose I fancied myself as a mentor. Later on, we had a bit of a bust up and I decided to leave the writing group. I'd managed to steer clear of him until the night Darcie died.'

'You can't have been best pleased when he turned up at the bookshop,' said Lachlan.

'You can say that again,' Mike sighed. 'Look, I've no way to prove it's mine. Back then I lacked confidence. It was hard sharing my work, so I stuck to shorter pieces. I put everything into that damned book and hardly anyone knew about its existence.'

'Couldn't an expert analyse the writing style or something against your other work?'

'That would never stand up to the might of a major publisher.' Suddenly, a wide grin transformed his face. 'I wrote a good book,' he said, happiness dancing across his face. 'I wrote a BLOODY good book.' The light dimmed from his eyes. 'And now I've got to watch that little shit take all the credit and live the life that should've been mine.'

'Dan doesn't know we've got this,' said Lachlan. 'If we can get a recorded confession from him tomorrow night, then we can take it to his publisher. The book can be withdrawn from publication and republished under your name. Otherwise, the resultant bad publicity could crush them.'

'You know as well as I do that a book's success or failure depends on so many variables,' said Mike. 'He's young and fit, a social media darling already, and who am I? Nothing but a jaded washed-up teacher. The same book would probably tank because

I'm not a product they can sell. If I really want to get this book out into the world, the only way I can see it happening is if I let things lie.'

'You can't mean that!' exclaimed Lachlan. 'We've got to take him down. He must still fear that he'll be found out. You know that you've got no other copies, but he doesn't. That's why he's waited so long before trying to flog it. This whole secrecy thing is because he's gambling on the fact that it'll be too late once the book's published. Maybe all we need to do is call his bluff and pretend you have proof of prior ownership. How fast can you type? I'll stick some coffee on. Run back and get your laptop. I'll make a start on mine. I'll call Beth, Morna and Chloe and get them to bring round their laptops. We can type up the book between us.'

Mike stood motionless for a few seconds as though frozen with indecision. 'You're right. He's not getting away with this. Sometimes you need to take a stand.'

FORTY-FIVE

BETH

The following morning everyone was bleary-eyed after the late-night session at Mike's house on Monday night. The tension in the air was palpable as they all realised that this would be their last chance to expose the killer before they went to ground. There was no way any of their book group members would be willing to cross the threshold again after what promised to be an explosive session tonight.

'Morning all,' Dave the postman smiled, plonking their mail onto the cash desk.

'Morning,' they chorused weakly.

'Blimey,' he said, folding his arms and staring at them. 'You lot look like death heated up this morning. Late night, was it? I didn't even hear our Chloe come in.'

'Thanks, Dad,' said Chloe, rolling her eyes comically. 'We all feel *so* much better now.'

'Happy to assist.' He grinned. 'Well, I'd best be off. These parcels won't deliver themselves.'

Beth waved to him but felt that beneath the banter he was making a fair point. Her staff had been working themselves into the ground lately, not to mention all the stress they had been under due to her own difficulties.

'I want you all to know how much I appreciate everything you've been doing both for me and also for the shop. I couldn't have got through the past few weeks without you all by my side. So, with that in mind, I've decided to close the shop tomorrow so you can all have a good rest. We'll stick a sign in the window saying "Closed for Staff Training". How does that sound?'

'Like music to my ears,' said Lachlan, his face lighting up.

Chloe squealed with delight. 'Beth, you're the best! Morna, how do you fancy a day shopping in Glasgow?'

'As long as we can visit a couple of games shops, I'm up for it,' Morna replied, trying to look like it was no big deal.

'You're on, as long as we can also do Primark. That's a deal breaker,' said Chloe.

'Fine,' said Morna. 'How bad can it be?'

The day dragged on with everyone's nerves increasing as the evening approached. It was too early yet for people to have started their Christmas shopping and the weather outside was dreary. The clocks had recently gone back, and it was getting darker earlier in the day. Beth wished she had nothing more taxing in front of her than an evening in front of the telly mindlessly eating snacks.

She was making some industrial strength coffee in the kitchen when she heard a plaintive miaow. Toby. She hadn't seen him for a while. Moving into the main part of the shop with her coffee she glanced around. That miaow again. Where on earth was he?

'Toby,' she coaxed. 'Come to Mummy!'

There was a snort of laughter behind her and she spun round to see both girls grinning at her.

'You talk to that cat like he's your baby.' Morna laughed.

'He *is* my baby!' she exclaimed, embarrassed at being caught out.

'He's up there,' pointed Chloe, pointing to the huge bonfire.

Sure enough, Toby, in the manner of cats everywhere, had decided that what went up couldn't possibly come down. He was wobbling precariously, balanced across two sticks at the very top that were giving way under the strain of one rather plump feline.

'Oh no, he's going to fall!' gasped Beth. She rushed through and dragged a chair from the kitchen and stood on top, but it wasn't high enough for her to reach the wobbling cat who was sounding desperately unhappy by now.

'Let *me*,' said Lachlan, tugging her down and leaping up in her place. With his superior height, he managed to reach the now hissing cat and grab him, getting some vicious growls and a few scratches in return. Once back on the ground, Toby stalked off disdainfully, his tail held high.

'Lachlan, I'm so sorry,' Beth said, horrified by the red welts springing up on his hands. Chloe ran to the kitchen for the first aid box and brought it through.

'He can be a little monster at times,' Beth said, administering to Lachlan who was mortified by the fuss and a most unwilling patient. After that the mood lightened for a while but as the clock edged towards five, all conversation ceased. Sombre now, they all filed out of the shop and went their separate ways to have a bit of a break before the fireworks started later.

FORTY-SIX
CHLOE

Chloe hammered on the bedroom door in frustration. 'Let me out!' she yelled. 'You can't just keep me here forever!' Frustrated, she looked out the window over the back garden. The window was stuck fast and even if she managed to smash the panes of glass, there was nothing to break her fall on the way down. Her mother would have a fit when she didn't come home tonight. What a mess! Feeling panic bubbling up once more, she took herself off to the ensuite bathroom and splashed her face with cold water then took some deep breaths. What she wouldn't give for her phone right now, but that had been taken from her. She was also absolutely starving. Although she had access to water, her captor was obviously loath to bring her food in case she managed to overpower them and get away. Her stomach felt like it was going to eat itself.

So much for the November book group meeting tonight when they were hoping to smoke out the killer. She could save them the bother, she thought glumly. No one would panic if she didn't turn up. They'd just assume she'd flaked out on them because she couldn't face going. It would be hours before anyone even thought about sounding the alarm. Her mother would assume she'd stayed at the shop with the others to get things ready. If only she'd thought to text Morna to let her know where she was going.

With a sigh she flung herself back down on the bed. What was her captor's end game? she wondered uneasily. Letting her go would be out of the question as her first port of call would be the police station. So why wasn't she dead already? What were they waiting for? Jumping back on to her feet, Chloe paced up and down, her mind whirring. She couldn't just languish here waiting to be rescued. It was clear no one was coming to her aid. She had to figure out a way to escape.

FORTY-SEVEN
BETH

This meeting tonight would be her last chance to extract a confession from the killer. If it didn't work, then she had absolutely no idea what she could try next. The waters were further muddied by the fact that she suspected Darcie had hit several nerves that night with her unwise remarks about splashing a secret all over the tabloids. However, there could only be one killer and, after her research at the library yesterday, she now had a fair idea about who it could be. Tonight was going to be a desperate gamble that would either smoke them out and bring this whole nightmare to an end, or the killer would hold their nerve and the police would never discover the truth, which would most likely lead to her spending the best years of her life incarcerated for a crime she didn't commit. Not to mention the fact that Darcie Baxter's killer would evade justice. Her poor mother would be turning in her grave if she could see her now.

Lachlan and Morna walked through from the kitchen, carrying a tray of steaming mulled wine and plates of sausage rolls to join the savoury snacks already on the table. Beside each plate was a copy of a book wrapped in flame-coloured tissue paper with a sparkler tucked into green ribbon, which they'd all contributed from their own collections. Chloe had wrapped them this afternoon. Place names were in front of every seat to give them control over how they were all spaced out. Each of them was going to surreptitiously record the night's proceedings on their mobile phones.

'Are you ready?' asked Lachlan, glancing at his watch.

'As ready as I'll ever be,' she replied, with a wan smile.

'Let's get this done,' said Morna grimly, her words and expression at odds with her Guy Fawkes costume. 'I can't believe that Chloe hasn't showed. I texted her and she never even replied.'

'That's really not like her,' said Beth, a bit worried. 'Maybe it all got too much for her. I sometimes forget how young she is. All that business with Dan's book last night, it's been intense. We'll just have to manage without her. Maybe she'll come by later. If not, then I'll phone to check on her once we're done for the night.' As Beth walked away to collect a few more bits and pieces from the kitchen she suddenly froze. It really wasn't like Chloe not to show up, still less phone. She thought back to recent conversations and had a horrible feeling that she knew where she might have gone. At least no harm was likely to come to her when all of the suspects were going to be here for the better part of the evening.

The bell above the door rang and they instantly switched into party mode, welcoming the members of the book club as they traipsed in off the street.

'Welcome, everyone.' Beth smiled, stretching her lips over her teeth until they ached. Moving amongst them, pouring the deliberately lethal mulled wine into glasses, she was alert for signs of tension or anxiety amongst their guests. Mike was doing his best not to glare daggers at Dan, though she could tell that he wanted to by the way his eyes kept slithering across to him then darting away again. There was music playing quietly in the background so as not to interfere with any recording.

'Beth, turn this one up!' yelled Ronnie, and she started shaking her hips as a pop classic came on. A few of the others joined in so she had no choice but to comply. How could they all look so carefree and relaxed, she wondered crossly, when all of them were harbouring such pernicious secrets? The alcohol was starting to take effect now. Turning the music back down after a few minutes, she clapped her hands for attention.

'Right, everyone, let's all take our seats. Our delightful festive Guy Fawkes will continue to top up your glasses and there are loads of snacks on the table. Now, it's time for each of us to open our bonfire surprise and start the bookish conversation.'

'Gee, I wonder what it can be?' asked Ronnie, holding up her book-shaped present and drolly rolling her eyes.

'I might keep mine for later,' said Harriet quietly, getting her bag up off the floor.

'No, no, we can't have that,' said Lachlan, his voice a pitch higher than normal. 'Let's do it now!'

They all grabbed their parcels and ripped the paper off.

'Wow!' said Mike. 'Look what I've got!' He held it up for them all to see. 'It's Dan's book! I can't wait to delve into this.' With that, he opened the book and started to read.

'How did you get that? Give it to me!' Dan snarled, as he lunged across the table to try and grab it, knocking over his glass in the process.

Mike jumped out of his chair. 'You cheating scumbag. You've been trying to pass my book off as your own work. You broke into my house four years ago and stole it off my laptop. I knew that something was way off with your so-called book deal. I taught you at school and I've never seen such stilted prose.'

'I certainly remember that he was never any good at English at school,' said Harriet, nodding along.

Dan suddenly sat back down, after struggling to regain control of himself.

'He's mad as a hatter,' he said dismissively, looking around at the others. 'He's never even mentioned writing a book before. Pure sour grapes because he's a washed-up teacher who resents the success of a younger man. It's pathetic,' he jeered.

'I told *you*,' Mike said. 'And what made you think that was the only copy?'

Dan's face drained of colour. 'You're lying, you son of a bitch.'

In response, Mike lifted up his battered briefcase from where it had been sitting under the table and pulled out a large sheaf of paper. He passed his copy of the book to Harriet and started to read out loud from the thick pile of papers with her following along. After a few minutes she nodded and smiled.

'It's the same,' she announced, 'almost word for word.'

'I'm arranging a meeting with your publisher and my lawyer,' said Mike, 'to see how we can resolve this situation.'

Dan slumped back in his chair, all the fight leaving him. 'You were so bloody talented, and you weren't even going to submit the damned thing anywhere,' he said. 'I thought if I kept the contents of the book secret until it was published you might not even try to do anything about it. I couldn't resist. I'm sorry.'

'Sorry you got caught, you mean,' said Ronnie, looking down her nose at him. 'Well, it's been fun and all,' she continued, her voice dripping sarcasm, 'but I'm afraid I've got better things to do with my night than sit at this dirge of a party. And I won't be back either.'

'Wait!' commanded Beth. 'I'm afraid that's not all. One of you has been harbouring an even worse secret than that. A secret that you were prepared to kill for. Darcie met her death here because, rightly or wrongly, you thought that she was about to make it very public.'

'Well, it wasn't me,' snapped Dan, folding his arms.

'And it certainly wasn't me!' said Mike, his eyes darting around from one to the other.

'This has gone too far,' said Harriet, struggling to her feet. 'I'm too old for this nonsense. Are we engaging in some poor taste murder mystery evening now?' she said, her tone scathing.

'Look,' said Ronnie, her eyes narrowed into slits. 'This is all some ridiculous smokescreen to disguise the fact that it was you who killed Darcie because she was about to reveal your own murderous past. The whole town knows what you did.' Her eyes were contemptuous.

Beth's mouth went dry. She was losing them. One of these people had killed Darcie. There was nobody else in the frame. She had to try one last desperate bluff to extract a confession. She'd backed everything on a long shot that she hadn't even told her staff about.

FORTY-EIGHT

'Harris, get in here, please!' shouted Beth.

Duly summoned, he strode in from the kitchen where he'd been concealed behind a curtain.

Looking at their shocked faces in turn, Beth said simply, 'Miss Pringle told him everything. He's already been in touch with the Law Society and their auditors will arrive to conduct a thorough investigation in the morning. She didn't know anything about the blackmail and was horrified to learn what had been going on.'

'You're bluffing!' shouted Ronnie. 'Why would she do that? My mother would never betray me.'

'Your mother!' exclaimed Mike.

'She didn't know it was you,' said Harris. 'I left her no choice. I found evidence buried deep within my father's paperwork suggesting that she and my grandfather had an affair many years ago. The product of that affair was you.' He waved a birth certificate in the air. 'It was agreed between them that she would leave the office before she started to show and then come back to work after she had placed the baby for adoption. The affair continued until his death. She was a cashier for most of her time at the firm and helped my grandfather cover up the embezzlement of funds to keep the casino's muscle men off his back.'

'Darcie was about to destroy everything I've worked for just to get her pathetic byline in a national paper. I had to do something!' Ronnie shouted, her eyes sparking with rage.

'So, you killed her,' said Harris, 'then started blackmailing me to ensure that Beth received poor representation and so was convicted of your crime. Only then would you be able to relax.'

'You lot deserve everything you've got coming, looking down on the rest of us from your ivory tower when you're nothing but thieving crooks,' she spat. 'Your grandfather seduced my poor mother when she was still a teenager. It was hardly a relationship between equals. He made her give away her own bloody baby. She was so damned happy when I finally tracked her down yet, even after I moved up here, the secrecy continued. She was worried about your precious family's reputation. Can you believe that?'

Beth couldn't help but be touched by the pain and vulnerability in her voice, but she steeled herself against it and continued. 'But that wasn't the only reason that you killed her, was it?'

Ronnie froze, shaking her head in denial. 'No, that was it, I swear, there's nothing else.'

Everyone looked at Beth in confusion.

The bell tinkled as the door to the shop opened and closed. They all turned their eyes to the person walking towards them with expressions varying from horror to pity and compassion as the woman took off the scarf wrapped around her face and revealed what lay underneath.

There were collective gasps as they took in her scarred and distorted face, a lifetime of pain etched into it.

'Remember me, Stephanie?' she said, in a coarse rasping voice, her eyes locked on to Ronnie.

Ronnie turned away from her. 'I don't know who you are, but you've clearly mistaken me for someone else,' she said, the sheen of sweat breaking out on her brow belying her words.

'Look at me!' the woman shouted, her voice stronger now. 'How dare you turn away from me. I've had to look at this face in the mirror every day so you can at least look me in the eye now.'

Ronnie's eyes turned back to her.

'You did this to me twenty-two years ago. At least have the grace to admit it. Your knock-off products caused such a severe reaction, I almost died. My skin was so badly burned it was peeling off in strips.'

'I didn't have insurance,' Ronnie whispered, collapsing in on herself. 'I cut corners to survive. I'd been dragged up in the care system and was slowly carving out a life for myself. I was young and desperate. The only thing I could think to do was run and start a new life elsewhere. I couldn't afford to pay you the amount of damages a court would have awarded. I figured I'd learn from it and move on.'

'Some of us didn't have that luxury,' said the woman, her bitterness bursting out.

'How did you even find her?' snapped Ronnie, turning hate-filled eyes on Beth.

'It was something Morna said,' Beth replied. 'That she'd found no presence online for you before twelve years ago. Since you're in the beauty business, I searched for newspaper reports of negligence in Glasgow for twenty years before then. In only one of them had the person responsible shut up shop and disappeared, leaving her victim high and dry. Once I had a name to search against, I found some old photos and identified you that way. You were using the name Stephanie Pringle back then. After that it was easy to connect the dots.'

'I didn't want my mother to know,' Ronnie said, her eyes anguished. 'I thought that if she found out about my past, she'd be ashamed and reject me again. How could I take that chance?'

'You've been through a lot, I can see that,' Beth said, 'but, in all probability, Darcie was talking about a different secret entirely. There's no way she would have mentioned it otherwise. But who amongst us doesn't have secrets? We all heard her words speak directly to hidden, dark parts of us but only one of us decided to kill her for it.'

Ronnie raced for the door. Nobody tried to stop her.

She wouldn't get far.

FORTY-NINE

'You don't think she's got Chloe?' asked Lachlan, jumping to his feet.

'No,' said Beth, sitting back down and staring across at Harriet. 'I don't. Give it up, Harriet, we know you're keeping Chloe at your house. And we know why.'

'I don't know what you're talking about,' Harriet spluttered, her wrinkled blue eyes watchful.

'Each of my staff was going to visit one of you to check whether you had a burner phone which was being used to blackmail Harris. Chloe was assigned to visit you, but Morna mentioned she hadn't managed it the night before. Chloe is nothing if not conscientious. She would've come to see you today on her way home from work. You panicked and prevented her from leaving, didn't you?' Beth's voice was like chips of ice. 'If anything has happened to that girl—'

'Alright, alright!' Harriet shouted, her voice breaking. 'I admit it. I caught her snooping around in one of the bedrooms and I panicked. Instead of sending her off with a flea in her ear, I ran up and locked the door. I didn't think it through and then I didn't know how to get out of the mess I'd made. I was going to wait and see what happened tonight before releasing her.'

'If you've harmed her...' growled Morna.

'I haven't touched her,' said Harriet, shaking her head. 'Though she might be a bit hungry. I couldn't figure out a safe way to get food in there.'

'Right, let's go,' said Beth decisively. 'Morna, come with Harris and me to get Chloe, and Lachlan, could you please lock up behind Mike and Dan? Also, could you call DS Hunter and tell him that one of the three stone statues in the small courtyard at Glow is most likely the real murder weapon.'

All three men stood and stared at her slack-jawed, but Lachlan quickly snapped out of it and hurriedly took out his phone. Dan beat them to the door and took off in the direction of his flat, shoulders hunched, his dreams of being a bestselling author now in tatters.

In silence they trudged through the town. The wind was getting up and Beth welcomed the salty breeze cooling her hot cheeks. They could hear the bangs and hisses of early fireworks exploding against the dark canvas of the night sky in vivid pops of sparkling colours.

'Wait!' said Morna, and she dashed across the street to the fish and chip shop. Beth shook her head in disbelief. Fancy thinking of food at a time like this?

Five minutes later she ran back to them clutching a tightly wrapped paper package. 'Right, let's go,' she muttered.

Soon they were all outside Harriet's house, waiting impatiently as she fumbled with her keys. Harriet opened the door and led them up two flights of stairs before stopping at a door. She took out a key and then swung the door open.

An angry Chloe rushed out, arms swinging, and then comically slid to a stop when she realised it was them. 'This crazy woman locked me up,' she yelled, pointing an accusing finger.

'I'm sorry, Chloe, I panicked and then couldn't see a way forward,' said Harriet shakily, handing Chloe her phone back. 'I never meant for this to happen.' Harriet's complexion was grey. She staggered back against the banister.

Chloe sniffed the air like a bloodhound, her eyes shining with rapture. 'What is that divine smell?'

'For you,' said Morna, pulling the package out of her bag. 'I thought you might be hungry.'

'Morna, you're the bomb, you know that?' Chloe smiled. 'Come on, let's get out of here, my mother will worry if I don't get back soon.' She cast a last furious glare at Harriet then made her way out of the house with Morna by her side.

'Harris, can you leave us, please?' said Beth, her voice brooking no argument.

'I'll be outside if you need me,' he said, and followed the girls downstairs.

'We need to talk,' said Beth, her newfound assertiveness surprising her. She helped the older woman downstairs into the lounge and made her a cup of sweet tea. Harriet lifted the cup to her lips with shaking hands but seemed to draw strength from the ritual.

'I suppose that you're going to inform the police,' she said. 'It's no more than I deserve. Chloe's always been a good girl. She didn't deserve that.'

'That will be up to Chloe and her parents,' said Beth. 'However, I know why you did it. You may not have killed Darcie, but you did kill someone else, didn't you?'

Harriet froze, her cup halfway to her lips. Big fat tears started to roll down the creases and folds of her skin. 'I had no choice,' she whispered. 'It was him or me. The mood he was in that night he'd have killed me for sure. Years I'd suffered his abuse, but that last year his drinking had got worse. He was jealous of my position in the community. The hatred in his eyes, it was terrifying. Towards the end he became a monster. That night I knew he was going to snap completely. I had nowhere to go. I'd hid the abuse for so long I felt no one would believe me. I felt powerless. I had to pay my salary into his bank account, and he doled out meagre housekeeping money. I acted in fear of my life. I had to stop him coming home that night. Whatever it took. I waited in the shadows until he staggered out of the pub then caught him with a brick from behind and he fell down unconscious. I didn't mean to kill him, I just wanted him to be taken to hospital, so I had time to escape.'

'Did you think about going to the police?' asked Beth.

'I didn't think I'd have to, I thought they'd come and arrest me. I can't even remember getting home that night, it's all a blur. But amazingly, I never even fell under suspicion. It was ruled an accidental death.'

'You do know that you would most likely have been acquitted due to effectively acting in self-defence?' said Beth. 'Your medical records would have corroborated your version of events.'

'I thought I had got away with it when Darcie dropped her bombshell.' She grimaced. 'As you can imagine. I assumed she was talking about me.'

'But you didn't kill her,' said Beth.

'No! Of course not! I always knew that this day could come. She didn't deserve to die for simply doing her job, no matter what the consequences were for me. Although, I'm ashamed to admit, I did feel relief when I discovered what had happened which makes me a terrible person, I know.'

'It makes you human,' said Beth. She stood up to go.

'I'll get my coat,' said Harriet, getting up.

'Why? Where are you going at this time of night?' asked Beth.

Harriet turned and looked at her in surprise. 'Why, to the police station of course!'

'Look, I believe you about what happened that night. There is a witness who was in the pub that night who can speak to his behaviour. I doubt very much that you would be prosecuted after all this time and in those particular circumstances. Maybe you've suffered enough? I can't tell you what to do either way, but no one will hear about it from me.'

'Thank you, Beth, that means more than I can say, but I've come to a decision. I'm stronger now than I was back then. I also feel I owe it to other victims of domestic abuse to come forward. I'll attend the police station first thing in the morning. It's time I stopped hiding and faced up to the past.'

Beth gave her a hug and took her leave. Harris was waiting for her on the street outside.

'What was all that about?' he asked.

'Oh, this and that,' she replied airily, a bubble of happiness rising up within her. Arm in arm, they headed back into town for a night cap.

It had been quite a night.

FIFTY

Two weeks later

Beth woke up and stretched luxuriously. All was right with her world. Detective Sergeant Hunter had received instructions from the Procurator Fiscal to accept her plea of not guilty and that had been attended to last week. Ronnie had been apprehended and charged. Although it had been wiped clean and exposed to the elements, specialist examination had found a few tiny flakes of blood clinging on underneath a small stone Buddha. Clearly, Ronnie had lifted Beth's fingerprints from the glasses of water and prosecco that she'd consumed on her premises then transferred them onto the smooth surface of the paperweight.

It transpired that Darcie Baxter's big story had nothing whatsoever to do with the book group. The rat that she had found in the shoe box was a threat sent by an influential organised crime group in Glasgow who had been aware she was close to blowing the lid on their entire operation. The additional phone that Beth had found in the flat had contained a treasure trove of information and recordings that were now with specialist analysts in Glasgow. It was going to be an enormous story once it broke in the press, but sadly the byline would not be Darcie's. Instead, she would be an important part of the narrative, which Beth felt would be some consolation.

It felt good to be a free woman. For once Toby hadn't woken her, accidentally on purpose, demanding to be fed. Gosh, it was cold. Shivering, she opened the curtains, and her mouth gaped in surprise. No wonder it seemed so quiet, the snow must have been falling all night. She lifted Toby off the bed and the look of disgust when she showed him the snow made her laugh.

She fed him and sat wrapped in a throw on the couch as she contemplated the pain and joy that this year had brought to her. 'I love it up here, Mum,' she said, dropping a kiss on the framed photo on the table beside the couch. 'I wish you were still here to enjoy it with me.' Her eyes filled with tears and she hurriedly jumped up to go and get ready.

Due to the depth of snow, she opted for wellies and carried her shoes in her bag with a bottle of wine and some chocolates. Rounding the corner on the way into town she heard shrieks of laughter and came upon Morna and Chloe each pulling a plastic sledge. She'd decided to keep the shop closed today on account of the snow.

'What age are you guys?' she asked, laughing.

'Come with us, you know you want to,' said the irrepressible Chloe.

'I do want to, but I have somewhere else to be,' she smiled, continuing on her way. As she climbed up the hill to where Harris and his mother lived, she turned back to look over the small town nestled in front of the bay and felt a strong sense that this was now her home. The snow came on again and her view was quickly obscured as she panted up the remaining distance to the house at the top of the hill.

She rang the bell and Harris's mother instantly appeared, enfolding her in a warm hug, closely followed by Harris.

'Welcome, my dear, it's wonderful to have you here.'

'Come away out of the cold, Beth,' said Harris. 'We've got a surprise for you.'

They led her into the sitting room where a tall willowy blonde woman was waiting to greet her with a welcoming smile.

'You not only have a new brother but a new sister as well,' said Harris. 'She's starting work as a doctor in Oban after the New Year.'

'Fiona Kincaid.' The woman introduced herself, her eyes moist. 'Welcome to the family, Beth.'

Her heart full, Beth accepted a glass of wine and looked round at this new family of hers with a full heart. It was all exactly as her beloved mum would have wished.

Later, sliding back down the snowy road into town, Beth marvelled at the winter sun now setting in a fiery display towards the right of the bay even though it was only a little after four. As she rounded the corner onto George Street, she crashed into someone and ended up falling backwards into the snow, the breath forced out of her lungs in an unseemly grunt. As she squinted upwards, she realised to her chagrin that it was Logan Hunter. Trust him to catch her at a disadvantage!

'Daddy, Daddy! You've hurt Beth!' a little voice squealed. Poppy's small gloved hand gripped hers and she tried ineffectually to pull her to her feet, before landing in the snow beside her and bursting into tears.

'Poppy!' Beth said, scooping the sobbing girl into her arms. 'Don't cry, I'm absolutely fine! It's so easy to slip in this fluffy snow. It feels like sitting on a big cloud, doesn't it?'

'A cold cloud,' the little girl answered, her huge brown eyes fixed on hers as she sat on Beth's knee.

Logan Hunter looked completely at a loss as he stared down at them before coming abruptly back to his senses.

'Beth, are you alright? I'm so sorry,' he said, bending down to lift up his daughter and set her back on her feet before extending two hands to Beth to pull her up. She was almost up when her feet slid again and he hurriedly grabbed her to him. Startled, she looked up into his warm brown eyes, her heart thumping so loudly in her chest she thought he might hear it.

'What am I going to do with you?' he muttered.

'I know!' said Poppy, taking him literally. 'Why don't we all go for a hot chocolate?'

Beth looked at Logan and they both laughed.

'You up for it?' he asked, his eyes crinkling with merriment. 'My treat.'

'I'm up for it.' She smiled back, wondering if they were still talking about hot chocolate. Beth took one of Poppy's gloved hands as Logan took the other.

'Hot chocolate it is, then.' He grinned.

They slid their way towards the chocolate shop as the last trace of the sun dropped below the horizon.

A LETTER FROM THE AUTHOR

Dear reader,

Huge thanks for reading *Murder at the Wild Haggis Bookshop*, I hope you were hooked on Beth Cunningham's journey. If you want to join other readers in hearing all about my new releases and bonus content, you can sign up here:

www.stormpublishing.co/jackie-baldwin

If you enjoyed this book and could spare a few moments to leave a review that would be hugely appreciated. Even a short review can make all the difference in encouraging a reader to discover my books for the first time. Thank you so much!

I wrote this book because Oban, in the western Highlands, holds a special place in my heart. I first visited it on holiday as a young student and fell completely in love. The next morning, I took a fistful of change and found a red telephone box. I rang round all the local solicitors' firms and managed to secure an interview for a legal traineeship. The firm was quaint and old fashioned with huge windows overlooking the bay. To make ends meet, I also worked part time in Aulay's Bar where it wasn't uncommon to discover a sink full of shellfish behind the bar because the fisherman was having a pint on his way home. As for Beth, I lost my own mother at the age of eighteen so I could identify with the loss that helped shape her character. I also had a fantasy bookshop when I was young. The cat in the novel is based on a real feisty black cat owned by my son. He has plenty of cattitude in real life as well!

Thanks again for being part of this amazing journey with me and I hope you'll stay in touch – I have so many more stories and ideas to entertain you with!

Jackie Baldwin

www.jackiebaldwin.co.uk

instagram.com/Jackie.baldwin.1088
facebook.com/Jackie%20Baldwin%20Author
x.com/JackieMBaldwin1

ACKNOWLEDGEMENTS

Writing the first draft of a book is a very solitary occupation but once it has been submitted it becomes much more of a team effort. I'm very grateful to have the wonderful team at Storm working hard to ensure that each book is the best it can possibly be before it arrives in your hands. Special thanks go to my editor, Kathryn Taussig, and her co-editor, Abigail Fenton, for the structural edit, the copyeditor, Liz Hurst, for her meticulous attention to detail, and proofreader, Amanda Raybould. Credit for my beautiful cover must go to the talented Dawn Adams. I'd also like to thank Elke Desanghere for her beautiful marketing materials. I'm also grateful to Alexandra Begley and her assistant Naomi Knox for their roles in production of the book. In relation to the audiobooks, I am so happy that Samara MacLaren agreed to be the narrator as her wonderful voice fits beautifully with the characters.

Finally, my thanks, as always, to my husband, Guy, for his unwavering support. Marrying him was the best decision I ever made!

Made in United States
Troutdale, OR
10/07/2025

35254041R00146